The Moonbathers

After studying English at Cambridge, Deborah
Lawrenson worked as a journalist, including
three years with Nigel Dempster on the *Daily
Mail*, and a further two as his deputy editor on
The Mail on Sunday. She has also worked for
Woman's Journal as editor of the London section.
She has written two previous novels, *Hot Gossip*
and *Idol Chatter*.

She now lives in Kent with her husband and
daughter.

Also by Deborah Lawrenson

Hot Gossip
Idol Chatter

Deborah Lawrenson

The Moonbathers

ARROW

Published in the United Kingdom in 1998 by Arrow Books

1 3 5 7 9 10 8 6 4 2

First published in the United Kingdom in 1998 by William Heinemann

Arrow Books Limited
Random House UK Ltd
20 Vauxhall Bridge Road, London, SW1V 2SA

Random House Australia (Pty) Limited
20 Alfred Street, Milsons Point, Sydney,
New South Wales 2061, Australia

Random House New Zealand Limited
18 Poland Road, Glenfield
Auckland 10, New Zealand

Random House South Africa (Pty) Limited
Endulini, 5a Jubilee Road,
Parktown, 2193, South Africa

Random House UK Limited Reg. No. 954009

A CIP catalogue record for this book
is available from the British Library

Papers used by Random House UK Limited are natural, recyclable products made from wood grown in sustainable forests. The manufacturing processes conform to the environmental regulations of the country of origin

Phototypeset in 10/12.5pt Century by Intype London Ltd
Printed and bound in Great Britain by
Cox and Wyman Ltd, Reading, Berkshire.

ISBN 0 7493 2434 1

Prologue

The women were in the garden: Rose where the clematis grabbed at every purchase; Veronica beneath the spreading hawthorn.

Would they begin to smell soon, from their makeshift graves? And Annette was still out there somewhere with an unforgiving look on her face.

Lara stared out at incipient summer. Through the fumy city dusk she could see vigorous dark-leaved cottage geraniums springing from their shared bed. The newly planted busy Lizzies. The sharp shovel leaves of the hollyhocks.

How well would nature cover up for her?

And for how long?

The murder of men and women by men was a common or garden crime; the murder of men by women increasingly well understood. But for a woman to be in possession of a woman's body (a dead one, at least) . . . now there was an abomination against all personkind.

Lara sniffed experimentally, hardly daring to smell. The air in her nostrils was a cocktail of diesel and clammy day, black dust and an entirely misleading ordinariness.

So she went inside. In her kitchen overlooking the garden plot, she brewed a cup of herb tea, and calmly consulted the Encyclopaedia of British Plants and Flowers *for expected growth rates of ground cover.*

As if nothing had happened.

Certainly nothing in Lara's previously well-ordered and cautious life had prepared her for this. The past few months had, in so many ways, been nothing to do with her, or so she felt. But then, she was not the ideal woman; she had never come close. That was why Will had gone, wasn't it?

As Lara sat over her purifying weed tea, a persistent ache in her lower back attested to the hard physical labour of burial.

How much had other people sensed, even before the deed? How much that was buried in her own nature, that had made the others come to her?

And, more importantly, how much had Mrs Allbright seen? Mrs Allbright, in the moonlight, pressing her billowing jowls to the window-pane above the scene of the crime, how long had she been there?

As Lara straightened up from the last body, Mrs Allbright, behind the glass, was an eerie deformation in a formaldehyde jar.

Rags of cloud tattered across the two-thirds moon.

Her elderly upstairs neighbour raked up the sash window on the first floor. 'Is someone there?'

Silence.

'Who's down there? What's going on?'

Lara cursed inwardly.

'I can see you – down by the bushes!' called Mrs Allbright sharply.

Lara stepped forward.

'Lara?'

'Ye-e-s. It's only me.'

A sigh of long-suffering exasperation. 'Well, what on earth . . .? What are you doing down there in the dark?'

'I . . . er . . .'

Large as life Annette lay outstretched on the plot, her

plump body silvered by the stars and sprinkled with glittering drops of rainwater.

Lara jutted her face up to the cold ball in the sky and closed her eyes.

'We're moonbathing,' she called up.

'Moonbathing . . .?' said Mrs Allbright.

'Coming out of the sun. Sunbathing's too dangerous now. You can't spend too long in the sunlight these days. It does you no good . . . you achieve much better results in the dark, this way . . .'

'There's a thing! Although I can't see how that would work . . . have you tried it before?

'Well . . . a bit.'

'Does it work then?'

'I think it might this time, for me,' said Lara.

The Moonbathers
I

1 The Ideal Woman

All her life, it seemed, Lara Noe had been striving to be good enough: a trouble-free daughter, loyal partner, trustworthy worker and Wonderbra feminist. All her life so far, that was.

Because there came a point when Lara Noe realised that virtue and values were no good to her. When she looked around it was plain to see: her life was in shreds because she had never dared to be bad enough.

The moment of realisation snatched away all her certainties with the swiftness of a terrible accident.

'It's true!' she hissed to the woman whose stomach bulged in protest against a straight beige skirt. And that blouse was too hideous for words.

The woman gave Lara a disgusted look.

You've done this, it's all your rotten fault and I hate you for it, the look said. Where's your self-control?

The skirt fell to the floor and was kicked into the pile. The blouse followed. Brown hair (style overdue for overhaul), then desperate eyes, bare of make-up, staring brown eyes, red rimmed, and finally an inflamed dry patch of skin near the mouth – all this loomed at her as Lara approached the mirror on the wardrobe door and peered inside.

The green dress.

The tan suit with black trim.

The burgundy trouser suit.

The khaki jacket, never worn.

The clothes which hung in the wardrobe, the clothes folded on the shelves, the less likely ones pushed on to the top space above the rail, and even the garments consigned to the muddle of shoes in the bottom, these all disappeared into a scowl as the mirror swung back. None of them would do.

In the glass, the woman Lara would rather have had nothing whatsoever to do with at this moment was showing signs of battle fatigue. Her hair, once so expensively styled, hung like hanks of horse bristle. Her face, blotchy with effort now, emerged clashing, from a red striped shirt.

The stand-by black had seen better days.

The split skirt was all wrong.

The cream cashmere made her look like a lumpy polar bear.

Lara looked at the clock on her bedside table: just after nine thirty. She wouldn't get to the office until gone ten now and she had nothing to wear.

Across the room stood another wardrobe.

Lara opened it and stared in at the striped shirts and silk ties, cord trousers and jackets, and the row of dark suits. Why had he left them anyway? To keep her in a state of uncertainty? If so, then she should hack his clothes to pieces!

She did not.

Not for Lara the ripping madness of the abandoned lover, the glorious voodoo surgery on his suits, the gleeful recitations. Lara was a good woman.

It would be a crime. Or perhaps she feared his anger, should he return.

But she stared at the possibility.

Then she pulled herself together.

The wood could do with a polish, she thought. Amazing, the amount of dust which could accumulate in two weeks.

Back to the pile.

The pile of clothes on the floor, I mean, not me, thought Lara. I am an independent woman of satisfactory means. I have intelligence and a career – an interesting career, even – and I am more than capable of standing on my own two feet. I do not need a man as a prop. I am taking control of my life on my own. I have lost five pounds in the last fortnight.

And when I am dressed up properly, I can look extremely attractive. I can!

She reached into the wardrobe. The stand-by black would have to do.

The pang came when she had slapped on her make-up and was brushing her hair. It fell straight to her shoulders, then curled up irresistibly in a fashionable fifties flick that said Hi-Honey-I'm-Home!

Was thirty-four so very old to start again?

She slammed the front door and struck out towards the underground station. Another kind of anger caught at her throat as she confronted, yet again, the space on the street where her car should have been parked. That had disappeared a week ago, simply vaporised between dusk and dawn. Just when she needed some constant in her life she could rely on.

The police had trotted out all the usual platitudes, but it didn't seem they would be putting out too many calls to track down a two-year-old Metro with a nice pair of boots in the back and a selection of George Michael tapes.

Bloody London.

It was sod's law that Lara had only just shelled out for a new car stereo after the old one had gone a month before in a shower of glass.

9

Righteous annoyance propelled her on to the tube at Victoria.

In the four years she had worked for *Reflections* magazine, Lara had never felt comfortable with the lift. It rose with a powerful surge, then fell back with a lurch on to the twenty-second floor, where the landing place seemed to buckle and roll under her elastic legs until she was some way beyond the swing-doors marked 'Editorial'. To suppress the feeling that she had begun her day with a bungee jump in reverse, she would invariably look straight ahead and fix a smile.

Level with her gaze each morning was a row of perfect cover girls in frames.

Lara knew from first-hand experience that not even Linda Evangelista looked like the Linda Evangelista on the cover of a magazine, but that never seemed to help one bit.

Reflections magazine was produced in a tower by the Thames that needed expensive upkeep – like so many of the images it purveyed. The corridors to its offices had an insubstantial, impermanent look. Dated synthethic walls were hidden behind cardboard boxes, dog-eared designer-label carrier bags and grimy fingerprinted old in- and out-trays. Inside, the maze of partitions was sand-bagged everywhere with posters and glossy covers and plans and layouts and lead time schedules. Press releases dripped from trays above open desk drawers. Inevitably, there were clothes draped over racks and slung over chairs in defeated layers. In short, the offices of the Thinking Woman's Magazine had all the sophistication of the bedroom of a fourteen-year-old girl.

It was a place where women spoke in low, tense voices of the struggle to reflect what would be happening at the end of a three-month lead time. Outside and far away, war and famine may have raged, but at the cutting edge of the style agenda, the big question was whether basket-weave heels would last until June.

After four years, Lara could have told them it hardly mattered.

In her files, she already had four articles about 'Springing into Spring', three on the theme of 'Preparing for the Season', at least three on 'Daring to be Yourself'. And if in doubt, the nautical look was back.

Lara sat down behind a partition at her desk, trying to pretend everything was normal.

Among the stack of features in Lara's cuttings file were:

'Get in Step with the Times!' (This from the current April issue, out 10 March.)

'What Do You Think You Look Like? What your image says about you . . .'

'Interior Design: Remake your body from the inside out!'

'Result Wear: Get the clothes you need to suceed!'

And now Ella the editor had commissioned 'Take That Risk!' which, in Ella's book, probably meant wearing a colour other than black, brown or beige.

Lara shifted uncomfortably in her swivel chair and sensed that she was part of some great happiness embargo inflicted on the nation's women. Why not give it to them straight?

'Improve, You Slob!'

'Get Skinny: Unsightly fat is an affront to designer clothing.'

'Get Happy: If not, bloody pretend!'

'Get a New Life: Cheat and lie and manipulate like everyone else, sucker.'

But then Lara had always decided not to take the risk, of course.

The position of features editor had gone to someone else two months ago.

*

11

As editor of the 'Metropolis' column (her other monthly curse), Lara had her finger on the pulse of the capital's shopping news. That was the idea, anyway. In truth, she was a processor of press releases and favours: which exciting store was opening now, who was making hand-made shoes, where to see unaffordable antiques, where to gaze faintly outraged at the prices and pretensions on show at certain Mayfair galleries.

Other people had done their tour of duty with 'Metropolis' and then handed it on to the next reluctant guardian, but Lara was good at it. She was so good at jazzing up the bits and pieces that were sent in that she had never been allowed to shake it off. Not for the first time she pondered the wisdom of trying her best, no matter what.

She sifted through a pile of material but a theme for the column in hand eluded her.

A nationality?

A colour?

P-lease.

Waifs and strays?

Crime and punishment. Now that was more her mood these days.

The quest to give the nineties a recognisable identity was over half a decade old and going through a more-than-usually silly phase. That morning the newspapers, to which she had turned for inspiration, were full of thin elongated things – allegedly models for the rest of womankind – wearing schoolgirl kitsch and weighted down by satchels. It was as if the grown-ups were throwing up their arms and begging to be allowed to start again.

And here, right on cue, was Tigi – Antigone Kerslake, deputy fashion assistant and all of twenty-six years old – *actually wearing her hair in bunches.*

'I've got something for you, Lara,' she said, marching

on the 'Metropolis' desk until Lara could see she had completed the look with white ankle socks.

'Yeah?'

Tigi held up a rope noose.

'God, do I look that miserable?'

'Eh?'

'Nothing. Er, thanks Tigi. What is it?'

'What? Haven't you see the new Longlon collection?'

Lara shrugged. 'Nope.'

'It's Raff Longlon.'

'And?'

Tigi shook her head in evident despair. 'It's a belt. It's *the* belt!'

'Ah. Naturally.'

'Of course. That's the thing – everything is absolutely natural this season. Their PR gave it to me for you, as a thank-you for the plug in last month's "Metropolis".' The deputy fashion assistant appeared loath to hand over this object of desire.

This was a thank-you? Lara wondered what she might have been sent if the fashion house had taken against her comments.

'Mmm. "Metropolis" turned out to be more tactful last month than I'd intended,' she said. 'My less-than-complimentary comments about those less-than-fabulous sheep-blanket jackets and dried conker buttons didn't survive the first reading in Ella's office.'

Tigi bridled.

'Not that that was the worst of it,' went on Lara. 'That accolade must surely go to the string-bag cardigans and the hospital gowns – no, wait . . . the strait-jackets. Which leads one to the only possible question: Where *could* one get *those*? Every fashionable reader should have one.'

'Really? Whose were they?'

'I was being funny,' said Lara.

'Oh.'

13

'Have you ever thought that we could do with a few injections of humour around here? Yes . . . like collagen injections. Goodness, we'd have people hitting each other with bags – queueing up to get the latest joke . . .'

Lara stopped. Tigi was questioning her sanity with a look.

'I don't think . . . I heard Ella told . . . someone . . . that *Reflections* doesn't do funny.'

'That's what she thinks,' said Lara grimly.

Lara brooded on her mounting dissatisfaction over a cup of coffee. Percolated Colombian failed to hit the spot – until, that is, she caught the rim of the plastic cup and sent the liquid streaking over a contact sheet of photographs. She watched the spreading brown mess quite dispassionately.

Since when had her unhappiness spilled over into every aspect of her life? Work was supposed to be the great saviour of the broken-hearted, wasn't it? This was the time when she would channel all her energies into her job, leaving no time for negative thoughts and emerging confident and triumphantly renewed. Wasn't it?

Why, even a style bible like *Reflections* knew that was the answer – as well as preaching the acquisition of lots of expensive new clothes, of course!

But then . . . If Lara was honest (and she always tried to be), maybe she had stopped believing all she wrote a while ago. However great it looked on the page thanks to the new art director, what they produced was so much fluff and nonsense. Then again, why should that matter? Fluff and nonsense cheered everyone up, didn't it? That was what she had always believed, anyhow.

Sometimes Lara caught herself wondering what exactly had happened in the last decade or so which had made it unsafe to believe in anything – anything except the definition of the self, that was. And then again, was this really a facet of the age she lived in or merely a facet of her *own* age? Was it possible that she had reached the stage in life when suppressed cynicism had emerged triumphant over hope and frivolity?

This was the age when women were told they could have it all, whenever they wanted it: worldly success, beauty, men, sex, children. The problem was that some women believed that, while others – perhaps older or wiser – did not.

Lara had believed it once.

Once she had been only too happy to work for *Reflections* magazine. The job gave her a certain glamour and a good salary and elicited envious looks from other women at parties. She was lucky to have it, everyone agreed. And it *was* fun, although not as much so as other people assumed. Most of all, though, it made Will proud of her. That had always been obvious from the way he introduced her to those he wanted to impress. Perhaps, now that she had been forced to twitch this particular cover, it even defined her as the woman he wanted.

'Lah-rah!'

She looked up to find that Ella had succumbed to a shrunken knit.

Give me strength to carry on, prayed Lara, as the editor advanced. It was one thing for an expensively starved middle-aged woman to pulsate with HRT and wear her hair like a shiny black warrior's helmet, but quite another for her to imagine that it gave her the divine right to wear skinny rib.

'*Lah*-rah!' A distinct change of tone indicated that Ella had seen the coffee slick. It dripped hypnotically into a steel waste-bin.

Lara made no effort to save the sheet of photographs. Instead she said, 'Coffee. Coffee brown. That's one we didn't think of.'

The previous week the quest had been on to come up

with new words for brown. A year of brown, and editorial descriptive powers were becoming ever more strained. 'Slate, stone, brick, mud, earth, bay, tan, marron, chestnut, hazel, umber, bronze, berry, nut, fawn, khaki, fox, mink, mole, bear, bambi, dapple, cinnamon, nutmeg, chocolate, twig, roast and rhubarb ... *coffee*,' intoned Lara. She had thought then that it was all cr— ... but had had to bite her tongue. 'I can't believe we never thought of that one.'

The editor had begun to dab ineffectually with the nearest press release. Then she remembered her position and stopped. 'Too late. Black is back.' She gave Lara a look of hard appraisal and produced a fistful of photographs. Lara took in their significance with a cursory shuffle. Most of the pictures featured six-foot supermodels posing as knock-kneed schoolgirls on some fashion-show runway.

'Milan,' said Ella.

'They cannot be serious,' said Lara.

Ella's look said they were.

'Most of this will never get into production,' sighed Lara.

'It's directional. What does it *say*?'

'I think it says it all,' said Lara.

'*Right*,' said Ella.

Lara stayed silent and waited, fixated by the way that the editor's dark brown lipstick seemed to make strange slime of her mouth.

Ella was having an affair with the publisher, so illicit that only eighty per cent of the magazine company knew about it. She was into one-upwomanship, even if that did necessitate performing unspeakable practices (or so the gossips had it) in the Strand Palace Hotel with a man who looked like a hammerhead shark. He *did*. His head was an odd blunt shape: it looked as if it had received a heavy blow with some industrial press and never been treated. But it was the curious pitted grey blubbery skin that did it. That and the small sharp teeth which he bared in a smile that was too wide.

So, Ella ... as an ambitious woman in the media what attracted you to the millionaire publisher Martin Skelton, the most powerful man at Incorporated Magazines?

'I want you to do the Hyper Red show this afternoon. Three o'clock at that place off the Brompton Road. Then a round-up of London shops: where to buy the nearest approximations, and as many special offers as you can charm out of them.' The editor laid special emphasis on the word 'charm'.

Lara took an audible breath.

'Lah-rah, I really don't know what's got into you these last weeks, dear. But do us all a favour. Get it out, will you, eh?'

There was a heavy pause.

The hammerhead shark ... does he bite?

Then, looking Ella straight in the eye, Lara said carefully and evenly, 'You're right. We should blaze the trail, inspire women with the knowledge of all that is possible, even if, in this instance, it looks very much as if we're advocating gym knickers and the threat of detention. It's our job to assimilate it all and think about where it's leading and what it all means.'

Ella actually looked relieved. 'That's the spirit,' she said, without a trace of irony.

That afternoon the Hyper Red fashion show lived up to all expectations. It was a carnival of the absurd, not that anyone else seemed to have realised.

At a minute to three Lara took her seat. From her prime place in the front row she felt the heat of white lights. *Reflections* always demanded an unobstructed view. Sometimes they got it, sometimes not.

Women in black and brown lined the catwalk, twittering aggressively like rows of vicious birds on telegraph lines. The one next to Lara finished squawking into a Nokia phone and snapped it away. She flinched when Lara took out a large bar of chocolate, broke off a chunk *and actually ate it*.

Lara waved Fruit and Nut vaguely towards the stage. 'What's this?' she asked, meaning the action about to begin.

The woman tapped her press pack. 'This is all about lips. *Frosted* lips. For the autumn.' Her voice was chilly.

Lara licked her own lips and ate some more chocolate. Then the real show began.

Creatures from another planet – long, long, etiolated strings of woman – picked their way down the glossy white runway. They were fragile stalks wrapped in dazzling colours: vibrant orange, peacock blue, violet, peony. They swayed in a rock beat so hard it seemed it would blow them off course.

Lara watched from miles away as pantomime dames and elves and witches and spacemen came on parade.

And then it advanced towards Lara. The fashion statement to silence all the rest.

It glinted first in the arc lights, so that she looked again.

The model wore ethereal grey. Her mouth was dropped open and in the void was a vertical steel pin holding the pale lips three inches apart. She advanced in a state of steel-clamped trauma to a rustle of excitement in the audience.

It looked to Lara, stock-still in her seat, as if the shining pin propped up the roof of the girl's mouth after cruel surgery. In expression, she was the living embodiment of Edvard Munch's painting *The Scream*.

The other women in their sharp black suits did not react as Lara wished she could. A few sisterly screams of derision would have been all she needed to encourage her. But no. All around hands flew but it was not to incredulous mouths. Their pens moved frantically on the pages of notebooks.

Afterwards Lara asked the designer, 'Why?'

It was to recreate the face of death in disasters, he told her.

As a symbol, Lara found she could not improve on that. The noise reached a pitch all around her in the room. Mainly it came from the mouths of shorter women in black and brown. They fussed around bright maypole women and fought over the men who had dressed them.

Lara stood back and watched them: moths butting at flames.

A rival at *Vogue* looked at Lara's dress in passing. 'Oh dear . . .' She smirked, and was gone.

Funnily enough, it didn't upset Lara as much as it might have done.

These past few weeks . . . it was as though lightning had struck, illuminating the dark so it was clear to see. Was she herself still one of these women who were running scared that they would be judged by the clothes on their backs and be found wanting?

So she stood there and wondered some more.

The backstage area was full of cigarette smoke; these women did not eat, they puffed away their appetites on Marlboro Lights. For the most part, the bright catwalk clothes had disappeared in favour of baggy cardigans.

Through the melee, Lara could see a famous photographer giving the full treatment to the tallest and blondest newcomer. She couldn't have been older than seventeen. She couldn't have weighed more than seven stone. Gerry Day, fashion iconograper and professional sixties survivor, sprawled even as he stood. Beside him was a slight woman, in her forties, wrapped in a shawl of glorious colours.

The shawl drew Lara's eye. It was an ethnic weave of

blues and golds and oranges. Above it was a sweet lined face which smiled brightly – perhaps too brightly – at the girl.

Day paid no attention to the older woman.

Lara battled with her malaise, pitting disinterest against a possible story and an empty notebook. On heavy legs she went over to the little group.

'Lara Noe, from *Reflections* magazine,' she said. She regretted her move immediately.

'I know who you are,' said Gerry Day. His head, too big for his body, was a great pig's head on a platter, jaw stoppered with an apple. He was eating some model's lunch.

Lara smiled at the model and then at the older woman. 'That's a beautiful shawl,' she said pointedly.

Then, as no reciprocal introductions were forthcoming, the woman added, 'I'm Penny. Gerry's wife.'

'Trouble and strife,' said Day, as Lara had known he would.

Her clothes grew limp in embarrassment under his gaze. He was staring for longer than was strictly necessary to workout that she was six months behind the times and therefore a person to be treated with caution.

'*Reflections*. I've got an idea for you,' he said at last.

He led her away.

After many pleasantries, during which she wondered what Day was after, Lara asked, 'Who's the blonde model, by the way, the one you were talking to?'

'Name's Agnetha something.'

'Scandinavian?'

'Somewhere east of Oxford Street.'

Lara kept her patience. 'Tell me about her.'

'Scrubber.'

Out of all proportion to the situation, Lara felt a surge of fury which took her aback. Under normal circumstances she would have given up then and walked away, her head ringing with what she should have said.

But for once, she did not. To hell with her usual deference – the man had just proved what a self-important little git he really was. A shocking wave of boldness overcame her. She looked him straight in the eye and said, 'The models in all your really famous pictures, the ones you were taking back in the sixties . . .' (Was the put-down too subtle?) 'Did they really look like that?'

He didn't get it.

All around the room, head and shoulders above the fashion folk, there were huge painted eyes and jutting cheek-bones and fantastical hair and perfectly powdered backs.

'Do you ever feel *responsible* for women beating themselves up to look like one of the models – models that *you* think of as scrubbers?' asked Lara.

'Sorry,' he said, 'I just take the pictures, that's all.'

And only a man, frowned Lara, would have said that.

'It *ought* to be all, but it's not,' she snapped.

For hours afterwards she wondered how it started. And how she should have handled what happened next.

'You need to relax more,' said Day, moving towards her. 'You seem uncomfortable.'

'Not particularly,' lied Lara. 'You haven't answered my question.'

They had been standing in front of a screen on which was hung the running order of the show. Photographs of models were matched with designs and fabric samples to aid the dressers. It was only when the face of Agnetha came round for the third time, that she realised what was going on.

Scamper, scamper went Day's surprisingly small feet towards her. 'There's something about you . . . I can get very turned on by aggressive lady interviewers . . .'

21

Lara was reversing deftly, keeping the distance between them. He approached again.

Ridiculously Lara kept going, unsure how to stop – until Day was chasing her around the table. Violets and yellows and greens in the fabric swatches swirled past – and then once again.

'You're full of it, aren't you?' panted Lara.

'I think we understand each other.' The photographer ran a slug tongue over his protruberant bottom lip.

Lara was sure they did not. Even as she backed away she was mesmerised by the succulent redness of that lip which had pressed itself (everyone knew) against so much icon flesh. By the time they went round again she could see the glisten of a saliva trail down his chin.

He lunged in a parodic pass. One pudgy hand squeezed the seat of her black dress while the other reached for her neck.

Lara gasped – and slapped him off hard.

Neither of them made any attempt to retrieve the interview.

Day was singularly unrepentant. 'You can't come in here, looking like that . . . and not expect me to react.'

'Looking like *what*?'

'All sorry for yourself – that dress. Staring at me. Begging for it!'

'Wha-a-t?'

'You women . . .' he said out loud, leaving his hooded eyes and scruffy brows to go on: *I know what you want, all of you.*

Lara turned to him, full on. 'You know . . . *fuck*,' she said.

Then she walked out. Outside there was a clash of horns and gesticulations as she ran out into the traffic to hail a cab which was bearing down on her. Lara gave back as good as she got with two fingers.

The taxi sailed past.

Rain had fallen on the dim pavements outside. But the only rainbow out here was a spill of petrol coiled around a drain on the Old Brompton Road.

The supermarket where Lara might once have shopped for dinner for two was expensive and nasty even by Pimlico standards. It gave her pleasure to pass by the ageing aubergines and escalopes and herbs without the faintest compulsion to buy. She bought another large bar of chocolate and a tub of Rocky Road ice-cream, and put them in the largest and tackiest cardboard box she could find in the pile by the door. The slogan on its side might have been an omen: 'Orzal Bleach, For All Your Cleaning Needs'.

A five-minute stomp and she was home.

The garden square at this time of year was still all pustullant grey branches and wind-lashed evergreens. Trees of some kind that Lara couldn't name. (She hadn't as yet become seriously interested in gardening.) And opposite was the blank stare of tall white terraced houses, almost all divided into flats like this one, their windows lit up randomly in the dusk.

Strange, she thought, that Eccleston Square felt like home for the first time.

She cannoned off the walls as the staircase turned downwards. Gracious the house may have looked from the outside, with its brave white frontage and portico which crumbled into Stilton cheese only in the very dampest patches, but inside the stairs narrowed meanly on their descent to the basement floor.

First the letting agent, and her and Will's subsequent change-of-address cards, had proudly proclaimed it to be the Garden Flat.

Lara let herself in. On the doormat was an airmail letter postmarked Tokyo from her best friend Liv. Liv –

the person Lara always called when the going got tough – had just gone to Japan for two years. Bad timing, Liv.

The flat had been *his* choice, of course.

As had the stripped polished floors. The vermilion and russet and indigo rugs had arrived only after he had left. She had brought them in to mark his leaving, out of a Saturday-afternoon terror of sliding alone into a colourless existence.

There was a large sitting-room with a pleasant-enough marble fireplace and bookcased recesses either side. The selling point of the flat, in fact, which meant that this was as good as it got. The large windows let in light but only helped by the white-painted wall six feet away. The square was certainly out there, but once in the property, this became an article of faith, like the continued existence of Mars or Pluto.

Another door led into a passage which could be crossed by a single stride, and there was the kitchen. From here, a french window opened on to a surprisingly big garden, which might have been a pleasure had it been less of a festering yard. A so-so-sized bedroom and bathroom were two steps down the passage. And that, apart from a deep cupboard inhabited by a frightening gas boiler which wheezed and juddered and shot foul flames like a sick dragon in its lair, was it.

During the two years that she and Will had lived here together, her dreams at night were full of arrivals and departures. Usually the means involved were trains: thundering, steaming great iron locomotives, or unpredictable roller-coaster rides liable to slip away down precipitous slopes with her. This had scared her when she read somewhere that trains in dreams signified death.

It was only recently, while lying awake at dawn, that she had realised that her subconscious had been penetrated by British Rail announcements floating south through the still air from Victoria station, and the dull rumble of carriage wheels.

On the bedroom floor, the morning's abandoned clothes lay like pools of colour on an artist's palette. Some were thick swirls, some lay clashing together in careless strokes. More dripped from a chair. For a moment, Lara gazed at the meltdown of brightness. It was another forgotten facet of living on one's own, the way whatever mess was left in the morning was there untouched in the evening. The best part was that there was no one else's either.

Lara scooped up the clothes and dumped them in the bleach box.

She would decide what to do with them later, however much later it took.

2   Subversion Blues

The clothes thing happened again the next morning, but
Lara managed to struggle into a Chinese-look jacket and
ignore the unsettling implications. For a woman who was
supposed to know who Rei Kawakubo was, and what's
more *care* about the effect of this designer's weird
Japanese deconstructionist creations on the Comme des
Garçons collection, this wardobe problem was nothing
less then culturally subversive.

When she arrived at work there was a message on her
desk from Ella:

> *Gerry Day has retro exhibition in June (see press
> release) – sat next to him at dinner at Coast party last
> night and promised him we'd do a pre-piece – Metrop-
> olis? Can you get round to his studio in Kensington at
> 4 p.m. today? Annie has the details.*
> *E.*
> *PS He asked for you!! Get him talking about the
> models in his life.*

Great, thought Lara, just great. She sets me up with a
famous fashion photographer, on the day I look like
a Maoist revolutionary. And the day after he tries to grope
me. What was he after – another slap?

The morning's first press release had a refreshing lack of

false bonhomie. 'GET MEAN,' it said. 'And you *will* get even.'

'Ouch,' breathed Lara. Blood oozed from a finger. She had cut it on the paper's serrated edge. That was a low trick to gain attention.

What *was* this? First the noose belt, then proactive post . . . Since when was getting shop addresses right for the Metropolis column 'The Year of Living Dangerously'?

She read while sucking the wound:

Terminally Nice is a syndrome which wrecks more lives than alcoholism!
Sufferers live with FEAR and TERROR of saying NO.
Sufferers feel POWERLESS as they watch others with fewer SCRUPLES surge toward their goals.
But the good news for TN sufferers is that they can learn a little
CONSTRUCTIVE NASTINESS.
They can FIGHT BACK!

It was a flyer for a group workshop session of the kind Lara would have imagined catered for displaced American executives and a certain breed of angry London housewife.

That was what Lara *would* have imagined, because now, all of a sudden, as she was half-way to throwing it in the bin, she was thinking it didn't sound such a bad idea after all.

She paused, hand in mid-air.

It was certainly more interesting than the heated dispute raging at the other side of the room between the editor and the diet correspondent over the beauty department's annual exhortation: 'Slim for Summer: It's Not Too Late'. Or as Lara had come to think of it, 'July's Guilt Trip Special'.

Face it, it was a *hell* of a lot more interesting.

And what if—?

27

Lara drummed her fingers in a tattoo on the edge of her desk. It left a little smudge of blood.

'Hi, Lara. Just the person.'

It was Annie with her interview instructions. She waved a sheet of paper feathered with yellow Post-its.

'Uh-oh, it's the features editor,' mocked Lara. 'Coming to chase me up.'

OK, so Lara had been passed over for the job even though she was the obvious choice, and Annie had got it. But Annie was a friend, as far as colleagues went, so where did that leave Lara? Being nice about it, that's where. Even though she had been at *Reflections* longer and more conscientiously. Even though she knew full well that Annie had enhanced her CV beyond the bounds of fair play. Lara had had other worries at the time, what with Will acting up and all that. She didn't see any way round it now; she had missed her chance to put her case.

Annie grinned.

'Gerry Day,' sighed Lara, signalling surrender.

'You've got it.'

'Resistance is useless, I suppose?'

'Utterly. Ella is taking Bruce Oldfield to lunch and is on a self-importance kick. Quite apart from the fact that she's desperate – *desperate* – to get Day to do her editor's portrait for next to nothing,' warned Annie. 'And in kindly light . . .'

'Hell.'

The features editor pouted conspiratorially. 'What's up?'

Lara bit her lip. 'I am having another Bad Clothes Day and I've realised something,' she said. 'There is no point in being good.'

'No?'

'Absolutely not. All my life I have been striving to be good. Made dogged advancement – or so I thought – by being careful and pleasant and clever, and playing the game and modestly proffering ideas . . . and look what it's got me.'

'A wardrobe full of bad clothes?'

'It's symptomatic,' said Lara.

Annie looked around quickly and twitched a grin. She was all baby curls and softness in the latest pink. Even her perky steel-rimmed glasses seemed soft on her powdery heart-shaped face.

'I live in a state of terror,' went on Lara, 'that I will never be good enough.'

'Good enough for what?'

'That's just it. I have no idea.'

'This,' said Annie, 'is a subversive conversation.'

Lara nodded.

'Want to resume over lunch?'

The wine bar (SE1 macho) was the kind of lunch-time venue where men went to be the men they would have liked to be. It was where Lara and Annie held their 'subversive conversations' in a spirit of truancy from what their women readers might have liked them to be. On a noticeboard over the pine-panelled dado was tacked a large Xerox of an advertisement: 'For Sale. Complete *Encyclopaedia Britannica* no longer required. Bloody wife knows everything.'

For some reason, it always made them smile.

Annie resumed without preamble. 'Is this about that bastard again? Have you heard from him?'

Lara shook her head. 'Nothing to do with him. It's over.'

Silence and a look.

'It *is*. You know, it was when I caught myself humming. It was ages ago, but that's when I knew.'

'Humming?'

'Yes,' said Lara. 'It was always the same song: "The Party's Over Now".'

Annie smiled.

'I've decided that this is my chance for a fresh start, and the more I look around me the more I see that I have to wise up first.'

'I see.'

'It's nothing more than a vague feeling, but I sense that something is seriously wrong with the way I have been looking at things. Don't ask to me elaborate. It's something I *feel*. It's something to do with finally realising that virtue is not its own reward.'

'Phew,' said Annie. 'It's taken you a while.'

Lara raised her hands. 'I was in the Girl Guides. They have a lot to answer for.'

'Especially that uniform.'

'I'm serious. I don't think I'm any good at all this any more. Maybe I never was.'

'But you *were* good. You *are* good.'

'Of course. But in the way you mean it, that counts for nothing, I'm afraid,' said Lara. 'You mean that I can produce the goods with a bit of imagination and without cocking up and on time, and I get on with it without making waves around the office.'

They exchanged an empathetic smile. Neither was going to admit what this was really about.

'Would be nice if more people were like you,' said Annie.

'And there you have it . . .'

'Uh?'

'Why should I carry on quietly—'

'Not that quietly . . .'

'I only moan to you.'

'You're being remarkably calm about this.'

Lara shrugged. 'It's very simple. I've decided to stop being everything that is expected of me. The nice one.'

She dug into a mixed grill, something that a month ago she would no more have ordered than a pint of stout.

Annie gazed at her with indulgent concern. Then she grinned. 'Hey – who said you were so nice?'

A weak smile.

'Of course I only know what a bastard Will is from what you've told me about him. In the nicest possible way, naturally.'

Lara chewed more meat, then said, 'Who cares? I've told you. I don't want him back. I've taken a step away from all that in the past few weeks, and I've seen rather more than I let myself before. Like how long it had been going wrong . . .'

'You have seen the secrets of your soul in your wardrobe mirror, you mean,' laughed Annie. 'Now that might not be a bad feature.'

'You are entirely wrong,' said Lara, with a fierce glare, 'if you think I'm not serious. And to start with, I'm not bloody doing Gerry Day. Get someone else to glorify that . . . that sleaze ball.'

Lara had loved clothes, even as a small girl.

In the anxious suburbs where life was regulated by train timetables, where the trees between the paving stones sprouted and then lost their leaves again, and the householders yearned for spring, then summer, then, tired of watering gardens, began to wait for winter, Lara's green life was gaudy with home-made clothes.

Often, these days, when she thought of her mother, the picture which popped up was of a woman smiling above ripples of colour. Either she would be kneeling before a pool of her favourite greens and turquoises, laying paper patterns on the fabric, mouth metallic and whiskered with pins, or churning at the Singer sewing machine above a cascade of jaunty blooms.

Every garment her mother made was beautifully hand finished.

'What does it matter that you can't see the stitches, they're on the inside!' Lara would say. 'No one can see them.'

31

'*You* would know,' her mother replied. 'And *I* would know. And if a thing's worth doing, it's worth doing properly.'

Lara had hairbands to match her summer dresses.

Her mother had urged her towards the sensible option.

Naturally Lara had resisted. 'I went to university – I have a degree in European literature! Why on earth would I want to do a secretarial course?'

Her mother had looked up then from some complicated cross stitchery. 'And what do you want to do, Lara, apart from read books?'

Well, that was just it. With no clear idea how to go about doing the right thing, armed only with negative feelings and gut reaction, what would she do?

At the end of six months, she graduated top of her secretarial course. Even now, Lara Noe could command a hundred words a minute shorthand. Her mother's good sense had prevailed. If a thing was worth doing, it was worth doing properly.

It took her through an insurance office; a shipping brokerage; an advertising agency (very temporary, that one); a small publishing company (even more so); to a weekly woman's magazine.

Of course, the secretarial course was a great advantage. No one had ever wanted to know whether she had actually read Balzac in the original (she had, *avec grand dictionnaire*) or in translation like everyone else, because – now as then – it simply made no odds to anyone but her.

Her mother had loved the idea of a fashion magazine – how could she not?

Lara had come to hate talking about it.

She kept her head down at work for the rest of the afternoon. At three fifteen she left the office – and went home early.

*

Her feelings about the state of the world were reinforced by the early-evening news on television.

Pictures flicked to pictures. The convicted burglar had a mouthful of teeth that looked as though squatters had moved in – he had been awarded compensation for injury after being set upon by the householder he had tried to rob. Several government ministers were skidding on lies they had spread, and a famous prison had been praised by a government inspectorate, said the newsreader, 'for the constructive and professional relationship between prison officers and inmates'. So, thought Lara, even convicted offenders are now accorded respect as professionals.

That became even more apparent when the main documentary that night was an unctuous affair detailing the heroics of the gangster underworld. 'I mean, you were as big as the Beatles, back then,' said the man with the microphone, positively drooling.

Lara pressed a switch and consigned him to a rectangle of blackness.

On the Conran table by the arm of the sofa was Icarus: a lamp on a gilded wooden stem from which spread gunmetal wings beneath a shade made of pheasant feathers. She had found it in a shop in Venice, years ago, and knew that she could not leave Italy without it. Unfortunately Will's opinion of it was not quite so positive. It had only just come out of its box. Decisively, she clicked its light off now too.

Then she went into the bedroom and glared into the bleak depths of her wardrobe. On the floor next to it was the bleach box containing the proven failures. She ran her hand along the hangers on the rail, gave the unappealing clothes a cursory appraisal, and bundled some of them into the box. Then she stomped out of the flat and went upstairs.

*

Lara knocked on the door of the top-floor flat. The white paint was black with scuff marks towards the bottom of the door. It was a front door which belonged to a busy person who always had her hands full and had to kick her way in.

'Any good to you?' she asked, pushing her burden at the woman in saggy leggings who answered.

'More?'

Lara shrugged. The woman – Val – accepted the box graciously.

'How's it going?'

'I'm tired,' said Val. 'I'm always tired when I'm resting. And it's Thursday.'

'Thursday?'

'The *Stage* is out. Which means I can't help but read all about which useless cretins are about to open in which new production I auditioned for.'

For a brief moment, Lara felt a pang of what it must be like to have a so-called glamour job even less appealing than her own. Which was undoubtedly why Val and her husband Sam, now both officially knocking forty, countered the diminishing returns of age in the acting profession with peddling old clothes and pieces of bric-a-brac they called antiques.

'I buy junk. I *sell* antiques,' Val would say. 'But the clothes are bread and butter.'

The clothes aged fast, too, in her temporary care.

They went through into a room festooned with even more old clothes which would soon be transformed into collectors' items, or cleverly packaged as the antiques of the future. Val dumped the box.

'Coffee? Drink?' she asked. Offscreen, she chose the gentle hippy-dippy look which went so well with fine lines on a gamine face. She had once had a well-reviewed part in a Jane Austen adaptation on television and decided to hold on to the mannerisms.

'Not staying, thanks.'

'You OK?'

'Fine,' said Lara. 'Really.'

'It's just that . . . we haven't seen Will around lately . . .'

Lara wondered if her neighbour was fishing as much as it sounded, or whether she already knew for certain. Two years of noncommittal hellos on the steps or in the entrance hall had developed into something approaching friendship during the last month or so. That hardly meant it was time for life histories. 'No,' she said. 'We've split up.'

'Ah,' said Val. 'I did wonder.'

I bet you did, thought Lara. For all I know, you've been trying out my facial expressions in the bathroom mirror. And then she felt mean.

So she said what everyone always said in the circumstances: 'No. It's all right. It hadn't been going well for a while. It's better this way.'

'Bullshit,' said Val.

Lara surprised herself by laughing.

'When did it happen?'

'Oh . . . nearly three weeks ago.'

'Figures,' said Val.

'Sorry?'

'Sam and I were coming home late one night. We couldn't help hearing . . . raised voices.'

'Hmmm . . . sorry. There was a lot of jumping up and down and stamping of feet . . .'

'So we could make out.'

'But, honestly, it's all right. Now. We both know it's over, and that's that. I don't harbour any disturbing thoughts that he might come back.'

'Hmm.'

'Don't look at me like that. I *was* upset, but I went through that and then I suddenly realised that any more moping around feeling sorry for myself would just have been acting up. I'd known for ages. And anyway . . . he's got somewhere else to live – with someone else.'

Val smiled sympathetically. 'It's clear-out time, then.'

'Exactly.'

'A fresh start. Live for yourself for a while.'

'Funny you should say that.' Lara studied her neighbour's expressive grey eyes.

'Still walking and tubing everywhere?' asked Val.

'Uh-huh. It's gone for good. I never realised how much I'd miss that bloody car.'

'No news from the police at all?'

'Nothing.'

'You'll get the insurance.'

'Yeah.' Lara supposed she ought to do something about that. She was still fuming after the fact. Against all reason she was still hoping her car would be found and returned to her. She wanted her wheels back, and her black hat and boots which were behind the driver's seat. She wanted the tapes in the glove compartment. She wanted divine justice that she hadn't replaced the stereo for nothing the previous month. Quite apart from the ransom she had only just paid to Westminster Council for the residents' parking permit.

Bloody bloody London.

'Go on, have a drink,' said Val.

Lara was reassessing the state of the trees in the garden square from the unfamiliar vantage point of someone else's view when Val returned with two glasses of white wine. Lara hadn't noticed her leave the room.

She gathered herself. 'No Sam tonight?' she asked.

'Haven't you seen him? He's thesping again. Got a part in some fringe translation at the Man in the Moon. Opens next week so the company will still be emoting over pints at the bar.'

Thesping, thought Lara. 'Well, cheers to him, then.'

They drank.

'Hey,' said Val, 'have you seen who's moved in across the way?'

This was why she liked talking to Val. 'I thought it was still empty, that flat.'

The bruised little blonde, barely out of her teens and alone – shrilly, sanctimoniously alone – with two tiny children had upped and left in a brand new BMW.

That had made them wonder. As had the unlikely procession of male visitors and the way no two stories of hers had added up to anything but murkiness.

Val shook her head. 'Get this . . . another one with mysterious means.'

Lara bit her lip.

'A Mrs Allbright. Otherwise known as Madame Isadora, Clairvoyant and Spiritual Healer.'

'That's all we need,' said Lara.

'I think it's great news,' said Val. 'If she's any good, I mean.'

'Oh?'

'Well, presumably she wouldn't have moved in if the house was about to fall down, or there was going to be a fire here, or a lightning strike, you know.'

'It's one way of looking at it,' agreed Lara.

'I thought you'd want the bright side,' said Val. 'And you never know . . . she might even be able to tune into your car . . . on one of her wavelengths.'

Lara smiled glumly.

3 Bare-faced Chic

Naturally Ella went ballistic. As the editor of a successful women's magazine in which articles entitled 'Take That Risk: Be yourself' lay cheek by jowl with 'Sheer Perfection in Ten Days', it was entirely predictable that she would retaliate with all the force of the wronged.

'Bad day, bad week – bad *mistake*,' she hissed.

Odd, thought Lara absently, as she stood before the desk in the office with the best view of the Thames, that it had never really registered before how this woman was a person in constant flux. In essence, Ella was a small, dumpy person who was currently shrinking as she did at the onset of every spring before expanding gradually back again throughout the rest of the year.

Blood-red lips were broadcasting this morning's tirade.

'I don't know what you thought you were doing, Lara! If I set up an interview with one of the most important figures in the London fashion world – in the *world* fashion world – then I expect my staff not only to show enthusiasm and gratitude, but to do the job!'

'Oh dear . . .'

'Annie had a *frantic* search to find Tigi somewhere between Joseph and Harvey Nicks. Half the office had to hit the telephones, and the work-experience girl was sent out in a cab. And *then* she had to get Tigi disengaged from Gucci and pacify the Wolford tights people to rush

38

her over there in time to take over when she realised that you hadn't gone!'

Her friend Annie had spared the editor no details, then.

'You simply don't let down a man like Gerry Day! And then I learn what was behind it. Tigi tells me that he told her that you were extremely rude to him the day before yesterday and he is very far from happy about it. Very far indeed! I have had to apologise to him. Thirty years Gerry Day has been in the business, and no one has ever questioned the integrity of his work!'

'Oh, I can't believe that,' said Lara.

The lips were confrontational, clotted and pursed as prunes. 'Shut up,' said Ella. 'Have you any idea what you have done? What did you *think* you were doing, making your personal feelings known like that? I can't imagine what you thought you could possibly achieve! What about the reputation of *Reflections*?'

Lara shrugged, schoolgirl to headmistress. It seemed too obvious to explain.

The editor would not let it drop. 'When a professional of Day's standing agrees to talk to a magazine like *Reflections*, it is because of our good reputation. Our *understanding*. Do I make myself clear? I had to spend *half an hour* on the telephone last night begging to be allowed to apologise for *your* behaviour. It was so . . . *humiliating*! Have you any notion, Lara, of the damage you have done through sheer, momentary pig-headedness?'

Lara hadn't, really.

'You've made him look ridiculous!'

'He *is* ridiculous,' said Lara.

Ella opened her mouth to respond.

A knock at the door came instead.

'Come,' rapped out Ella, with a seminal flash of the eyes which implied she would relish a public flogging, a scenario that was indeed now a logistical possibility with the arrival that morning of the rest of the Noose Collection by Raff Longlon.

A procession of gesticulating black-clad arms and legs followed a man with a photograph.

'It's impossible!' shrieked Dominic the art director, slamming the photograph down on Ella's desk.

'It's fine!' screamed Victoria the fashion director.

'It's obscene!' howled Dominic.

'It's a statement!' yelled Tigi, acid-yellow gymslip riding up as she waved her arms.

'Yes, and what is it saying?' struck back Dominic, stamping his foot.

Victoria stood firm. 'So, as far as you're concerned, underarm hair is a political issue?'

'It's outrageous!'

'ENOUGH!' Ella stood up and dropped an atlas-sized Coco Chanel retrospective on the floor to gain silence. Carefully, she fixed the deputation with a laser look and gave her decree. 'Airbrush time,' she said.

The group, semi-disgruntled, exited right. Pursued by a bare woman, thought Lara, as the offending photograph scudded after them, thrown at the heels of the retreat.

Ella resumed her offensive before the door had slammed. 'I have handwritten a letter of abject apology to Day, Lara, and I would like you to do the same.'

Silence.

'What's got into you, Lara?'

When there was still no reply, she changed the tone of her voice to that of someone used to dealing with petulant children. Apt, in the circumstances. 'Haven't you been having fun with the shops and celebs, Lara? Haven't you enjoyed the opportunities you've had here – and all the beautiful clothes . . .?'

She was waiting for an answer.

'I've had a lot of fun here,' said Lara at last. 'But it was someone else's idea of fun.'

40

'But – the chances I've given you . . .! This is the perfect opportunity – most *normal* women—'

'No,' said Lara. 'I sometimes wonder whether . . . No, I *know* that most normal women aren't like us. They don't snip the buttons off Marks & Spencer jackets and sew on Chanel ones instead. They don't mix different mineral waters and call them cocktails. They don't agonise between shades of cinnamon and nutmeg, mud and sludge. They've given up on perfection. And if they haven't . . . they're doing themselves no good at all.'

That clearly called for an explanation which she was unable to provide.

The editor waited, then asked coldly, 'Have you finished?'

Lara nodded her head sadly. 'The Empress has no clothes, Ella.'

Lara had had enough.

She found Annie and exploded her anger, loose limbed with conviction and startled that it had taken her so long. 'I *told* you I wasn't going to do the Day interview.'

'You're overreacting,' said Annie.

'At least,' said Lara, 'I *am* reacting.'

Annie struggled to look sympathetic.

There didn't seem any point in asking why she hadn't stood up for someone who was supposed to be a friend. 'The problem is,' said Lara instead, 'that it's not terribly relevant, is it?'

Her colleague didn't get it, but then Lara knew that this was never going to be the moment, not with half the office getting off on the drama, and Ella hovering like a swarm of maddened wasps.

'I mean, it's not like any of us are building houses for people, or teaching them . . . or rescuing them from poverty and deprivation, or – or even clothing them . . .'

Annie scratched her head. 'Was it ever supposed to?'

'It doesn't mean anything,' shouted Lara, not caring any longer, 'and yet it's so easy to get caught up with it all, to think that any of this *does* matter. But how does it start? You're frightened of the consequences if you ever stop trying for a moment – because you know what? You might stand still and realise that all you've been doing for years is going round and round in pointless circles!'

Then she calmly walked out to the lift without a word, past the incredulous dropped faces of the faithful, and past the pictures on the wall of the women who were not themselves, and she slid down an artery of the glossy tower to the street below where women had bellies and underarm hair and wore clothes without needing pegs at the back.

She jiggled, rolled and clattered her way home on the Circle line. She was light-headed when she emerged from the station, but she walked home with a growing confidence. When she let herself in, the house sounded – no, felt – empty.

She made herself a coffee and drummed her fingers experimentally on the jam of the kitchen door. She stopped. Silence. It was as if the world had stopped, or so she felt. It was bliss for about twenty minutes.

Then she seemed to come back into herself.

What *had* she done?

'Singularly happy. Single-minded. Singularity. Single,' wrote Lara, cross-legged on the floor of the sitting-room. A tablespoon balanced in the ice-cream tub by her side:

Single life: its attractions and pitfalls:
Living for myself.
Freedom.
Independence.

No dinner to spoil: eating choc biscuits for supper if I want.
No waiting for the sound of his key in the lock – God I *hate* that!!
Stop fretting about the cleaning.

As luck would have it, there was an article about 'Singles Survival' in the current edition of another magazine. Lara, according to a tame psychologist quoted in the feature, was still in a transitional phase, not happy every day, but using this time as an oasis when it was not necessary to bother about the needs of anyone else. 'Making plans is the single most uplifting thing you can do,' urged this professional know-all. 'Start right now by making a list of all the positive benefits of your situation.'

So Lara did:

Listening to old records without fear of ridicule. If I want to listen to a group of old dopeheads going through the desert on a horse with no name, *then I shall*.

No more dirty socks on the floor (unless I want to chuck them there myself).

No more pools of water in the bathroom. [Why do all men claim that bathrooms mop and dry themselves by *evaporation* . . .?]

No more arguments about empty packets left in the fridge, and open packets not put back. [Because none of the rows were really about these transgressions at all.]

No more one-inch heels.

Now that *was* an uplifting thought. Decent heels at last! Will had hated her wearing high heels because Will was somewhat— No, laughed Lara to herself – Will was *short* and at last she could say it: size *did* matter.

It was only when she had put the finishing touches to the list and polished off the ice-cream that it occurred to Lara that walking out of her job was a pretty stupid way to redress the balance for Will's walking out on her. But it still felt good.

She would have liked to talk to Liv. But she doubted that Liv, in Tokyo, in the middle of the night, with two small children and a husband finding his feet in a new job, would want to hear her troubles.

After a while, she thought she would see whether Val was in. Lara climbed the stairs to her door at the top of the house, but there was no answer. As she went back down, past the door which belonged to the exotic new neighbour Val had told her about, she gave a rap on the knocker. She might satisfy her curiosity in the form of offering some small service. But there was not a sound in reply.

Lara was unwilling to examine her motives in seeking out the other women who lived and worked around her. Perhaps at this moment they were less acquaintances than constants, but that was as far as she wanted to push it.

She wondered whether it was always like this on a midweek afternoon with everyone out at work or pursuing their daytime activities.

She would soon find out.

4 Single-mindedness

The morning Lara Noe got up and dared to live defiantly, the sun shone. The ragged winter pansies outstaying their welcome in her window-box were brown and singed by the spring sun. They nodded their heads sadly in a dull wind. A sulphurous light fizzled through the kitchen window and put extra sparkle in her glass of champagne.

Champagne for breakfast? Why not.

From now on, not taking the risk would not be good enough.

For the first time in weeks, she was satisfied when she saw herself in the wardrobe mirror. The black sweater, black jeans and black boots made her feel like a commando on mission.

The problem was, what mission?

If Lara was stripped of all convention – by which she meant the conventions that had kept her meek and striving – then what would she be? She suspected that a simple reversal of all previously held convictions would not, in itself, be enough. There was another dimension, one with its own customs and accepted boundaries of which she knew nothing as yet. It was as if she had woken up in another country where the strangeness grew from superficial similarities.

But she felt the tingle of a new beginning.

She had walked out of her good job because she felt

powerless: powerless against Will and his decision to leave; powerless that this person who had gone had taken with him all her visions of the future; and powerless to remake herself in the image of the perfect independent woman who would now move onwards and upwards.

So she had exercised the one power she did have. She had walked, and soon they would see what they were missing at *Reflections*. If they didn't – well, she hadn't been enjoying herself there any more anyway. It had all become too silly for words.

Or so she rationalised.

Onwards and upwards. Although ... Even as she repeated the words to herself, what she realised all too clearly was that even by having this notion, she was condemning herself yet again to constant struggle.

She stared out at the new day.

What she required now – as a matter of some urgency – could be summed up in one word. *Fearlessness*.

Lara, who had always been grounded by an over-active imagination, was preparing for take-off. She looked beyond the boundaries of the garden fence, higher than the dark prisons of the drain-veined houses beyond that. By a trick of the light, the moon was still visible, white against the morning sky.

She spent the day purposefully by going nowhere, an experience so unusual as to seem entirely new.

'Things must be desperate,' said Lara aloud to her sitting-room the next morning at a time which should have seen her strap-hanging east on the Circle and District line, 'if I am hanging on grimly to the notion that Mars in Scorpio will see me all right.'

She chucked the astrology page of the newspaper over a dirty plate on the floor. Lara was eating again. She must have been. The evidence against her was all around the sitting-room and the kitchen: cellophane bread-bags and buttery smears, crumbs and jars with no tops, half-finished packets of biscuits and chocolate wrappers.

She ran her finger across a knife lying on the arm of the sofa and put her tongue to the glob of redcurrant jelly congealed on the blade.

Sometimes, especially on grey days like this, the heavy security grilles on the windows and doors of the Garden Flat made Lara feel like a privileged prisoner. She lived behind diamonds made of steel. She grappled with the metal and flung open the back door to the garden. She stood on the threshold and said aloud, 'I am free!' and perhaps she even felt it for a fleeting second.

So she said it again, a bit louder.

She breathed deeply, as you were supposed to do in the fresh air. She persevered, and after a while she had a sense of the atmosphere lightening, or maybe it was the cold which stirred the winter fur of her inner tubes as they braced themselves to throw off the bleakness of winter's long drag. Outside, the sharpness was positively tangible, a thin metallic scent of receding chill. A stirring in the air. For perhaps the first time in her life, Lara wondered about the sap and surge of new life.

She strode out into the garden, and kicked around the forlorn yard.

Controlling the garden had been Will's chore, not that he had often risen to his responsibilities. He solved the grass problem (it grew, to his disgust, come what may) by putting down flagstones. Lara, romantically, had favoured the idea of an urban meadow, had suggested sowing poppies and other wild flowers among the waving fronds. His answer to that was a sneer and, some days later, a delivery of old stones from a salvage yard in Camberwell.

She wobbled on one of them now. The slime and grimy moss which gripped and dripped over the stones was like

47

the after-effects of a nasty cold. Chipped and grey, thrown down to suffocate the grass's vigour, the stones lay like a half-hearted mosaic over what had once been the lawn. He hadn't even done the job properly. There was no measurement, no precision, no cement. Under the flag she lifted was compacted brown degeneration and sleepy worms.

She dropped it back.

But she had decided that the scheme suited her purposes. It would be her first positive action.

Positive action – when she was up to it, that was.

She heard the sounds made by the other residents of the building, but she made no effort to contact any of them. The telephone sang to itself as she read and ate and padded around the flat, and the answering machine recorded her callers:

'When are you coming back, Lara? I mean . . . you *are* coming back?' This was Annie's voice, counterpointed by shrill demands which came unmistakably from the editor's office.

'Haven't heard from you for a while, love. Hope you're all right. Give us a ring, will you, when you can?' That was her mother.

'Hi Lara! It's Fi. A group of us are meeting up on Thursday at the New World in Golden Square. Eight o'clock if you can make it. See ya!'

And so on.

At this stage, she fully realised, she was in a state of detachment. Detaching from her family. Separating from every part of herself that had ever sought security. Cutting off from the person they all thought she was, even.

How could they know her, when she didn't even know herself?

All they knew were the parts of her that they thought they understood.

After days when their messages went unanswered, the voices of her friends returned. Now the voices were intense, conspiratorial, worried:

'Lara . . . are you there? Will you pick up the phone, Lara?' That was Mary, a friend from way back.

'Come out . . . you must get out. Would you like to talk? Come on over. There's wine . . . we can have supper. Let's have a long chat about what bastards men are.' Fi again.

'Rang you at work but you weren't there. Is everything OK?' Sue.

Still Lara did not pick up the telephone. She did not want these confiding tones; she could not have endured long nights of confession – their own, naturally. For after Lara's own woes had been examined over the first bottle of Valpolicella, she knew that would lead inexorably to dissection of another woman's relationship with its attendant disappointments.

She did not want their sympathy. She did not want to talk about Will, nor have him the absent guest of honour at a quiet, well-intentioned gathering.

Neither was she ready to launch herself, remade, back into company.

How could she know what to do next, if she didn't even know what she wanted to be?

The half-remembered philosophy seemed ever more apt as she unlocked the french windows and threw them open to the dangerous freshness of the air. Then she went into the garden and got her hands dirty for the first time. *'Maintenant,'* it went, *'il faut cultiver notre jardin.'*

The words played around in her head, settling into her rhythms as she pulled and tugged at dead stems and roots and began to clear the wilderness outside her kitchen window. As she worked – and this was real, physical work – the questions grew more insistent.

Where was Will now, and what was he doing?

Who was the unknown woman who had stopped telephoning – occasionally leaving a number but more often hanging up when Lara answered – now that he had moved out? Had it always been the same woman, even?

Was he with Janey now?

What about Jennifer, the bitch? Was she still busy tipping her poison darts?

And why had Will been whispering on the stairs that time to that little tart who'd just moved out?

In the garden, Lara dug around and turned over what she could: soil and stones; questions and answers. She came no nearer to finding whatever it was she sought.

When Lara thought of Will's final departure (and generally, she tried not to) it induced a feeling of torpid dissatisfaction. There had been no clean break, but months of atmospheric tension relieved by slamming doors. At the end, when the front door had simply never reopened from the other side, the effect was that of a bodged execution, messy and painful although missing, of course, the actual death certificate necessary after the heart has stopped beating.

No, it was a small exit, a slipping away. Perhaps this was due to a fear of sharp knives and damage to property on both sides, but more likely it was a mark of tiredness with the whole business.

Nothing to warrant fireworks.

The void was emphatic. He left no forwarding address, no telephone number. For days afterwards Lara moved through her days like a clockwork toy. She smiled brightly, and sometimes, she even felt she might mean it.

Will, the theoretical, historical Will, that was – for he had come under heavy revisionist scrutiny since the

Great Departure – was an attractive, intelligent, successful man. But if Lara were honest with herself, now she had nothing to lose, she'd had plenty of notice that he was no great long-term prospect.

By which euphemism she meant husband, of course.

They had met at a wedding. Didn't everyone who was unattached at thirty?

Will Radcliffe – she could see ever more clearly – had all the swagger of one who came from a wealthy, perhaps even landed family, but none of the fatalistic resignation which befitted those whose forebears had lost it all again, as indeed his had. The crash of a South American mining company in the thirties had done for them, and what was not already lost was then finished off by a V2 rocket in Chelsea. The tale had a certain glamour, retold in romantic circumstances. In the light of Lara's own background, it positively gleamed with a patina of old gold and jewelled damasks.

His mother's side had had the social connections and a certain amount of old money; his father's the company and the business nous, the latter a legend which survived more or less intact despite the evidence to the contrary when all went to the wall. Will's father, the odd one out, was a painter. He occasionally sold a canvas or two – these were large and vibrant with the reds and oranges of equatorial climes – but there was nothing left in the coffers for him to be able to pursue this wholeheartedly. He taught at Camberwell Art School.

Will talked up the sunny, bohemian aspects, and down the smallish Victorian house on Telegraph Hill (a district most other people called New Cross). He referred to the fact that he had attended the local inner-city comprehensive as if that were merely proof of his enlightened upbringing.

He saw himself, though, as having inherited the golden

touch in business. He took care to dress his achievements with all the right accessories; he knew all the codes of expensive wrist-watches, tables at restaurants, cuts of suits, models of cars. These things mattered to him. They had mattered to Lara, in the beginning.

But it was *this* Will who grated on her nerves now. And perhaps what grated the most was that Will was one of the few impulses on which Lara had ever acted rashly. She had bought the whole shop-window.

Normally, when Lara made a decision she took a long time to mull over what it was she truly wanted, and then, when the conclusion had been painstakingly made, pros counted, cons countered, only then would she make her move, cautiously. Lara's previous boyfriends had been an altogether stabler crew. She was both intrigued by and in awe of Will, amazed and flattered that he could be interested in her.

For three years they were happy, or so she thought.

One of their first arguments was sparked by his late arrival – by some hours – at a dinner party she had been preparing for days. She could not understand how he could have done it to her: the tenterhooks when he was due any minute; the affected nonchalance as the food spoiled; the unvoiced sympathy of the other six guests; and finally the humiliation, mixed with a relief that horrified her, when he eventually appeared at nearly half past ten, drunk and unrepentant.

'How could you *do* that to me?' she sobbed over the sink when the others had departed.

'Come on, Lara . . . it wasn't that bad.'

'What do you mean, not that bad? Why couldn't you have been there when you said you would? Surely that's not too much to ask! If you couldn't come, you could have said so in the beginning!' And so on – and on.

The problem, as would be articulated far better later

on – for there were to be many more contretemps which proceeded along similar lines – was a question of order. Order as opposed to chaos, that was.

'You think that the world can be organised,' said Will, 'whereas I know that it can't be.'

'And *that*,' Lara would spit, 'is extremely convenient for you and your chronic unreliability.'

'There is no universal order. The world is chaos, and as soon as people come to terms with that, the happier they can be,' he would explain, in various ways and guises of excuse. And in varying degrees of annoyance with her annoyance.

And so they went round and round.

Lara prided herself on her perception, especially where people and their motives were concerned. This may have been the result of a childhood misspent in books and long hours alone, or of a terrible insecurity which manifested itself in overwhelming caution. Whatever its origins, it usually held her back.

That was the trouble, Lara found, when you decided to take yourself in hand and go against the grain. Take some actual action. It was profoundly unsettling.

Now she was alone. She would not think about Will. She wouldn't.

The next day, she booked a session at the most subscribed hairdressing salon in the city to kick-start her new image – and then she called and cancelled when she realised what it was she was doing.

What had given her a measure of worth for years had been revealed as meaningless. The goals she had been striving for were part of a game that was not worth playing; she kept score only out of fear of losing. She told herself that, angrily.

Maybe what she had now – for once in her life – were some genuine options.

In a sweater the colour of fury, she launched herself into the grey outdoors. It was mid-morning, a time when she should have been at work, buzzing with coffee and interruptions. She felt like a submarine bobbing to the surface from the ocean floor.

Eccleston Square was still there, as she'd thought it must be. It was bleak, abandoned by everyone but a stray down-and-out in an army-surplus coat. Armoured by her determination she passed through the familiar streets, slid along them, as if transported behind bulletproof glass. Or as if she were seeing everything around her through the lens of a camera. Or watching it on a screen.

Maybe this was what the others felt, those who cared less, those who weren't always striving. Lara felt ungrounded, detached, as if at any moment she might leave the pavement and float away to who knew where.

She reached the noisy dust bowl of Victoria station. People were coming at her from all directions, all cutting their own trajectories across the forecourt. Twice she was bumped, by an arm, by a bag, as she strayed into someone else's line. It was as if she had been up all night drinking or maybe sleeping rough. She was there, but not there.

It wasn't long before the feeling began to panic her. Lara had never liked feeling out of control, had always needed to feel safe.

Maybe that was the key to it all.

Lara had only ever applied the maxim 'Nothing ventured, nothing gained' to the most cautious of steps forward. And here she was on the rise of her giant leap, weighted down by fear.

Days passed after that, and Lara sitting in the flat, felt depression seep into her foundations like an invasion of wet rot. So she switched on the radio. News of an outside world filtered only patchily through the fog in her brain. She was angry with herself now, for wasting all this time – time far beyond this present week of self-indulgence. She had wasted years in which she had achieved nothing: years of being subsumed by desperate anxiety that she might do the wrong thing.

The sugar-pink jacket in the wardrobe was still in its dry-cleaning bag. Lara ripped into the polythene and released it from the transparent chrysalis. It might do. She appraised it critically, extracting a tag of paper from the top pocket. It bore the cleaner's warning legend: 'Chocolate and grease marks'.

So life hadn't been *that* great with Will.

In the end she marched into the bedroom. She threw open his wardrobe and wrenched a suit and jacket from their hangers. Then she went back to her own wardrobe and swept shirts, skirts, sweaters and trousers from the shelves and thrust the lot into two black dustbin bags.

Then, without faltering, she heaved them into the world upstairs and see-sawed down the street, with a grotesque vision of herself as the scales of justice with one balloon of vengeance in each fist. She puffed round a couple of corners, and this time dumped them on Jo.

Jo, with her palour and cheek-bones, was the Dietrich of Tachbrook Street. She ran a second-hand clothes stall in the market in sometime partnership with Val upstairs.

The merchandise on Jo's stall swung above the rotting detritus of other days and other lines of business. Discarded cabbage leaves were veined green rags in the gutter. Small detonations of grape and tomato starred the roadway. The street smelt of potatoes and tobacco and drains and cars and, despite Jo's best efforts, old dust in old clothes.

Ever since Lara had swooped on a gold fifties original, they had chatted over the rows of garments. Some she recognised from Val's handiwork. Others were stiff with age now, like the bodies they had once encased.

If Jo couldn't use them, she'd pass the stuff on to some good cause. Lara suppressed a smile at the thought of one of the down-and-outs who hung around the market – or more particularly, the pub on the corner – soiling Will's pristine Armani jacket.

Jo examined the haul. 'Definitely no more Will, then?'

Lara shrugged and wondered when people would stop asking. 'Looks like it.' Why *had* he left that jacket, anyway – to intimate in language he knew she would understand that he might come back at any moment?

'You look good on it, anyway, you really do. Rather serene,' said Jo. The nails on her long fingers were painted black. They were commas and quote marks in the air, punctuating her conversation as she waved her hands in emphasis.

Lara accepted the compliment.

'I mean, and please take this the right way . . .'

Here we go, thought Lara.

'Less *striving*, somehow. I think it's the clothes.'

Lara looked down at her plain black jeans and white T-shirt under the second-hand suede jacket. 'I can't find anything trendy that I want to wear. I don't know whether it's my mood, or my age – or whether it's permanent or not – but I look around at the shops and the magazines and the advertisements, and it all seems faintly ridiculous.'

'Hmm.'

'Apart from anything, it's a bit awkward in my line of work.'

'I can see that.'

'Not that I'm going in at the moment.'

'You're off sick?'

'I suppose I must be.'

'It could be post-break-up trauma,' counselled Jo.

'Oh, for goodness' sake, I am not a victim. Can't you see? That's part of the problem.'

A slightly perplexed pause.

'Put it this way,' said Lara. 'I haven't got an eating disorder, I just can't stick to a diet. I'm not suffering from a challenged metabolism, I'm just lazy like most of us, given the chance. And I am certain now that there is no way I am ever going to look like a victim of child abuse.'

Jo looked startled, but less at the sentiment than the vehemence of its expression. 'What brought this on?'

'Everything,' said Lara.

It wasn't really to do with bruised Lolitas staring out of every fashion page and fourteen-year-old girls with giraffe bodies made up to look as if they had spent the night shooting up and sleeping rough on the Embankment, although clearly that didn't help one's sense of perspective. Or the sense that men did not like real women very much. Lara recognised all those as the symptoms.

But did the malaise have much, in the end, to do with being left alone and car-less, either?

Jo lent on the railing. 'It must be age, I think. Or it is in my case.'

'Sorry?'

'This clothes thing. I know what you mean – it's happened to me a bit lately . . .'

Around them flapped chiffon and taffeta, tweed and twill.

'It's a state of mind, being young,' said Lara.

'It's the state of your thighs.'

They laughed, but then mulled that over companionably for a moment.

'The word "mature" strikes terror into my soul,' admitted Lara. 'It sounds like a mixture of matron and manure, don't you think?'

'I'd rather not.'

'Do you hear anything from Tom these days?'

'Talking of manure. I can't think how you made the connection with *him*,' said Jo.

'Have you, though?'

'Not really. He's got a new woman. One of these skinny bitches who say, "I eat whatever I want," then go wild and have more lettuce.'

Lara smirked. 'How do you know?'

'I had the misfortune to bump into them, at the theatre of all places. He *hates* the theatre. Used to say it was – get this – too stagey. Four years we were together, and he took me to the theatre twice in all that time.'

'Men are such phonies. And the worst thing is that they think we don't know.'

'Women are great at reading between the lines. We have to be.'

'Birthdays are good,' said Jo.

'In what way?'

'They have a party – you can meet all their friends in one fell swoop. No one usually invites people they don't know fairly well to a birthday party. Well, not at our age, they don't.' There she goes again, thought Lara, with the age business.

'And you can tell a lot about a person from the company he keeps, right?' she said.

'Right. But not as much as you can from the cards. That is where birthdays come into their own.'

'You've got a theory?'

'Believe me, it works. People always send in-jokes,' expounded Jo. 'Beware the man with nothing but willy jokes on his mantelpiece. He's a jerk. Ditto the one with a selection of Now-You-Are-2 badges.'

'I think I'm with you.'

'There's many a truth said in jest. Equally, watch out for the birthday boy whose cards are full of funny animals saying "Cheers!" and getting pissed. Any reference to this one's great personality is likely to be a euphemism for "drunkard". Proceed only if you require a lot of time to yourself while he's in the pub with his mates.'

'And what about art repro, or good photos – tasteful, in other words?'

'Gay, I'm afraid.'

Gloom descended once more.

Lara pressed on down the street.

There were choices all around, she realised. There were new flats in the estate agent's window. Next door at Lunn Poly there were cheap weeks in Tenerife (depart Sat). The newsagent had a display of cards advertising yoga classes and friendly slimming classes and second-hand cars. There was an old Metro for £1,200.

Lara went inside, where an altogether more radical impulse spiked her blood.

She emerged with a packet of Silk Cut and a plastic lighter. She would take up smoking.

She lit up in the Eccleston Square garden. She choked (she had never smoked in her life before) but persevered. Nicotine was supposed to help you think, wasn't it?

It was becoming difficult to remember the very last times with Will. When Lara looked back over the past weeks, she could remember the few precocious spring blooms straining at the bud to show off, and the bare branches in the square, and the rush of silence in her ears when she returned to the flat, and even – in obscene detail – the ludicrous selection of tank tops she had been required to assemble for the long-suffering readership of *Reflections*, but nothing of the wider circumstances of his departure.

Why, they had even been close to agreeing how awful his mother, and his mother's sister and her daughter Jennifer were. Now that had been a seminal moment.

Lara hadn't known what was wrong. Only that *she* was.

Face it, she'd known that for a long time.

Of course there was no one else, he'd said.

Of course there was.

Lara dragged on her cigarette. No, she was not going to get het up again about Will and Janey. She was on her own now. Sitting on a peeling wooden bench, Lara burrowed down inside her jacket like a large animal testing out a hibernation spot. The wind raked through the trees. Despite the March sun, the cold was sharp as a volley of knives hurled across the square's garden.

She watched as a man walked a dog around the perimeter, on the pavement. A woman with a small child clapped her hands. By high summer, the roses would be the pride of any London square. As yet they were unpromising stumps.

'Won't be long to wait for the mock orange and the bluebells will be lovely. And *there* – there are going to be beautiful roses.'

The voice sliced in with the wind, but Lara still stared deeply into the woodland patch. She knew the bluebells there. Last year, now she came to think about it, she had spent time here, staring morosely at their elfin progress.

It must have been going wrong then.

She knew nothing about flower language, apart from the obvious – red rose for love. In her mind, though, each delicate bell was betrayal. Fury with Will had driven her out here. It was only now, when it couldn't hurt her any more, that she let herself remember the truth in such detail.

'You saw them last year, then?' asked Lara, her tone flat, turning slightly at last to focus on a currant bun of an elderly woman.

'No, dear, I wasn't here last year.'

Lara looked quizzically at her.

'I just know.'

Lara said nothing.

'You feel alone, but you're not, you know.'

'Sorry?'

'Alone. In the sense of the only one.'

'I'm—'

'Everyone is looking for the answer these days. All life will be perfect when they find what that is. But then – what happens if their idea of what is perfect is wrong? It makes everything skew-whiff, doesn't it!'

Just my luck, thought Lara, shifting on the seat. Spare me from batty, chatty old down-and-outs with theories.

'You may think I'm batty, but I'm no down-and-out,' said the woman. 'I live here in the square. You can't get in here unless you do, can you? That's the rules.'

Lara met her eyes for the first time. They were brown, more conker coloured than her own, merry and mocking. She held the gaze as she coughed and put out the half-smoked cigarette. 'What's the theory, then?'

'You can't have it both ways. You can't hate her for doing what she has done – and then hate yourself for not doing the same.'

'No.'

'If you must persist with these destructive thoughts, you should use her as a spur to drive yourself on. Not as a whip to flail yourself with.'

Lara considered this. 'You are absolutely right,' she said. Then, after a pause, 'How did you know it was a she?'

'Well,' said the woman, 'I don't suppose you're quite ready to start blaming *him* for everything.'

Back inside, Lara wrapped herself in a moth-eaten sweater, curled up on the sitting-room sofa, and tried to lose herself. Neither books nor tapes nor CDs transported her. And the only mystery in the late-afternoon film on television that day was where the leading man's Russian accent disappeared to half-way through.

Something was nagging at her.

Absently she put her hand to her mouth and touched with her tongue the ripple thread of the scab on her thumb. It tasted of salt and resolve.

And her own passivity.

For if she did nothing, all this would represent was yet another nettle she had failed to grasp.

After a moment, she scurried into the kitchen and pulled open a drawer. There was no frantic search. The invitation was there, waiting for her where she had put it for safe keeping.

Safe keeping? Lara grinned as she pulled the paper tight as a drum between her hands. She tested it. The edge was still sharp enough to inflict another cut.

The words were bold: 'Don't Get Mad . . . Get EVIL.'

It was then she made the decision.

She would go.

After all, she had taken the trouble to book herself a place and pay the £500 fee on *Reflections* expenses. Was she learning, at last?

Perhaps she had always intended to go and to grab what she could.

Perhaps she had needed the extra courage that taking control of her life the past few days had given her.

Perhaps timing was all.

The workshop for people who were too nice to survive this world unscathed would begin at ten o'clock tomorrow morning, and she would be there.

5   To the Workshop

Leaving home for the workshop, Lara walked once more past the spot where her car should have been parked. The anger that still induced drove her down into the warm roaring catacombs of the Victoria line.

During the clanking journey she wondered how many of her fellow passengers were desperate people leading desperate lives. She watched a man with a quarter bottle of whisky in his gaping jacket pocket, and a middle-aged woman whose varicose veins wound around her thick legs like a root system. Lara, light-headed, heavy-hearted, tried to count her blessings.

Her anger, at last, seemed to be a Good Thing. It was driving her out to take a risk for once. And the time was right to confront her inner self, the one that was causing all the trouble.

Lara emerged from the Angel tube station feeling adventurous. She marched purposefully towards the Pentonville Road, looking for her turning.

It was cold enough after the fug of the underground to make her hurry towards the grey bulk of the Gothic hall booked for the Terminally Nice workshop. It looked as if it had once been used as some kind of evangelical centre. Judging by the forlorn atmosphere, it had promised much, but delivered very few. But that may have been more to do with the feeling Lara always had when she found herself in fashionable Islington.

Inside, dust was a fuzzy galaxy in an unexpected shaft of sunlight from a high window. Plastic seats were set out in an arc on the scuffed wooden floor. An anticipatory murmur of conversation rose and fell as Lara looked around.

There must have been about twenty or so other people who had arrived for the workshop. They didn't look perceptibly any different or nicer than the average runner in the city's rat race – and some rather less so.

Lara felt the stares on her body and involuntarily smoothed her jacket. She slipped quickly into a seat in the back row not knowing what to expect.

The workshop began with a pertinent question.

'Do you ever have an overwhelming sense of what it is possible to accomplish, yet be quite unable to lose the fear of actually achieving it?' asked the group leader, addressing all of them.

Her name was Annette. She had splayed feet and a stare like a roadblock. She was reassuringly middle-aged and solid under a high pepper-and-salt hairstyle which she wore like a new hat. Best of all as far as Lara was concerned, she wasn't wearing large glasses with red frames. Lara had feared she might be. The ones she wore were violet.

Lara had taken the bull by the horns. She remained very sceptical indeed.

Annette was getting into her stride in a transatlantic accent: 'We are not offering answers but an opportunity for people to gain understanding of their own position . . .'

Somewhere way down there, Annette . . .

'This workshop will give mutual support, and we hope people will discover their own particular needs and the reasons why they do what they do. Stop the blame! Stop blaming yourself for being a nice and weak and pathetic person!'

She fixed her disciples with a Gorgon's glare.

'We are here to remove the shame and the blame. And if those who hear the message want something more ongoing, then there will be discussion sessions through the next month. This is not a quick fix. One workshop won't make it happen, but for some of you, it might be a beginning.'

They were ready to applaud already.

Annette gathered up all their insecurities and was off.

'How many times,' she asked, 'have you heard it said of someone, "He or she is absolutely ruthless, they'll do anything to get what they want. You can't help but admire them"? And you think, "That's right. That's the way of the world: Who Dares Wins. You can't take against someone who is only trying to get ahead and do the best for themselves, simply because you are envious of their courage."'

Lara, picking at stubborn grains of black soil lodged under her fingernails, was already beginning to feel herself in that uncomfortable space between the rock of her certainty and the hard place of her cynicism. She looked around.

The others in the draughty hall were listening intently. Disappointment or just plain disaster – what had brought them here?

To Lara's right was a frail woman of fortyish. She was well dressed and attractive, but looked worn. She sat miserably on her hard chair, head down, like someone perched on her suitcase at a station after a shocking farewell.

A pair of heavy women with a wary look in their eyes, who didn't glance up except shyly, but whispered together. They were a few years older than Lara, but not much.

One was dark and wore Camden market ethnic; the other, a redhead, was dressed in a sub-sporty ensemble.

Three or four quiet men in blue suits and ties, worn with shoes which gave away the fact that they weren't happy in either.

A rather older man, stocky with a full beard. It was impossible to make out his expression.

And a younger, far more determined woman, sure of herself in her deft movements, arms crossed, whom Lara immediately took to be a journalist. *Another* journalist, Lara corrected herself.

She caught herself in time. Let there be no doubt that she was here as an observer. This was purely research. Naturally there would be others who had the same aim in mind. It might make a good story, after all.

She would keep quiet and listen.

'Dare to say NO!'

This time the exhortation came from a softly spoken man with a faint lisp who had taken the floor, one of the men in blue suits. He might have been in his forties, or he might have been a lot younger. Thinning mousy hair was raked over his pate in the time-honoured manner. Lara was near enough to see that his hands shook fractionally when he unclasped them to stress a point.

'My name is Al,' he said, 'and I have begun to overcome my problems through positive choice.'

Was he some kind of regular, a convert on parade? A man in a permanent state of transition who lacked the guts to arrive? On his long face was the kind of expression which hinted strongly at a preference for quiet nights in.

'Stop saying that you're *sorry* when others ask you to do things that you really don't want to. That used to be me. I felt guilty about asserting myself because I couldn't bear not to be liked.'

This was evidently the Personal Testimony part of the
proceedings.

Lara hoped they would not be asking her to leap up
and proclaim, 'My name is Lara and I am a Pathetic Yes-
person.'

And then she thought: But I'm not, any more.

The lisping witness stumbled on. 'Now I realise that
not . . . asserting myself was . . . destructive. I . . . I was
demoted at work because I was not . . . assertive enough.
Other people took advantage of me . . . and I let them get
away with it. Now I know better.'

A helping hand of applause, initiated by the group
leader.

'I'm very passionate about . . . the main thing is . . . I
feel strongly now about . . . the most important question
is . . .'

Yes, yes?

' . . . is that I want to be *me* . . .'

Poor chap, thought Lara.

At noon there was a break in the proceedings. There were
wholemeal sandwich rolls, fruit and apple juice for lunch.
Strung out by curiosity, Lara hung back as the others
drifted towards a small kitchen at the back of the hall,
and watched them emerge again with plastic glasses and
food.

Were these people like her? And if so, what kind of
people were they?

The confident woman identified by Lara as another
journalist had already slipped away. There formed a wary
huddle of men in suits. The bearded man had buttonholed
Annette.

Nearest to Lara, the two wary-looking women were
chatting by the coat rack. Clearly they had come together.

'I told him,' said the dark one. 'But did he take any
notice?'

'Do they ever?' asked the redhead.

They exchanged a knowing look.

The redhead had an outdoor complexion. Under a lilac sweatshirt, she wore the bottom half of a tracksuit which strained over Valkyrian thighs. She was broad shouldered and her face above had a plump eagerness to please. Lara responded immediately to her lack of artifice.

Her friend the black-haired woman – in an Indian crinkle dress – was equally round of face, but with marshmallow chins and an incipient moustache. Her flat broad feet were planted in the type of plastic shoes which broadcast a radical aversion to meat eating, but this was combined with the timid air of a woman who feels she takes up too much space.

Intrigued, Lara moved closer. Then closer still, with a smile, when she realised that Al the positive-choice man was closing in on her. She could hear what they were saying now: the women were swapping recipes and talking about their husbands. From the tenor of the discourse Lara wondered how far they would get, daring to say no.

'Moussaka,' suggested the sporty-looking one. A hunk of her short red hair fell as a fringe on sky-blue eyelids. Her hands were studded with bulbous rings.

A grimace from the other.

'Useful though. All those Greeky herbs and a hint of the unknown . . .'

'The *unknown*, in the sense of . . .'

'Umm.' An emphatic nod.

'Surprise him . . .'

'Might even . . . you know . . . manage a bit of the other . . .'

Now Lara got it. She managed a polite smile at the vision this produced of the substantial moustachioed one transformed unexpectedly into a belly-dancer, say, for the big night, chiffon scarves trailing, sex on the menu. It was almost too much to contemplate the husband's reaction to this spicing of his supper. To think that magazines like her own might actually encourage this kind of marital scene!

They noticed her then. The redhead returned her smile. 'I'm Cass,' she said.

'Sandra,' said the other.

'I'm Lara.'

'I'm telling you,' went on Cass, neither excluding nor deliberately including Lara in the conversation, 'get yourself up to Crouch End or Hornsey, wherever, to one of those delicatessens. Go for the exotic bits and pieces they put in little bags for you. Very . . . indeterminate.'

'Aahh . . .' The point of the exercise was taking longer to dawn on Sandra.

Lara waited, intrigued by the foreignness of other people's lives.

'You see what I mean, Sand?'

'I'm getting there.'

More fat wet stirrings of passion inspired by aubergine and mince galloped across Lara's mind. She could just see Sandra – pink with effort, bursting from a black basque and stockings, perhaps – serving her husband's supper by candlelight, holiday bazooki music plucking at the edge of the picture.

At last there was a shriek of laughter from Sandra. The two women wobbled together in a shared moment of mirth.

They were more cheerful than they had been, by far, thought Lara.

They listened with a hungry intensity to her recipe for beef madras.

'Now . . . we welcome Colin to our forum. Colin is going to share with us how he dealt with his noisy neighbours.'

The session had resumed.

He stood up awkwardly, a stringy pale man with receding light hair and a prominent Adam's apple. When he stood, he seemed to slope, with his head bent forward from the shoulders like a number seven. He crossed his arms and began his tale. 'For years I had suffered, my life was on a downward spiral. My neighbours made my life a misery. The couple in the room upstairs . . . the television on full blast, the all-night parties, the dog . . . I lacked the courage to confront them.'

'But *this* time, Colin . . .' prompted the group leader.

'I went up stairs. Shaking and sweating.'

'Tell us what you were carrying, Colin.'

'An axe.'

'You dared to be bad . . .'

'And I got off with a conditional discharge,' said Colin triumphantly.

There was a bright smattering of applause.

'My husband is an adventurer,' said the woman who was asked to speak next. It was the worn-looking woman, risen from her baggage.

Something in the way she got to her feet snagged on a sharp part of Lara's recent memory. She was slight and pretty, Lara could see now, with a chest like a rack of lamb. The pink V-necked sweater which revealed it was the finest cashmere. Her voice was even softer. Waves of hair were pulled back austerely by a clip.

She cleared her throat nervously. 'My name is Penny. I'm forty-two . . . and I have had enough . . .'

Murmurs of sympathy unfurled around the female parts of the room.

'Good for you . . .' called out one of her audience.

'Go on, Penny.' In every way the group leader was short and to the point.

' . . . I look after two children, three people who come to help in the home, and several distraught ex-mistresses

of my husband's ... who turned out ... you know, not to
be so bad after all ... when you got to know them, after
he'd moved on to the next ... Helen, she's his latest, only
she's gone off with someone else and he's desperate to get
her back ... although that doesn't stop him—'

'*You* ...' prompted Annette, brows knitted, arms
crossed. 'We want to hear about you.'

Penny swallowed and nodded slowly. A deep flush crept
up from her neck. 'I can't say no to any of them. I end up
doing everything for them. And then ... it seems sometimes as if I live surrounded by perfect women.
Everywhere I look, there they are ... The only time I get
my own work done is when my husband goes away on
one of his trips.'

'Work?' asked Annette.

'He says it's for work.' A sigh. 'Maybe not.'

'No ... *you*. What's your work – how do you place a
value on yourself?'

'I ... I make things. I ... weave,' sighed Penny. 'When
he goes away.'

Portrait of a woman with a slime ball.

'Tell us more. What kind of things?'

A gentle shrug. 'Quite small things ... in the beginning.
Scarves and hats. Decorative bits and pieces.'

'And now?'

'Kind of ... quilts and rugs and bedspreads.'

'I see.'

'I sell them now,' said Penny. 'Mainly to people I know,
by word of mouth ... you know ...'

'You're passing on your pain,' pronounced Annette.

It *was* her. The photographer's wife, Gerry Day's
trouble and strife. Lara was convinced of it now.

The woman nodded dumbly at the group leader.

'Your pain,' said Annette once more. 'You are giving
shape and colour to your unspoken anxiety. You keep
yourself going stitch by stitch. You think as you work

about what is happening in your life. And then you push
your creations away. You sell them to people you know,
and you hope that they will see your pain.'

'I'm not sure that that's—'

'Bedspreads,' said Annette. 'I'm not happy about that,
not at all. You see what I'm getting at?'

'I . . .'

'Transference of emotion into inanimate objects has its
place, but in this case I really would advise a verbal
approach. It's hard, I know.'

Penny opened her mouth, but Annette put up a hand.

'It's hard. But if you can, you must start slowly with
the negation exercise. You must learn to say no. Stand in
front of your mirror. See what it feels like to say no, no,
no . . . Feel that it's good to say no . . .'

Penny seemed to be mouthing the word. Then her delicate face crumpled, dry and brittle as the tissue-paper
lining an expensive dress box. She was helped back to
her seat.

Lara wanted to go over to her, but there was no chance
of that.

The session rumbled on. Lara barely listened to a single
one of the men in blue suits who had been passed over
for promotion. Her sense of adventure had gone. It wasn't
funny any more. Lara was beginning to feel very uneasy
indeed.

They heard more from Al the positive-choice man, a
workshop regular, who revealed himself to be an
accountant on the verge of a nervous breakdown. He
described his unhappy marriage in terms of profit-and-
loss accounts.

Lara was anxious now. She fretted at her nails, wondering whether Annette would pick on her next. She
wanted to go. She should stand up and walk out!

Lara did not. She sat there stony faced, her usual

drippy self. As the minutes went by she could feel herself turning into a stalagmite.

Cass the exotic cook was up next. She said how she knew what she should do but always lacked the courage to go far enough.

Lara tuned in and out. She felt sorry for these people – but were their stories really relevant? But then the demon inside her, which goaded her constantly that she would never be good enough, played its master-stroke.

You're no better than they are, it hissed.

You think you're superior to these people, but you're not.

You think that if you can laugh at them you won't feel the same pain, but you do.

Lara suddenly felt sick. Her hands were sweating: she realised she was gripping the underside of her plastic seat.

'Lara Noe,' called Annette, consulting a large clipboard. She scanned the gathering beadily.

Lara closed her eyes and prayed for anger. Anything to quell the terror. She thought of Will and the massive electricity bill he had left, and Jennifer's 'Who, me?' smile, and Annie's courage (or perfidy), and her own treacherous demon inside.

Everyone was waiting for her.

Stolen car. No job. No money. Will. Jennifer. Gerry Day.

Lara rose unsurely to her feet.

'The way I feel is,' said Lara, feeling the words like pebbles in her mouth and hearing a stranger's voice, 'that some people just take what they want from life, regardless. While the rest of us poor idiots hold back because we feel we must play by the rules. Not use other people . . .'

There were murmurs of agreement. She saw the women Cass and Sandra nodding vigorously. 'I mean,' she continued, still haltingly, 'especially when you consider that it's just a myth, really, that bad women come to bad ends.

73

And it's a dangerous belief, because the only women who set any store by it are the ones, like me, who play by the rules.'

A sigh of recognition went round the room.

So Lara, encouraged, found it all coming out. She told them a bit about Ella, and Annie who she had thought was her friend, and Jennifer who never had been, and Will who had gone off with Janey. Once she had started, she couldn't stop.

The others heard her out, indulgently. Lara heard herself too, appalled by her own frankness.

'These people who always get exactly what they want – mostly to your detriment – they do it with sheer gall . . . Your jaw drops open with amazement – and *they* take that as a "yes" to whatever it is they want,' finished Lara, indignation congesting her chest. 'Well, I want to be like that, but I can't see how to do it without becoming one of *them*.'

She sat down, heart pounding.

Annette resumed her place at the head of the group and adjusted her confident stance. 'In the end, whether you approve or not of what someone else does, comes down to one consideration. Whether or not you like them,' she observed succinctly to the gathering in general. Then she turned back to Lara. 'But you knew that already, didn't you? What you're actually doing is finding excuses to *dis*like them.'

'I suppose you're right,' said Lara.

'Well, that's good . . .' The violet glasses bobbed.

'Good?'

'You're making progress.'

Lara shook her head. 'You see . . . the worst is, I know this is all a fuss over nothing. It's so unimportant . . .'

'What you feel is important, Lara.'

She tried to explain. 'No . . . there are people every-where who have real cause for rage and hate. This – what

74

goes on in my life – is nothing compared to that. So you feel ashamed that you even presume to feel hard done by . . . because all that proves is that you are an unpleasant and self-obsessed person too . . .' She tailed off, unable to articulate further.

'No,' said Annette in a tone calculated to inspire. Then she said, 'That is their greatest weapon.'

'I'm sorry?'

'Those who undermine you – they presume on your innate logicality and compassion. *Your* goodness. Because your goodness will stop you from retaliating in the same way as you are treated.'

Lara could see that.

Annette went on. 'You think that two wrongs don't make a right.'

Lara wasn't the only one nodding at that.

'Big mistake,' said Annette.

'Yes, but—'

'Get real.' It came out as a snarl.

'But surely—'

'What gives you the right to judge what is good or evil?'

That wrong-footed her. 'B-but . . . there *is* a framework, an accepted moral code, surely . . .'

'Maybe,' said Annette, 'it is accepted by *you* – but you cannot impose your values on anyone else. And *that*,' she added with a vicious flourish, 'is where you are losing it.'

Lara raised an eyebrow to show she appreciated the cynicism.

'Good and bad! Who is sitting in negative judgement of you? You *are* a good person, Lara. We are all good people, no matter what actions we take.'

A charged pause.

'I think that might be the crux of the matter,' said Lara, warm with self-conscious exposure now. 'I live in a state of terror that I will never be good enough.'

'Good enough for what?'

'That's just it. That's what I need to know.'

'Then that is what you need to discover, but you have to realise that there is no longer a right and a wrong in the way you have always imagined.'

They broke for coffee.

Lara cast around for Penny Day but could not see her.

The two women Cass and Sandra waved at Lara as she went for a cup of instant sludge brewed from a catering drum by a mournful male acolyte.

It was all very well, having a supportive friend to come along with, thought Lara warily, but these two exhibited all the signs of a child-like mutual dependence. Neither had been invited to speak. They had sat close together in the back row of the horseshoe, exchanging glances of shy encouragement when others were speaking. In fact, it was hard to tell where one ended and the other began. With their interchangeable bulks and plump faces, they could have been one person with two heads, one red, one black.

Even during this interlude, Cass and Sandra held themselves apart and huddled as one over a book which had been produced from one of their many bags. It was eye-catchingly entitled *Nasty People and How to Deal with Them*.

Lara felt heavier at the sight. She doubted it could ever be that straightforward.

That didn't stop her from edging nearer for a glimpse, though.

'Hello again,' said Cass, looking up.

'Hello,' said Sandra.

They waited for Lara to continue the conversation.

'Hi,' she said. What more was there to say after she had finished making public the realisation that she had lost faith in all civilisation's structures and natural order, and was close to feeling the same about all humanity?

They drank their tepid coffee more or less in silence, until Lara gathered herself enough to remember why she was supposed to have come.

'How did you hear about the workshop?' she asked. Surely not everyone had been sent a press release?

'Friend of mine,' said Cass. 'She always had a bloody awful time at work – until she signed up for this.'

Interesting . . . 'And now she doesn't?' prompted Lara.

'She's a headmistress now. She gives everyone else a bloody awful time!'

They laughed.

'So . . . are you a teacher?' she asked. Cass looked as if she might be. She had the critical darting eyes which took in many faces at once, assessing the degree of intervention needed.

'I've got four kids – dropped out of training college when I fell for the first. My husband's a teacher – God help us all. At least it's only metal-work now. It started off as pure biology.' She paused for effect. 'Like most things do.'

Lara would have like to ask more, to find out a little about the other quieter woman, but they were being summoned back to their places. They binned their styrofoam cups – almost all had been picked apart by anxious hands by the time they hit the metal bucket – and dutifully returned to their seats.

The final session consisted of a lecture by Annette in which she reinforced the great message. At the end there was an opportunity to sign up for further exploration and analysis. Lara hesitated.

The men hung back too. Penny the weaver was one of the first to go up to the clipboard on Annette's table and scrawl her commitment. She put down the pen with a sigh and caught no one's eye as she hurried out.

When Lara went up to the table it was more to see

whether she was right than with any intention of following suit. She was. The small neat signature read 'P. Day'. It might have been that which persuaded Lara to add her name, or it might not. For whatever reason, she did.

Behind her Cass and Sandra held a brief conference, mainly on the question of money.

'Let's do it,' said Sandra.

'Yeah ... well, they have it coming to them ...' said Cass.

'Too right,' concurred her friend. 'One day ...'

They moved off towards the exit. Cass bumped bulky bags against her legs.

'Night,' called Lara.

It was still light when Lara left the workshop session, but only just. Nevertheless she had the feeling she had crawled from the bottom of a dark disorientating cave and emerged blinking into the upside outside world.

He followed her to the Angel. She did not hear a sound or feel an unsettling breath until, at the ticket gate, he was close as a dance partner, his hand hovering above hers.

'Ah!' Lara started awkwardly.

It was the shy axe man.

'Hello ...' he ventured.

Lara resolutely pushed her ticket into the machine and snatched it up again as she passed through the gate. 'Er ... hello,' she said from the symbolic safety of the other side.

He fumbled before he produced his own pass from a plastic folder, then came through after her. 'Which ... way?' he muttered. 'Which way do you go?'

Lara stood, still caught off guard, in front of the bright certainties of the underground map on the wall in front.

The familiar intersections dissolved into a colourful tangle of party streamers.

The axe man did not wait from an answer.

'It was . . . quite interesting, wasn't it?'

'Quite.'

'It was your first time . . . there . . .'

'I have to go, sorry—'

'I don't suppose you might fancy . . . er, consider . . . coming out . . . with me . . . some time . . .' His thinning blond hair was scraped back from his forehead, which was studded with toy beads of moisture. Close up, Lara couldn't help noticing a couple of nasty shaving nicks around his neck.

'I'm afraid I . . .'

It was hard to believe she would be entirely safe to take him up on his entirely presumptuous offer. But there again, how safe would it be to refuse?

She made a move towards her descent without trusting herself enough to answer. The smutty platforms below exerted their clammy pull, and her feet were taking her to the down escalator, towards the tiled caves and the hot breath of human pores, down to the rush of engine smells on warm wind. Lara, poised on the edge of the under-world, paused a fraction too long.

'I have seen the possibilities, Lara,' he called.

Oh yeah . . .

'Colin . . .'

He was coming with her. On creepy crepe soles he was soundless and stuck to her side. 'You go this way, do you?'

Too late she realised her legs had been carrying her away towards the right platform.

'Me too,' said Colin.

They rode the train four seats apart. Lara fastened her eyes to one of the Poems on the Underground, and concentrated for dear life on the lines by Dylan Thomas.

Then the lights of Victoria station streaked across the windows and she got up. He stood with her.

'Don't tell me,' said Lara. 'Your stop.'

'Your stop too,' he grinned.

On the way up the escalator he told her about his humble abode round the corner from the Tachbrook Street market. Close enough for her heart to sink.

There was no way that Lara would have considered them neighbours, but it was clear he was going to.

6 Making the Moonscape

The workshop advice was wrong in at least one respect, Lara decided as she returned to work the next morning. She was dragging stones over to the back wall of the garden and depositing them in crooked piles. Mossy and misshapen, they made for a cemetery atmosphere on the far side.

To start with, she should not be saying no to anything. If it was possible, she should be exploring every avenue. Her current inertia, then, could be rationalised as mere hesitation at the crossroads.

She let go of another stone flag. It fell with a muffled damp crack.

She had begun to worry about the sustainability of her own life in the city – and she was not thinking, as before, of life*style* here. This was the nitty-gritty. She would need more than thin air and exercise to keep going: she would need money for food and bills.

Should she take in a lodger? And if she could find one (who was also sane and solvent), would this person have to take her room while she camped on the sofa?

In this more practical spirit, loose and strong from her gardening, Lara read the small ads in an old copy of the *Evening Standard*. Perhaps now was the time to find a job. A proper job.

What that might possibly be, though, was another question.

There didn't seem to be a great call for disillusioned perfectionists (shorthand, some typing) who could probably turn her hand to most things but couldn't see the point in trying.

Then she pulled herself up short. This was *precisely* what someone like Lara would be expected to do: to sublimate their wildest dreams for the sensible option.

'No,' she said aloud. 'No, no . . . NO!'

It felt good, so she said it again, only louder.

Then she equipped herself with some impressive paper and switched on the word processor which stood long unused, now relocated in the far corner of the room.

So she was going to be a different person with none of the old scruples, was she? She composed a highly imaginative curriculum vitae and an effusive letter of recommendation which purported to be from a leading theatrical impresario whom she'd once met.

Then she composed a letter to the head of drama at London Weekend Television, signing it from an agent she had not acquired, offering him an option on an award-winning play that she hadn't yet written.

After that she wrote a speculative job application to *be* head of drama at another station which began with the usual courtesies and continued, 'During a recent trip to Los Angeles, both Jack Nicholson and Michelle Pfeiffer expressed a wish to widen their experience of British television and they have signed an option on the series I propose to produce, details of which you may be interested in discussing.'

Hell, wasn't this just the kind of scam everyone else was up to?

She found some first-class stamps and went out to post the letters straight away before her nerve failed.

Of course the letters would be binned – no one could

possibly take them seriously. But that was not the point. The point of the exercise was daring to do it. Then she sat in the darkening sitting-room, gathering herself.

After a while her old sense of honour settled in too, a heavy arm around her shoulders like a persistent bore at a party.

Had she just made herself as ridiculous as all the other pie-in-the-sky merchants – she, who should have known better, who actually had something (or what was left of it) to lose?

No. For once – just once – instead of sitting seething that the world turned in favour of those who took crazy chances, she had actually sent up a rocket herself.

She felt better for half an hour.

What she felt, in the end, was resentment. Resentment that she had done something that was so alien to her natural inclinations. Granted, she was no candidate for canonisation, but she had been brought up to respect the rules and to accept defeat with grace. She did not habitually cheat and lie – in fact, to her own detriment, rather the reverse.

But here was the rub.

At some stage, while she was striving, the rules had changed. According to Annette, there was no right or wrong. It followed that if there was no longer good or evil, only differences in opinion, then she was done for. She was no good at schemes and politics and manipulations because she had never thought she needed them – and now she was all too easy to outwit.

While she had imagined she was breaking out on her own, all she had actually done was to run away.

In the end she spent a strange afternoon prompted by the urge to go back to the beginning and start again.

In the beginning, thought Lara, there was Berkeley Drive.

It was a sweep of bay windows and square edges in the outer reaches of South London. The houses were built in the thirties, and each little building was an interlocking part of the grand design, so that from the street they were matched as the vertebrae of some vast dead animal's spine and from the air the roofs made fern patterns and spiralled here and there into insignificant snails. On the ground it was a place where a flight of fancy was likely to involve a chalet-style extension or, in an extreme case, painted wooden shutters with punched-out hearts.

And this was where she and her dreams had been formed. In a place that was neither here nor there.

She wondered about going back. Of course she could return, but what would she do if she ever got there? She was seeking a place she could not reach again.

That was what rational thought told her; it was still grumbling more of the same as she walked to Victoria and caught an off-peak commuter train south into the suburbs.

The hardness of the paths and paving stones held no imprint of what had once been. There could never be treasure trove churned from history's layers here as there might in the moist renewing earth of country fields, nor evidence caught in the roots of ancient trees. In narrow fenced back gardens there would be, at best, chips of old crockery and pennies, lost plastic ephemera and bones buried by prisoner dogs.

And now, it was not possible to believe that the people were flesh and blood. She could not believe in them, that they had once led real, rounded existences. Here were the long straight streets of doubt.

Lives lurched on. Was anything ever under control? It was a failing of a particular type of character, she knew, that argued a belief in order. Will had been right all along. The only logic was the supremacy of chaos, and human reconciliation to it. She passed the corner where she had once crashed her bicycle. There was no possibility of a tidy suburban universe. Roses in the uniform patch gardens may have been carefully pruned, ready for summer, but the care they were shown was as yet only in hope and not certainty of sun and warmth.

She walked for a long time, reaching nowhere and no conclusion.

She had not yet told her parents that Will had gone and she was jobless. They of all people: even now she couldn't let them down. Not yet. But she would have to call, would do it that evening, just to let them know she was alive. And busy.

Back at the flat, Lara returned to the book.

She had found it on the book shelves in the sitting-room, had never realised it was there. It told her that success was all a question of perspective. Tricks and illusions. That was what the book recommended for a tiny urban garden. *A Treasure Trove from Dirt*, it was called. Create a garden full of surprises, where a little inventiveness could provide unexpected lushness and secret corners to amuse and delight.

How lovely it sounded.

Lara wiped the back of a muddy hand over her forehead. And so in tune with her mood. Why, she didn't even care when the dirt smeared over the page she was reading.

Maybe she couldn't manage false doorways and *trompe-l'oeil* vistas, but as far as she could, she was on for a game of fragrant green deception. It wasn't much, but it was a beginning.

She assessed the dankness of previous half-heartedness in the garden's history. A large tree – it might have been a sycamore – hung over the far corner from a neighbouring plot. It blotted out half a street of brickwork and quite a bit of sky. Last winter's leaves rotted and curled in its shadow and beyond. On her own side, a hawthorn was out of control. She would have to build up beds – the stone slabs would be useful there – and take down other levels. What she had in mind, if only she could achieve this, was to give the impression that it was not a grimy brick wall which marked the end of her garden and separated it from a stony tradesman's path no one used, but that this was only the beginning. That her patch was merely an antechamber to a much grander garden; much much more lay beyond, if only one knew how to gain access.

The idea fired her arms as she began to dig with a rusting spade which must have been left by some long-gone gardener tenant. It wasn't the answer, but it would do for now.

Her work in the garden quickly became a routine. Even now, there was an entirely instinctive orderliness to her dissent. On her own, she dug and uprooted and replanted and burned. Wanting company one morning when she stopped for a coffee break, she switched on the television.

It proved a mistake.

For there was Jennifer, the loathsome Jennifer, leaping uninvited into Lara's home. It was just like old times.

There must have been plenty of actresses who hadn't made it big but couldn't blame that on their traumatised childhoods – but these were not the actresses who seemed to rate an interview on the *Top of the Morning* show.

It was that kind of show.

In the eighties the *Zeitgeist* was: If in doubt, go shopping.

In the nineties it was: If in doubt, blame someone else.

Somewhere between the two, Lara decided that both options made her feel like throwing things. Especially on daytime television when Will's cousin Jennifer lit up the screen with her sympathetic smile.

Daytime television viewers thought Jennifer Gould was marvellous. They wrote her sackloads of fan letters and clamoured to put their sad lives before her. Or so Jennifer said.

For Jennifer, she who had presided with such blood-lust over the death throes of Lara's relationship with Will, had carved a niche for herself as the champion of the victim.

On this particular morning an unfortunate old woman was to be tranformed inside and out. Or, as Lara could clearly see, put through two hours of further victim-isation.

'It hasn't been easy for May Cartwright to come here today,' purred Jennifer to camera. 'She's seventy-three and she lives in a high-rise on a notorious inner-city estate. She's been burgled five times in the past year. But she's fabulous, isn't she?' she asked the main presenter. Then she summoned the fashion consultant, the hair-dresser, the make-up artist and the therapist to make it all better.

May Cartwright sat lumpen under a plain suet expression as these too-eager elves danced around her. Their bright smiles went on and off like flash bulbs.

'So what are you going to do for Maisie today?' asked the plump blonde anchorwoman.

'She does look fabulous, doesn't she,' said Jennifer, 'but she's getting rather fed up of woolly hats and camel coats, so we're going to do something special here today. That's right, isn't it, Maisie?'

Patronising git, thought Lara, hating herself for having switched on. It was ten thirty in the morning and she was drinking Irish coffee – the version without the Nescafe and milky froth.

The old woman on TV nodded obediently.

When Lara had first watched the *Top of the Morning* show a couple of years ago to see what Jennifer was like – the Jennifer Will was so taken in by, his mother's sister's daughter – the set had been powder blue, the kind of do-it-all deluxe so favoured by television to patronise the homely masses. Now, even when it wasn't actually powder blue any more, it was in spirit.

Jennifer had been presenting a consumer spot then, and it was clear from the patronising calm with which she warned the nation of the perils of pressure cookers that she believed she was destined for television greatness. And so it had come to pass.

'And still to come,' said a dummy of a male partner on the sofa, 'in the week when fifteen died in the tornado in the southern states of America, we'll be asking what you can do about the effects of wind.'

Lara could barely listen to this drivel. So why did she?

The answer to that was Jennifer, of course.

And truly Jennifer *was* an inspiration for Lara as she sat in limbo, watching, waiting, in front of the television. In the past months she had not lost her horrible fascination for Lara: in life as on screen she embodied a magical malevolence. Whoever would believe this was the woman who had once stolen two expensive suits from Lara's wardrobe? (Will didn't.)

Jennifer was the ultimate spur, if one were needed, to send Lara bounding towards another session at the TN workshop.

It would do no harm, surely, to turn up for the post-one-day-session discussion session. After all, what was the point of beginning a task if you never saw it through?

She went.

Annette held forth bullishly on self-assertion for some time until someone dared to tell her they had got the point. She was beady with triumph; the heckler feted.

Then Annette expounded her ritual theory.

It was crucially important, she stressed, to mark the freedom from old constraints. There should be a ceremony, a solemn moment of no going back.

What kind of ceremony? she was asked.

'It could be anything that has meaning and form for you as an individual,' replied the group leader. 'It could be as simple as lighting a candle and watching the flame of an old obsession run its course and burn itself out. It could be the planting of a tree or a shrub to represent the start of new growth. It could be as elaborate as . . . a pagan ritual to celebrate the solstice, or a version of a church blessing.' She beamed around. 'It's up to you. The only limit is that of your own imagination.'

That was rot, thought Lara. It wasn't lack of imagination that was the trouble. It was lack of daring to act on these exciting ideas in real life.

All around her, Lara sensed the others sifting through their own thoughts.

Letting her gaze wander, she caught the eye of Penny Day, the photographer's wife. There was a nice moment of mutual understanding – or was it recognition? Her face was paler than ever, almost translucent, but it rose above a riotous fiesta of a woven shawl.

A few seats away were Cass and Sandra.

The strangest thing had happened to the twosome since the first meeting. They had begun to evolve already, in appearance and, presumably, confidence. Or as Annette would have put it, they were finding themselves, growing into their own personalities. Visibly.

It was fascinating, decided Lara, and a little spooky.

Sandra, in particular, had blossomed in an unexpected way. No longer was the first impression made by the dark pudding body and rippling chin. She had unveiled the most disconcerting lynx eyes. These eyes – slanted and sooted and slicked blue and green – had sprouted overnight on Sandra the couch potato. It was as though she had grown butterfly wings.

Even Cass seemed a little startled. She didn't mention the eyes.

'She's been buying stacks and stacks of dog food,' she confided urgently to Lara during the coffee break while Sandra was consulting Annette. 'I saw her in Safeway the other day pushing a trolley full of the stuff. Nothing else apart from a cheap packet of fig rolls!'

'So what's wrong with stocking up?'

'She doesn't have a dog.'

Lara looked past Cass's ear, from which dangled a jolly parrot. She wanted to speak to Penny, to find out more – to talk to someone whose life might have brought her to this place for reasons similiar to her own. Penny Day, she was sure, was the person whose conversation would make the most sense.

But Cass had her pinned to the wall.

When they went back to their seats for the second half of the session, Penny's was empty. She had slipped away again.

'You want emotional growth? You gotta take risks,' expounded Annette. 'The very act of taking that risk, which seems so mentally terrifying, is what gives you the amazing burst of confidence you need.'

Sage nods all round.

'Comfortable does not give courage. Being passive means settling for the dregs of what other people are prepared to offer. Be bold! Take! Demand!'

For another hour, she fired them in this way.

Afterwards, as they discussed the next step forward, Cass said, 'I've never had a ritual.'

'You got married,' pointed out Sandra.

'I got *pissed*. I must have said yes at all the wrong moments.'

'Must have done.'

It was only natural then that they should ask Lara the same question. 'So were you married to this guy, then?'

'No,' said Lara.

It was interesting – or so she assured herself – how the idea of actually being married to Will had once been her forbidden fruit. It was a succulent temptation that drew her all the more for knowing she should not have it.

Now, she was stronger. She found that little by little she was coming to regard what had happened since as a lucky escape. Marriage to Will, she thought, could well have turned out more like a supper of tinned sardines: consumed out of desperation but lingering on unpleasantly.

'You're one of the lucky ones, then,' said Sandra unexpectedly.

Cass flared her nostrils in sisterly agreement.

'Course, you're younger so you didn't have all the pressure we did,' went on Sandra. 'God, I wish I was twenty now!'

It seemed a useful line of enquiry, if only to mask unhappy returns of Will. 'What would you be doing?'

Sandra shrugged. 'I know what I wouldn't have done. I wouldn't be getting ready to marry Barry at twenty-one, that's for sure. I wouldn't be falling pregnant for my first before I was twenty-two. And I wouldn't have made myself into a bloody miserable housekeeper, cook and bottle-washer – not to mention mother of three – by the time I was twenty-six. But that was it, you see. That was what was expected.'

Lara looked to Cass. The woman hoisted up a bra strap as if she were heaving on a rucksack. She was large breasted, with the same martyred air.

'And you, Cass?'

A sniff. 'Something like that. Up the spout with the first kid when we signed the papers at the Hackney registry.'

'It's hard, then, to—'

'Life's better now,' Cass said firmly, but from the way the pronouncement turned her mouth down at the corners it was doubtful whether she meant it was for them.

They were right about one thing, though. The rules had been abolished – even Lara felt that – while they had been striving to do the best they could. They looked around them and saw that there was no moral outrage, none of the fear of censure that had taken Cass up the steps of the register office with a man she had come to loathe, and they wondered how, if there was no right or wrong any more, there could be any such thing as a best either.

Perhaps it was because of Sandra's alarming display of independence that Cass asked Lara to join them for a drink in the Dun Cow. Lara, intrigued, agreed with a thirst for insight greater than that for warm drink.

'All we've been doing so far is muddling through,' announced Cass as soon as they were settled at a wobbly round table, having used tissues from the bottom of their bags to swab up pools of liquid left by previous occupants. A beery kind of pond life lurked in the bottom of the ashtray they pushed aside. 'We need a plan.'

Lara drank draught lager with them because the stained brown walls implied that it was that kind of pub. The gingery paisley mess of a carpet was a fair representation of the after-effects of too much beer and curry. Irrational bubbles of electronic sound from a prize quiz machine rose and popped through the conversation.

Sandra finished shredding a beer-mat and nodded vigorously. 'Life,' she pronounced, 'is not a dress rehearsal.'

Lara rolled her eyes.

'Lara?' They turned on her.

'Mmm.' She lit a cigarette.

'What do you think?'

Lara was beginning to wonder whether this was not all rather pointlessly self-indulgent. She said nothing.

'I mean . . . look at us,' said Cass. 'Cooking up a storm but never quite having the nerve to go through with it.'

'Mmm,' said Lara.

'All those exotic ingredients,' said Sandra ruefully. 'But those men, I tell you . . . cast-iron stomachs. Nearest we got to a death in the family was a bit of groaning and some nasty belching.'

'Sorry?' asked Lara.

'We've been experimenting for a while,' said Cass. 'Only it's been a bit haphazard. To be honest, we've probably never used quite enough weed-killer.'

'What?' asked Lara.

'It's more difficult than you'd think to mask the taste. And he's always been a picky eater, my Barry,' explained Sandra.

'Is that lager all right, Lara?' asked Cass. The women stared at her, round eyed.

Lara had started to cough.

The recipes they had been swapping . . . Then she thought: No, they couldn't possibly mean that. Lara looked from one to the other.

Cass and Sandra exchanged one of their deadpan looks.

So Lara laughed. 'You had me there for a moment. I thought . . . I thought you were serious!'

These women were a hoot.

'To get back to the grand plan,' said Cass, suddenly businesslike, 'maybe we should begin like Annette said, by deciding on a ritual.'

'It should be something . . . arresting,' declared Sandra.

'It shouldn't be a freak show either,' said Lara. 'Surely it should be subtle, an act that means something to each of us personally.'

Sandra folded her arms and issued a militant glower with her startling new face.

Something in her demeanour made Lara backtrack rapidly. 'That's what I think will work for me, anyway.'

'*You* may see it like that, Lara. But some of us are actually getting in there as a force for change, making bold statements,' said Sandra.

'We need to ease ourselves into it,' said Cass, diplomatically for once.

This they seemed to agree on, as an agenda already passed.

They ordered more lager.

'I mean,' said Cass, assuming as always the role of leader, 'this is going well, but we need some DIY top-up sessions between workshops. To keep our resolve strong. Something to help us focus on ourselves and our goals.'

Lara thought that was fair enough. 'What did you have in mind?'

'Something pampering.'

Not all Lara's previous notions had left her. 'Sounds reasonable,' she concurred.

'Something more radical,' asserted Sandra.

'A flotation tank?' suggested Cass.

Lara vetoed this. 'I did that once. It was very salty. Tons of Epsom salts and it's you against six inches of Dead Sea and creepy underwater music . . .'

'Reflexology?'

'Too ticklish.'

'Shiatsu massage? Colonic irrigation? Come on – you're the one who knows about all this stuff.'

Lara made a face.

'Hypnotherapy, what about giving that a go?'

'Forget it. I sent off for this hypnotherapy tape *Slim in your Dreams*. I lay down, followed all the instructions . . .'

'And?'

'I dropped off to sleep, and woke up an hour later feeling ravenously hungry.'

'Aromatherapy, then. Have our natural positive impulses confirmed and recharged.'

'What *have* you been reading?'

'Oh, come on.'

Lara grinned in defeat. 'The Sisters of Perpetual Hope and Indulgence.'

Lara went home and considered her ritual options. Perhaps, she thought almost smugly as she drank hot chocolate standing by the kitchen window through which the neglected garden was a pitted moonscape, I worked that out for myself.

But the next night after another day in isolation, if anything her life seemed stuck in reverse. The bonsai tree was dead, for a start. Lara considered the ex-tree of her ex-lover in its Japanese dish on the bathroom window-sill. 'I just don't have the commitment for bonsai,' she was forced to admit.

Nor the restraint, she added resentfully to the tightened, curtailed coils of a life lived in miniature.

No longer.

This was confirmed, yet again, half an hour later when Lara chose mainly C answers to a self-analysis quiz in a magazine. She turned the page for results and advice. 'Be proactive!' urged the psychologist whose opinions were expounded. Her photograph appeared by the boxed solutions, and Lara noted the hard salt-and-pepper hair and the set jaw of her face – Annette's face.

Was that an omen?

Had she at last met the right person at the right time?

Lara read on: 'Your response shows that it is all too easy for you to take a passive role and wait for others to come along and solve your problems. Expecting others

to pick up the pieces for you can be counter-productive:
it could lead you to be too much of a victim.'

It was up to her.

Anything Cass and Sandra could do . . .

It came to her eventually, what form the ritual should
take. There would be a private ceremony first, and then
a leaving party – call it a wake, if anyone liked.

The next day Lara spent less time choosing the definitive going-away outfit than she might have done a month
before. Obviously: there were far fewer clothes in her
wardrobe now. She wondered briefly about buying back a
pert little number she had passed on to Jo's stall but
decided in the end that she still had enough to go on.

The hardest part was making the body.

There were a couple of false starts when she experi-
mented with a foam-filled pillowcase, and then with a
plastic bin-liner. After that there was the problem of
fashioning the head.

Eventually she settled on the Venetian carnival mask,
making ingenious use of the handle as a spine. The
mask was deathly white with a rosebud mouth. Feathers
and fake jewels spumed gaudily from the smooth plaster
forehead. Lara sewed up the arms and most of the neck
of a red tailored jacket and stuffed that from the bottom
with a selection of the remaining clothes in her cupboard,
then she pushed the handle of the mask down the slit
she had left in the neck and stitched tightly all around.
She shook her creation by the shoulders. It held.

She propped the torso up on a chair and opened a
drawer to choose a pair of black opaque tights. She gave
them a stretch, then hunted around for something to
give them substance. Like a mother at midnight on
Christmas Eve, she thought, as she assembled a collection of knobbly miscellanea – and the notion sent her
scurrying into the kitchen for two satsumas. She pushed

them into the toe of each floppy black leg so that they formed a weight, and then began to cram in old underwear that needed mending, enticements in red and black lace which Will had encouraged her to wear (these were too flimsy to go far), a shirt of his that she had missed down the side of the airing cupboard, a blouse, and finally two rolled pillowcases which formed the thighs, perfectly slim and straight.

She seemed too floppy. She needed sustenance.

Laughing to herself, Lara stuffed her torso with oddments of food – a slab of pate, a Lean Cuisine, some yellowing broccoli – mouldering in the fridge. It was revolting. Strange and secretive too. She slapped in half a packet of streaky bacon, and rejoiced. She had rediscovered the sheer pleasure of naughtiness. Then she stitched up the full stomach and took the body over to the legs. She pushed them under the vermilion jacket and decided not to bother with a skirt.

Brave hussy.

More stitches and she was perfect: she was a life-size, silent rag doll.

Rose. She was Rose, the English rose.

Lara sat back to admire her handiwork; Rose stared back serenely, sitting upright on the bedroom chair, and startling in her red, white and black.

On impulse Lara picked up a pair of clip-on earrings, paste monstrosities which advertised their provenance in the form of the designer's logo, and attached them to the sides of the mask.

Was there anything missing? Some memento of Will, perhaps. Some symbolic tie, although he had left nothing of real value, she was sure. There was nothing in the bedroom. She stalked into the living-room and foraged in forgotten drawers and cupboard shelves. All she found was a file of papers, some typed, others covered in handwritten notes – a filming schedule, some accounts. She

pulled out a fistful, folded them resolutely, and then
stuffed them into Rose's jacket pocket. She clapped her
hands as she finished.

Then she wondered how to tackle the ritual itself.

She went out to buy candles. She wanted scented candles,
of cinnamon and dewberry, and lemon and opium. She
waved at Jo and a few familiar male garments in the
distance on the stall in Tachbrook Street as she breasted
the corner, but then hurried on with her mission.

The shop sold Indian dresses and brass artefacts; crys-
tals and aromatherapy oils with their burners; rugs from
the Andes and mats from Sri Lanka; china bowls from
Japan and painted silk screens from China. Lara found
her candles and splashed out on a mauve crystal to
harden her resolve.

Then she went, filled with purpose, to the off-licence
where she bought a bottle of good champagne for the
send-off, and then to the fruit stall in the market for
great bunches of black and white grapes. Suitably
equipped now, she had visions of bacchanalia for one – a
single serving of high decadence. She would prepare the
setting for midnight; she would play this music and chant
that anthem . . . And then she stopped.

It was wonderfully liberating to find pleasure in mis-
chief, but Lara was learning at last.

She would have to be practical. Some joys had to be
discreet.

There were curious eyes and ears all around.

When she let herself back in it was past six o'clock. She
put the candles on the table, the champagne in the fridge
and the grapes in the sink. She would consume them
when the deed was done, raising her glass alone to
misrule.

Then she put on her gardening clothes – simply the

ones she had not got around to washing – and went out
into the yard to begin the process.

As dusk came down, Lara churned up a flower-bed –
carefully, though, so that she could replant.

Then she buried Rose and all that she represented.

7 Transition

The morning Lara was due to meet Cass and Sandra there was a robbery in North London. The heist on the Northern Rock Building Society in Muswell Hill took place at 9.06 a.m. – a particularly vicious crime, said the police on the local radio news. It made the local television news at lunch-time, and would be embellished with the twin thrills of a bloodied handbag and a rhinestone pistol by the early-evening bulletin.

The gist was this: a raider pointed a gun at Ms Janice Rollins where she sat behind the third customer service window inside the building society on Muswell Hill Broadway. The society was relieved of £10,050 and a cashier's bag after the emergency alarm button beneath Ms Rollins's position failed to activate, and a second raider entered through the rear of the premises, having first immobilised the branch manager Mr Richard Heaton in his Ford Mondeo.

The raiders escaped with the cash in bundles of used twenty-pound notes, and an additional single fifty-pound note which Ms Rollins had thrust at the gunperson in the initial confusion. The getaway vehicle was a large motorcycle, which headed north at speed and was not recovered.

The film from the security video camera showed that the first of the assailants was of indeterminate gender, short to medium height, wearing black motorcycle leathers, a full helmet and a T-shirt which read 'Jesus Saves'.

The second was well over six feet tall, of stocky build and broad shoulders, again in motorcycle leathers and full helmet, and with long matted brown hair which hung down below the shoulders.

Both spoke with coarse London accents.

Ms Rollins, a twenty-three-year-old, and last November's employee of the month, told police that the raiders entered the premises 'like a whirlwind'. 'I hardly had time to look up to see who had come in when this shiny black gun was right up my window,' she recalled in her statement after treatment for shock. 'The raider said, "Give us the money." I said, "You must be joking." The raider replied, "No, I'm bloody not. Get on with it." You could hardly see the face, only these really dark-coloured lips, almost like black paint. That's when I thought that it might have been a woman, although I could not be sure.'

The traumatised ex-employee of the month was able to seek help and succour from the Reverend Barry Stubbs of St Leonard's Church, happily situated no more than two hundred metres away. The vicar was particularly concerned, he told reporters, at the vile subversion implied in the raider's choice of T-shirt.

Lara actually smiled. *Someone* was daring to be bad.

She switched off the radio, checked her bag and set out as arranged for an extracurricular session with the workshop women.

Sisters were doing it for themselves.

In the end Lara had come close to agreeing tactics with Cass and Sandra, although Sandra declined to join them for the first step. She had her own path to tread, she told them mysteriously.

*

The Heavenly Aroma-Massage Centre was above a heel-bar and key-cutting emporium. Crouch End's short cut to Nirvana was reached via a dark narrow flight of stairs. Cass met Lara outside and led the way.

Inside the Heavenly, there were paths of green carpet and nooks of pine which served as consulting rooms. There the clients were separated and introduced to the life-enhancing powers of essential oils. Lara found herself answering questions about her stress levels and work and domestic pressures. She could see how some clients would welcome the confessional, but she did not. Old habits died hard and she was under no illusion that she would undergo metamorphosis in a cheap wooden booth deep in suburban North London.

She gave the glossed-over version, polite but distant.

Then Lara thought of Rose and the ritual and the new beginning that was supposed to represent. She deter-mined to stop carping and enjoy the performance for what it was – the fantasy that there might be solace at the hands of strangers.

She found herself lying face down, being slicked with lavender and ylang-ylang by anonymous fingers. She emerged an hour later, sticky even after showering, but surprisingly relaxed. Perhaps that was the answer: never have any expectations.

Against the white of the reception area, Cass was beaming pinkly.

'Good?' asked Lara.

'Good,' confirmed Cass.

Their first recharged impulses on floating down to the street took them to the Mighty Veg Cafe a few doors away. Lara was coming round from the massage stupor over a workman's mug of hot chocolate, when Cass said, 'Wait till Sandra gets here and I'll show you, but you'll never believe what I've got.'

In the end, Cass could not wait. She produced a copy of the local paper over spinach and aubergine bake.

Lara pored over the story she indicated.

At first Lara was sure there had been a mistake. She clutched at the wooden table.

'It's Al!' she gasped.

Cass nodded excitedly.

Al! The quiet accountant was a shining example to the workshop faithful. He had dared to scream no to the world!

The full-page story was accompanied by a picture of Al as a staring gnome in a raincoat. A further photograph of a residential street told the rest of the story. Wonderful, vengeful, furious Al had let it all hang out. All over Styx Avenue, Wood Green.

Rolling against the kerbstones behind him were fragments of china; these were the tea services his wife had prized so highly, and the porcelain dinner setting for eight. Slewed across the road were framed pictures he had wrenched from the walls. Shards of glass glittered around his own gatepost, and the remains of a coffee-pot lolled against his neighbour's.

Most dramatic of all, though, were the bright flags of women's clothes which fluttered from the hedges and crenellated walls up and down the street. Even through the black-and-white press photo the colours could be imagined: sugar pink and mauve and baby blue and marrow green, some with obscene swirls and paisley patterns, some with dog-tooth check and gingham squares. Blouses fluttered victorious in a light breeze; a mischievous wind plucked at the hems of skirts and dresses.

Al had done this!

Lara rocked back in her seat, trying to judge Cass's reaction.

Cass was gleeful. She also seemed to know an awful lot about it.

*

The tragedy of Quiet Al, as told by Cass, was all down to the Fury.

'The Fury?'

'His wife. That what he calls her. It's all her fault.'

In the face of Cass's steamroller logic, Lara stood her ground shakily. 'It must have been a bit more involved than that.'

'Of course it was. She was threatening to leave him.'

Lara rolled her eyes.

But Cass was shaking her head. 'She wanted a divorce. She was working out a plan – had been to a solicitor. Half and half, that was the split.'

'Sounds fair to me.'

'No. He didn't even like her any more, but he didn't want a divorce.'

'I don't get it.'

'Half and half? Don't you see? The man's an *accountant*. After all that he'd worked for all these years ... why should she get as much as that?'

There was a fundamental flaw in the argument, as Lara saw it. 'Maybe there's another way of looking at this, though, Cass. What the Fury – Veronica – was asking for was a chance to have a new life for herself, after years of stagnation with him, and he couldn't bear that.' She reached for some handy therapy terms. 'I thought this was all about change and empowerment.'

Cass pursed her lips and kicked her feet up on to the empty chair at their table. She was wearing some strange soft laced-up shoes like Victorian boxer's boots. Her calves were formidable. So was her glare. 'There are other aspects to be considered.'

'But surely as women, we should be sympathetic to the positions of *other* women ...'

Cass produced a loud snort. 'Not *cows* like that!'

'Cass!'

'As I say, there are other considerations.'

Lara waited for them. 'Go on, then.'

'Like . . . I might, you know . . .'

'You might what, Cass?'

'It is possible that . . .' The other woman was suddenly peculiarly bashful.

The glare dropped away, and realisation dawned. 'Oh, no Cass . . .' This was quite ridiculous – but then hardly any more so than the events which had led up to this botched confession. Lara began to laugh.

'What? What's so funny? That he and I might find each other attractive, that someone might like *me* for what I have become?' cried Cass. 'We have an understanding, me and Al, and no one can take that away from us!'

It wasn't that.

'But – I thought you hardly knew him!'

'So?'

'So . . . OK.' Lara dropped that tack, and was trying to formulate the words when she was interrupted.

A formerly familiar figure had appeared in the doorway.

Sandra was late and proud – and very tall.

She was not so much dressed for action, she was dressed *as* the action.

She clomped up to their table, towering on thigh-high boots which seemed to demand a Wild West saloon-bar setting. Her hair contributed to the effect: the lank brown curtain had been raised to neo-punk heights.

And she was wearing black lipstick.

The smiles of general amusement in the cafe as she attempted to take a seat were not echoed on Cass's mouth.

'What the—?' was etched there. As was the worry and annoyance of waiting for someone who had not come as expected. Cass, it was clear, was the one who was used to taking the initiative. She directed a look of wide-eyed

105

disbelief to Lara. Lara responded with a noncommital shrug.

'You're late,' said Cass.

Sandra flashed her alien eyes – painted now so that they almost touched the electric shock of new hair, two exotic birds shimmering watchfully in a wild nest. 'I've been busy.'

Lara, still pleasantly limp with essential oils, felt a bubble of amusement rise into her throat. There was a sense that events were taking a distinctly peculiar turn over this cosy hot chocolate but this did not bother her. Strangely enough, she felt exhilarated.

For Lara realised that Sandra had conquered the first stage of a good woman's transformation. She had known what was expected of her, and she had fallen foul of it.

Good for her.

Over apple and blackcurrant crumble, Lara told them about her own ritual burial and, in turn, found out more about Sandra's domestic past.

'I had the kids, followed him around the country – lived in some dark holes, I can tell you – made the pennies stretch, put up with *his* constant pressures of life, kept everything together while he gave his all to other people – and what a shower they were, at times – and he refuses to let me work, says he needs me there all the time, putting on a show—'

'A show?'

'Of what a wonderful family we are. Three well-turned-out children, sparkling house, everyone's shoulder to lean on. And all the time, he can't see it.' She gave a hard stare behind which the dam threatened to burst. 'I've had enough.'

'What does he say, when you tell him this?' asked Lara. And what did he think of this vision?

Sandra blinked. 'As ye sow, so shall ye reap.'

'And that's crap,' snorted Cass. She lit a king-sized full-tar cigarette to the evident disgust of their fellow patrons. It was clear she had heard this many times.

Lara indicated the new image. 'So this is . . . the definitive statement?'

'Could be.'

'What does he think of it?'

'What do you imagine he thinks?' butted in Cass. 'He's the vicar of St Leonard's, Muswell Hill.'

They were half-way through their coffees when the clergyman's wife touched up her black lipstick in a pink plastic toy mirror with a small sigh of satisfaction and stood up. 'Come on, then.'

'Is it time?' asked Cass.

'Just about.'

Lara grinned hesitantly. 'Where are you two off to now?'

The women exchanged looks.

'We have to go to the workshop,' said Cass. 'Today of all days.'

'I'm sorry, I—'

'But we have to! It's a follow-up session this afternoon!'

'I wasn't going to go. I've had enough. It's been great today, really *great* . . . but you know, I need to find my own way.'

Cass blocked her way. 'For *Al*,' she said.

Sandra took her arm firmly.

So once again Lara found herself in the church hall with the workshop faithful. Colin gave her a shy smile and pointed at the empty seat next to him. Lara shook her head and allowed herself to be steered into place by Cass and Sandra. Any exhilaration at enjoying the unexpected had gone. She was back doing what other people wanted.

Her heart sank as Quiet Al (although his wife would no longer have recognised that description of him) stood at the front of the class and told his tale in a flat, slightly nasal London accent.

Quiet Al had a disconcerting face. It was as though a small boy and a middle-aged man were fighting for supremacy over his features. At any conversational point at which a reaction was required, a succession of faces would emerge, the expressions changing from innocence to enthusiasm, through thoughtfulness, and finally to a sagging dogmatism which was full of repressed longings.

Two days ago he had pushed away the remains of his breakfast at 8.12, according to the kitchen clock which measured out his mealtimes.

'Finished?' she asked.

Too right, she was.

Her name was Veronica, or had been, for he could not remember the last time he used it. The Fury, she was, in his mind, and now – daringly – in his conversation, too. He nodded perfunctorily and she cleared his place without a glance at him.

There she was, tied into the flowered apron, barren as the boiled egg he had just consumed. She stuck in his throat in much the same way, come to think of it. He had these strange thoughts more and more often; she had become an abstract. They did not touch.

But she was speaking to him.

'Only twenty-nine per cent of men regret getting divorced,' she said in that way she had, with a sniff punctuating the end of the statement. 'Half and half and we'll call it a day.' Another sniff. It grated into his backbone and he clenched his fists.

Silence hung.

'Half and half,' she repeated. 'That's what the solicitor said.'

He exhaled heavily.

He could have hurled her against the obscenely striped wallpaper she had chosen as one of her more subtle instruments of torture had he not been planning a more cunning end.

It was not that he wanted her any longer. But he had other plans.

His morbid preoccupation with scenes of death – hers, to be more precise – had begun as a calming measure in times of provocation. Now, he realised, he had come to depend on these vivid constructions as a pressure release. The violent imaginings had all the status now of an all-consuming hobby. As soon as he left the house, and put Styx Avenue behind him every morning to walk to his accountancy firm, the scenes danced across his day-dreams.

On his way to the office, he passed numbers stencilled on the lampposts. He noticed them still but had long ceased dwelling on them. Only ... he supposed there must be some kind of electrical charge beneath the con-crete and steel. Fantasy-involving-fatal-malfunction-of-lamppost-number-4356 on the corner of Styx and Lethe Avenues flared optimistically for a block or so before being consigned to the mental file marked 'Pure Escapism'.

An underground train.

Poison by stealth.

And a new scenario, inspired by a story on the local early-evening news: 'Dangerous reversing manoeuvre by a council refuse lorry.'

He was forty-eight now, and the clock was ticking harder every year. Would he ever be the man of his dreams?

Two evenings ago he returned from work at his usual time of 6.20. His wife checked him in by the second-hand of the kitchen clock on the wall and with a sniff pronounced herself moderately satisfied.

Then he began his task.

He opened the front door. He pulled her treasured

plates and pots from the dresser and hurled them into the street. Upstairs he wrenched her possessions from tidy cupboards and ran outside with them. He pegged up clothes on hedges, flew corsets from a fence post, launched hats from the bedroom window.

It was an hour later that his madness subsided. By then the house had been transformed into the vortex of the storm, and Styx Avenue outside was a foreign landscape.

In the best tradition of the neighbourhood there had been no overt opposition to his victory. The police were called – but from the sanctuary of a fox hole behind some unknown curtain.

They cautioned him, citing a breach of the peace.

Quiet Al was bellowing his ascendancy over the forces of his own nature – and the frustrations of *hers* – as an officer pinned one arm behind his back and marched him back inside Number 45.

'It was *wonderful*,' said Al. 'I'd never done anything like it before.'

The was no doubting the renewal of his confidence. He glowed before the assembly. He held his head high. Even his balding pate was flushed with pleasure.

'And your wife,' asked Annette, resuming control after this engrossing but lengthy narrative, 'has she come to terms with the quantum shift in your relationship patterns?'

Al rubbed his chin. 'If you mean, has it shut her up, then I would have to say yes.'

'What was her reaction to this release of your previously sublimated emotions?'

'Um . . . much as you'd expect, really.'

'Would you like to tell us, in your own words?'

'She screamed blue murder, the silly cow.'

There was a crude laugh at that, from the back. It came from Cass.

'Go on,' urged Annette.

The avenging husband shrugged. 'She was all over me. Clawing at me to stop. Grabbing my arms. Yelling her head off. As usual.'

'But you didn't stop.'

'I was enjoying myself.'

'And when it was over?'

'She was quiet then,' said Al.

There were still some details Annette was bent on extracting. 'When the police came, what happened then? What did she tell them?'

'Nothing. She didn't tell them anything.'

'She had already come to terms with the situation?' Even Annette seemed unsure that a solution could present itself this easily.

'You could say,' said Al.

The others certainly wanted to believe it. A few hesitant claps became a hearty round of applause for the hero of the hour.

'It was quite a night,' conceded Al.

Applause broke out again and he basked in his moment of glory.

When Lara arrived home at eleven o'clock she found herself checking the dark recesses of the flat. She had an unsettled feeling that was not assuaged by peering around corners and into the dustbin area outside.

The unease wasn't here, she decided. She had brought it in with her.

Those people, she admitted to herself at last, those people were *weird*.

8 A Leap in the Dark

One benefit of spending a mind-expanding day with the women was that other aspects of her life seemed reassuringly sane by comparison.

As early as the next day she began to wonder whether the big day out with Cass and Sandra had been some kind of depressive hallucination. She had momentarily lost touch with reality. Perhaps there had even been a spot of group hysteria.

Either way, Lara was more sure than ever that she needed to find her own way forward.

She tried to rationalise why she had spent time with them in the first place.

They had been the start, that was all.

She was testing the water before she plunged into her new life as a new woman.

Lara's friends were still leaving messages on the answering machine, but the tones were hurt and puzzled now. Either Lara was away, or their services, their years of understanding, were not required. Although, when Lara really listened to the disembodied voices, there were not as many friends and messages as might have been expected, given that the break-up with Will was still recent, set against their years together.

But then, he had gone in spirit long before that. Maybe

the simple fact was that everyone else had known that, long before she was ready to admit it.

In any case, she didn't want to talk to them and hear their advice. Neither did Lara seek out her women friends in the house and the market. They too would only ask about Will, and she did that herself – too often.

No, Lara had imagined it would be liberating to be with Cass and Sandra *because* they were not her friends: they had no expectations of her, and no prior knowledge of her viewpoint. They did not want to pick over the bones of her relationship with Will. They did not know her, they were not judging her, and so she was free to be whatever she wanted with them. They would be her release.

But then they had sprung into new life with a ferocity which had knocked her back while she was still feeling her way.

In no time, they were as slippery and frightening as the hordes Lara had left behind. What was more, she found increasingly – unsettlingly – that *they* were the characters who peopled her thoughts, whose voices rang in her consciousness, and whose shadows took rides on the roaring trains of her dreams at night.

What had made them so bitter and vengeful?

Yet, even then she was capable of considering Cass and Sandra, and poor Penny, and Colin the sad axe man, and her thoughts would lurch between the sense that it was excitement that bound them, and despair that it was only, after all, a terrible humiliating mutual inadequacy.

Which brought her back, unfortunately, to Colin. Colin was already determined on his own interpretation of the workshop ethos. He was not taking no for an answer.

Somehow he had acquired Lara's telephone number and was set on making use of it. That was disconcerting enough, but not as disconcerting as wondering how he had come by it in the first place. He told her that all numbers were on the course register but she knew that was a lie.

He wanted to be her support buddy.

He wanted to make sure she was all right.

He wanted to spend time with her.

They were neighbours, after all.

And gradually, despite herself, she came round to believing that there might be no harm in it.

It had been a curious sensation, the one of realising that he was right in one thing: there were many possibilities. Only, she had been conditioned for so long – by convention, by consideration of others, and by imprisoning fear – that there was a safe way to proceed, slowly and surely.

For once in her life, why shouldn't she break loose?

She gave in to Colin, as she knew she would. She hated to hurt the feelings of others. Suffer the meek, or however it went. Terminal Niceness again.

Besides, Colin was helping her in the garden. She had meant it simply as an excuse at first when she told him she was working in the yard, but he insisted that he wanted to see her. He even insisted that he wanted to help her dig and drag and fill. Besides, it would be good therapy, wouldn't it?

In the event, he proved usefully adept. Not to mention a very neat excavator.

At the kitchen table they drank mugs of orange workman's tea and pored over the plan she had sketched while they felt the satisfying ache of their muscles. They were building up and burrowing down, making beds and raising planting areas to catch the light. After two days the yard was a moonscape.

'What about that area by the wall?' he asked, prodding a grimy finger at the chart.

'Up, definitely.'

'And a ceanothus on top?'

She nodded.

'Grows pretty fast, that. Small tree in no time.'

'Good.'

'So it needs root space. Soil's poor there. Waterlogged. Slug infested.' He was surprisingly knowledgeable. Either that or he was mugging up before their sessions to impress her. She did not discount the possibility.

'What do you suggest?'

'Go down first. Sort out the underlying problem. Some grit and sand. Then you build up.'

'OK. Yes . . . good idea.'

And so they would rise and return to their toil.

In this situation, she thought, he was definitely at his best.

Certainly it was the only way Colin was going to make the earth move for her.

Once he had begun, he continued to come round to lend a hand in the garden. She did not invite him, but he would arrive intermittently and she did nothing to discourage him. They were sitting outside on two kitchen chairs one afternoon the following week when he asked her a question about herself for the first time.

'Have you always lived alone?'

She was suddenly aware of the cold dampness of her old shirt on her back after what had been a strenuous session of lugging and dumping. So used was she to their comfortingly terse exchanges when they took a break, that she had to ask him to repeat it.

'Have you ever been married . . . or anything?' His bony face was pink, although that could have been from exertion. Pale hair flopped, darkened and damp, over a moist smooth forehead.

She shook her head automatically. 'No . . . not married.'

'Anything, then?'

'You could say.' She didn't want to, though.

Birds wheeled overhead. A gust of wind pushed over a row of plastic flowerpots and they skittered around on the remaining flagstones.

'I just wondered . . .'

She wondered whether he would press the point, but he didn't. He finished his tea in silence, then stood up holding out his hand for her mug before going back to the kitchen. She heard water running and was touched.

'It's . . . still a bit raw,' she told him when he re-emerged.

He nodded and picked up a stone.

At night after these sessions she would sleep like a chalk giant on a hillside, flat out on her back, tired arms splayed. If she woke, her mind bursting with dream images, for the first time in a long age they would not be of Will; she was alone, but not lonely.

She went one day to a garden centre off the King's Road where she saw wonderful statuary. Wandering alone amid weathered stone urns and busts of the ancients, she was reminded of the time she spent with Will in Greece. But she did not think of him. The stab of memory was of another man, and it stole up on her like a mugger.

She had missed her chance once. Never again. In a trance she bought tray upon tray of seedlings, the new beginnings of flowers which would grow into summer's carpet. When they spilled from their beds and containers towards the sun and glory, so would she.

She felt she had to repay Colin somehow for his toil in her back yard. That was all it was.

The clock said it was gone five. She supposed she might bath and change before he arrived, but there seemed no necessity. She was utterly at ease as she scrubbed up and set about making a lasagne. Nothing too fancy.

It was hardly living dangerously.

On her doorstep promptly at eight o'clock, Colin smiled shyly.

Under an unforgiving light in Lara's kitchen he presented her with a bottle of Australian Cabernet Sauvignon and a profile that was unexpectedly sleek while he opened it.

He had a thin boy's body, which had that curious propensity to bend into the shape of a number seven – he was a slight figure, in other words. Or rather he was one of those men who seemed slight when standing on their own, but when they stood against others you were surprised to deduce that they were probably six feet tall. His blond hair was well brushed – it was real blond, not Will's wishful-thinking blond – and he was gentle looking, Lara decided, which was probably due to the slightly untidy mouth and evidence of the occasional pimple. A nice face, but a nondescript one with its share of unfairnesses.

Perhaps that was exactly why she decided she liked him.

There was a peculiar honesty, she thought as they drank some wine, about an acquaintance founded entirely on nihilism. They knew nothing about each other but the fact of their disillusionment. It made getting down to the nitty-gritty all the easier.

'How was it for you?' asked Lara. 'Before.'

There was no hesitation. He knew exactly what she meant. 'I realised it was all . . . the most terrible disappointment,' he said.

'Everything you'd always set such store by?'

'Couldn't have worked any harder. Days, nights. Always gave my all.'

'People like us always do,' she concurred.

People like us.

'I was confused. For a long time. Didn't know which way to turn, where to find the answers.' He looked ever more like a lost boy sunk into the deep squashy sofa, hardly touching his drink.

'What was the last straw?'

Colin sighed. 'There were so many.'

She warmed even more to him, to his brave silent battles.

'I was the target of several malicious incidents. In the block of flats where I lived. Terrorised in my own home.'

'The axe . . .?'

'That came later.'

'Go on.'

'Attempted arson, hate mail, dead birds and dog excrement on the doorstep. And then there was the home-made bomb through the letter-box . . .'

'My God . . . I mean, *who*?'

'He knew his rights,' said Colin.

'Don't they all.'

'Not normally this early.'

'Oh?'

'He was seven years old. Below the age of criminality. Nothing anyone could do about him.'

'That's awful.'

'And then there was his mother.'

'It gets worse?'

'Very much so. Bitch of the first order.'

'What did she do?'

'About the boy? Egged him on. Lied for him. Seemed unperturbed that he carried a Stanley knife – and used it to get what he wanted. Thought it was a laugh.'

'Bloody hell.'

'She came home from work one day to find I'd taken it away from him after yet another confrontation—'

'Was that wise?'

'There was a half-disembowelled cat on the stairway.'

Lara shuddered.

'Neighbours in uproar. Everyone taking her side . . .'

Lara frowned. 'But why?'

'She was a nurse. And they're angels, aren't they.'

'Everyone knows that,' said Lara.

'Then there came the day she comes home with this great brute of a trucker – shoulders big as his cab, you know? – and he says he's protecting her from the likes of me, they'll take her stuff and they'll get the hell out of my way . . .'

'So what was wrong with that?'

'She was my wife. I'd taken on the boy but he wasn't mine.'

Lara served the food with little ceremony. Colin seemed to have shrunk back into himself after this rendition of the facts as he saw them. Her sympathies sounded cackhanded. That could have been due to the way he had of leaving out crucial aspects of the story until he could use them as a punch-line – she had noticed the first time she heard him speak. It was unsettling, wondering what he was saving for later.

But then, they both knew that the course they had chosen required action, not words.

It was too dark to dig at the garden to disperse the awkwardness, so they chewed at the lasagne, then the salad.

'I am resuming my life,' he said at last. 'Taking steps. One day at a time.'

'Well . . . that's good.'

A shrug.

'Isn't it?'

'I suppose. It has been rather a revelation. I didn't realise I was into all this until I found the organisation . . .' He made it sound sinister. 'Other like-minded people, people coming from another direction.'

Lara searched for a suitable response. One that would lighten the moment.

'But you see . . .' He put down his fork and stared numbly at his plate. 'There is something burning inside me . . .'

'Could be the lasagne.'

As he raised his eyes, he was a supplicant for all the sorrows of the world.

Lara was forced to change tack. 'You're upset, but you *can* work it out. I'm sure you can,' she said gently.

He did not answer so she probed further.

'What did you do before all this – as a job?' She hadn't asked this before, deliberately. In view of her own situation she knew for the first time that the question was at worst an impertinence, at best an irrelevance.

'I . . . don't really want to talk about it,' said Colin.

Lara could have kicked herself. She filled his glass with wine, feeling a surge of compassion. 'OK then, you might as well know,' he rallied. 'I was with . . . a security force.'

She was taken aback. Had she assumed too little of him?

He went soon afterwards.

The next time she saw him, she made a grave mistake. She let him kiss her.

He arrived unannounced the following day bearing a tray of blue and purple pansies, and was standing, king of the castle, on a mound of stone slabs which she intended as a kind of wild rockery.

'It's going to be beautiful,' proclaimed Colin, 'just like you.'

Even in their best days Will had never called her beautiful. Parts of her, yes: her eyes, her shoulders, the nape of her neck for which he had always expressed an especial liking. But never as a whole.

So Lara looked up at Colin on his mound, squinted up in the afternoon sun and could not see his face. She could only feel it, as he bent and put his mouth on hers.

Then they worked together until the light faded, hardly exchanging a word more. They planted the pansies and raked over other beds they had constructed, and perhaps that made her bold. Maybe the effect on her dwarf confidence was to give her renewed confidence in nature.

After that they drank a bottle of wine together.

Later she washed and slicked foundation cream over her face.

He had left her to fetch something from his car.

Preparing herself in front of the mirror for Colin to return, Lara wondered vaguely what she was doing, but then turned the flutter of unease neatly into a small dilemma over which lipstick to apply.

She chose one which had been heavily advertised in *Reflections* for its softness and suppleness. It was no better nor worse than a hundred others. She made a face in the mirror.

Sometimes – even knowing what she did – she allowed the women's magazines to make her feel like a fraud, as if she wasn't a proper woman at all. She was a *real* woman, but that was something entirely different. She had dimpled thighs and no hip-bones and her breasts did not look like those in the magazines. Hers was not an advertisement body; it would only scrape into the editorial pages these days by way of the problem page.

It was thoughts like these that made her feel profoundly depressed at Will's leaving.

How would she ever have the courage again to show her imperfections?

She quite liked Colin, strangely enough. There could never be anything more than that, of course. But she was fascinated by his pimpled, inexorable *loserdom*, which somehow went hand in hand with his absolute certainty that prices would be paid. His wife – he had been *married*! – had discovered that.

He had said that she was beautiful.

He hadn't actually said that he was special agent in the security services. That something had gone horribly wrong and that MI6 was watching his every move. That he was a sad fantasist. He had said that he'd been *with* a security force, whatever that meant. He meant a security firm, surely; one with threatening notices and drooling guard dogs and lardy men in grey uniforms.

Colin was one of life's clerks. He probably did the wages. Events blew up around him, and still he filed and drank tea. So there was, after all, something admirable about the stance he was taking. He was weak, yet he was preparing himself to stand in the eye of the storm. So she convinced herself.

Together they were dancing with the devil.

Or so it felt.

Especially after another bottle of cabernet sauvignon. At last, it seemed, the drink was having an effect. It was making her feel quite ourageously attractive and friendly.

Colin revealed that he had taken the liberty of bringing with him a length of cloth. Half-way down the third bottle of wine, this did not seem strange. He began to acquaint her with its history. He had bought it in a wonderful shop near Brick Lane, he said. He unwrapped it and when he shook out the iridescent folds of green and indigo and purple and gold and silver it was like the wash of the South Seas.

'I have this fantasy,' he said.

Her newly slicked lips felt as conspicuous as a false nose.

'Drink?' asked Colin, pouring her another glass.

Lara thought they were going to need it.

*

'You *do* like me, Lara, don't you?'

That caught her off guard.

She was also off balance, and probably off her head. No sooner had she thought that than she had a strong urge to turn herself upside down to test the theory. She dropped to her knees and tried to do a head stand. It did not work, and she felt herself roll over soft as a baby on the rug.

She laughed and said, 'Now . . .'

'Yes?'

'I think you should know,' she said, 'that I am not the person I used to be. I am working on the principle that a woman could wait a very long time indeed for the right man to come along.' She paused. 'During which time she might as well have a good time with all the wrong ones.'

He didn't take that nearly as badly as she thought he might.

'*Yes!*' he cried.

Then he made his move.

When all was said, and she was undone, there was an awkward pause.

But she remained silent and strangely calm as he advanced in a billow of gold and purple and green, his head apparently balanced on the top edge like a ball on a magician's scarf. When they were eyeball to eyeball, a hand extended and he brushed her cheek with infinite gentleness.

He began to wind the cloth around her body, breathing heavily as he accomplished his task.

'How does that feel?'

'I feel a bit silly, to tell you the truth,' said Lara.

'This,' said Colin, breathing hard, 'is going to work. It's all falling beautifully into place.'

The declaration was accompanied by a strong pressure around her chest. He was tying her – in a standing position – into the gold and silver and sea-green fabric. She watched as though it was nothing to do with her. In a matter of minutes she was girdled, tall and as thin as she would ever be. She could not move. Ridiculously mummified, she stood in the middle of her sitting-room.

Colin stood back to admire his handiwork.

'How was it for you?' she asked drily.

He bit on his lower lip as he adjusted a fold of cloth to his satisfaction. 'Lovely ... lovely ... just perfect ...' he muttered, but more to himself than to her. Then he turned his back on her and bent to select another length from a paper carrier bag she had not noticed him bring in.

He began to caress her over her taut chrysalis. Involuntarily she lowered her eyes coyly. Under his strokes she felt reality slipping. She was no longer herself; she was silk swathed; she was a shy, beautiful Hindu bride ...

This was different; this was living dangerously.

He did not avert his gaze. His eyes were positively smoking.

'What?' she asked tenderly when his beatific stare became too spooky.

'You're here with me now. You can't go away this time,' he said.

'I won't go away,' murmured Lara, joining in the game and glad she was drunk.

'I'm going to get my camera now.'

WHAT?

She wouldn't want anyone to see her now, like this. No prisoners, no evidence ...

That woke her up from the madness. What the *hell* was she doing?

Colin's smile was gruesome. 'Beautiful pictures ... keep you like this ...'

There was something about the way he said it. She shook her head.

Lara struggled back to him as if swimming through weeds and shadow, lungs wrung of breath. Surfacing in the lamplit present, swathed in the sea-green, blue and indigo material in which he had wrapped her, she was the corniest of survivors, too dazed to tell the tale.

Her body was suffocating inside its glittering prison. Her heart was rattling at her ribcage. She elbowed at the inside of her bindings, fear apparently increasing her strength while the wine made her efforts as impotent as they were in bad dreams.

Colin continued to stared intently. 'Well?'

'Get this stupid stuff off me!' She was fighting it now, struggling against the glorious hues.

He waited long enough for her to be convinced her number was up at the hands of a madman and that she had no one to blame but herself. There was no mistaking the edge in his voice as he stepped forward and began, slowly, to release her.

She sank down dazed on to the floor, the fabric once again loose around her but covering her near-nakedness. He was watching her intently.

'Why did you do that?' she asked crossly, terrified of showing the extent of her fear.

He hung his head.

9   Casting Off

The debacle with Colin did it. No more other people, no more odd bods: Lara was going to get herself together by herself. She was on her own and she was going to do what she should have done weeks ago.

A surge of spiteful optimism beached Lara in a phone box which suited her purpose. If anyone wanted to trace the call, the code would tell them it had been made from Belgravia.

She was on one corner of a creamy stucco square which was hushed with money. Passing traffic did not grate and growl here; it positively purred.

Lara slipped a coin into the slot and dialled the direct line to the overlord of Incorporated Magazines.

Funny, she thought as the ringing tone began. She had never had reason to speak to him before, when he was controlling her life from his glassy suite high above the mayhem of headlines and deadlines. Lara pictured the man with the head like a hammerhead shark tipped back in his leather chair, sated after lunch or a feeding frenzy with his ambitious editor Ella.

'Martin Skelton's office.'

'I have a call from Ella McGuire,' said Lara.

'Putting you through.'

Seconds later, she was through to God.

Lucky, lucky Ella.

126

'I'm afraid this isn't Ella,' said Lara. 'I shall make this as brief and clear as possible. I would like you to tell your girlfriend Ella to leave my husband alone.'

'Who is this?'

'If you don't know, then I suggest you ask Ella to tell you. Goodbye.' Lara placed the receiver carefully on its cradle. Then she danced a little jig and clapped her hands together.

She spent the rest of the afternoon, much cheered, drinking gin and tonic in the pub where Lady Lucan famously staggered to raise the alarm that her husband had tried to murder her.

Two days later, to complete the job, Lara put on a head-scarf and paid cash at a West End florist's shop to send a single dried black rose to her former editor's lover, with the inscription on a card: 'Thanks for the ride (you were lousy), with love from Ella.'

Lara surprised herself by the ease with which she did it – and the glib way she made sure it slipped to the girl behind the counter that her own name was Annie, and she was acting for a friend.

Was she in touch with her hidden depths at last?

She concentrated on this for a while when the mission was accomplished and could only come up with one explanation. If it had been a fear of being unhappy that had kept her striving before, now she *was* unhappy and the recognition of that brought its own freedom.

Lara had learned to hide her strong opinions. Indeed, it would have surprised many people who thought they knew her that she *had* strong opinions. For surely part of being good enough was passing muster with other people, and that meant rarely contradicting them, certainly never knocking them off course. The theory had

127

worked a treat, through school and university, but especially well when she graduated to work.

Lara did well at whatever she tried. But then she had long ago discovered that 'She's good' was only another way of saying 'She agrees with me'. And one way or another, that had agreed with Lara. She had made her way forward in a way that was slow but sure, and she never rocked the boat.

No longer.

It was hard to tell sometimes whether some people got what they wanted because they behaved extremely badly – or whether they behaved extremely badly because they always got what they wanted. To achieve what Jennifer had, or Janey, or the girl upstairs with the tiny children and inexplicable lifestyle, or even Cass and Sandra, she decided, one had to have no sense of danger, or fear of failure. Perhaps one also had to have nothing to lose.

Lara had tried to explain as much to Will once, before she realised that he would never understand because he had never known what it was to be held back by personal integrity, or the remnants of a consideration for others. She had thought it extraordinary at the time that her point had slipped between his play frown and the serious way that he examined his own hands before changing the subject.

What seemed extraordinary to her now was that she ever assumed he would understand. Phrases came lightly to his lips, sincere meaning less so.

She had asked him straight, 'Does Jennifer realise what she does, do you think?'

'What do you mean, exactly?'

'The way she talks to people. She makes demands on them as if they should be . . . I don't know, flattered that she's noticed them or something . . . She never says or does anything without considering first what the return will be for her.'

'What *are* you going on about?'

'You mean you've never noticed?' countered Lara.

'Can't say I have,' he replied.

'Oh, come on . . .'

'Lara . . . I don't know what this is all about. If you want to say something, then say it.'

Lara thought she had, but clearly not.

'She called me today at work. She wanted me to supply her with three British designers who were willing to talk about suppression of the true self, and to have them with her in the studio by ten o'clock in the morning the day after tomorrow.'

Will was unfazed. 'And?'

'And, for once, I told her where to get off – with no suppression of my true feelings.'

'So you were rude to her then.' There was a quiet lethality about this interpretation of events.

'No,' said Lara, 'not nearly as rude as she was to me in issuing yet another of her demands.'

Will paused, then said, 'Sorry, Lara, but you have to stop this.'

'Stop what?'

'All this defensiveness. This . . . reading into situations what isn't there.'

'What?'

'She called me yesterday. Said she was worried about you – the way you fly off the handle with her. She wanted to know whether it was just her, or whether you had a problem in general.'

'What?'

'She thinks – and this was an explanation she was reluctant to come to – that you might be jealous of her. And she wants to help.'

'Oh, for fuck's sake,' exploded Lara.

'And I think you should apologise. She'd promised the producer that she could come up with this feature. The programme editor was giving it top billing – and she had to tell them that she'd been let down by someone who was practically family.'

Lara stood hot and trembling like a kettle coming up to the boil.

'You just don't get it, do you?' she said.

'No,' he said, 'it's you who don't.'

Making trouble between them soon turned into something of a hobby for Jennifer. She had an uncanny knack of choosing the perfect moment. Lara had to hand it to her; her timing was impeccable.

Will would be due to appear at a dinner party or charity ball or similar event in the magazine world where the privileges of coupledom were paraded, when Lara would be summoned to the nearest telephone to be informed that Will was unavoidably detained, and probably for some time. It was often Jennifer who did this informing. Lara could just imagine her, a light hand on his shoulder, saying, 'Never mind, darling. I'll let her know. You carry on persuading this film contact of mine of your genius, saving me from despair by being my partner at this opening or that final performance, being my rock, like you are.' At which point Lara's imagination would become fevered, although never far from the truth, had she but known it at the time.

As far as Will was concerned, Jennifer could do no wrong.

Lara decided to live a bit. Who was she kidding? She decided to live a *lot*.

She dared to make the arrangements.

Two days later she was steeled to see an old enemy.

Lara surfaced from the underground at Embankment this time and walked – positively jauntily – towards this meeting. She would cut loose and free.

She was ten minutes late when she arrived at the

wine bar in Wellington Street, knowing full well she'd be waiting longer on her own. Surprisingly, she was not the first to arrive. Her own demons, naturally, had preceded her; but there, in human form, was Jennifer.

Lara saw her through the plate glass, at a corner table.

Unpleasant manipulative people laid traps. You had to think as they did to outwit them – and even then they were skilled at making it seem as if you were the one in the wrong. They are very good at that, Cass had said.

The others had murmured agreement.

We all had dark thoughts and instincts, but they used that knowledge to make us feel that we were as bad as they were.

They lie. Well, we have all lied.

They are selfish. So are we.

They use people, but we have all asked other people to help us to achieve something, contributed a quiet man at the back of the group.

They hurt people. We have all been guilty of that.

They have no qualms about turning ourselves against ourselves, all the while smiling with superior human knowledge.

You must never show bullies you are scared of them, Annette said in Lara's head.

Lara went into the wine bar and smiled at her old tormentor.

'It's good to see you,' said Jennifer, raising her glass. There was a bottle on the table. The implication was that Lara might need it for an update on Will.

'You too.'

'Don't – before you say anything – don't mention May Cartwright.'

'I wasn't going to,' said Lara. 'Who is May Cartwright?'

131

'She was a fucking actress. Can you believe it? We were set up. We're suing, of course.'

'Naturally.'

'She came on the show for a make over – pretending to be a defenceless old lady. We were set up by the *Sun*! Have you seen the piece they wrote? Outrageous!' Having established her own precedence, Jennifer poured Lara a glass of wine. 'You haven't changed a bit!'

That reassured Lara. Now she knew she had.

Lara smiled, more confidently than she had for a while. 'I saw the show today,' she said. 'I thought it was very . . . telling.'

'Well, thank you.' Then Jennifer sighed. 'The item about thirtyish women picking up the pieces when their lovers leave them – it was scheduled for the show last week. I had no idea I'd be seeing you, Lara.'

Lara waved that away.

'How *do* you feel?' asked Jennifer, seizing the opening.

'Relieved, I think. Yes. I feel relieved.'

'Oh? In what way?'

'I don't know what I think any more,' said Lara matter-of-factly. 'I'm having to question everything.'

'It's only natural. The break-up. The end of the struggle.'

'What *has* he been saying?'

'Will? Oh . . . I haven't really wanted to ask in too much detail.'

Lara lit a cigarette and kept quiet.

'You know what he's like,' said Jennifer, clearly relishing the moment.

'You're his cousin.'

Jennifer took a breath, waving away smoke. 'OK . . .'

Actressy, thought Lara.

'He's been . . . Now Lara, you know I'm being honest here because I know that's what you would want, right . . .'

'Sure.'

'He's . . . he seems *happier* now . . .'

Lara felt tension grip her.

' . . . than he's been in quite a while.'

Lara took a gulp of wine.

'I'm sorry if that's not what you wanted to hear from me.' Jennifer twisted a thick gold bangle on her slender white wrist. The insides of her arms, Lara noted, were as pure and dewy as freshly cut lilies.

'Well, I—'

'Only when you called . . .'

'I was the last person you expected to hear from,' said Lara.

'I wasn't sure that we'd ever . . . hit it off, exactly.'

'We were never friends,' confirmed Lara. 'Maybe because we are very different people.'

Jennifer was a picture of soft blonde vulnerability, with eyes as hard as flints. Lara was certain she saw relief register on her creamy face.

'No. The reason I wanted to see you was to tie up everything.'

'Meaning?'

'Secure the end. Make absolutely sure that's it's over.'

'Oh?' she said. She was whiter than white, with a hint of hurt.

'And you can cut the crap, Jennifer. I *know* what you say about me. You didn't control him completely. And I know it was you who set him up with Janey. Great friend of yours, isn't she? Was there a point to that, or just a bit of malicious fun?'

'They are *such* a sweet couple,' purred Jennifer. 'They're deliriously happy, I'm afraid.'

The surge of pure fury must have registered on Lara's face.

Jennifer affected concern. 'This can't be an easy time for you, Lara . . .'

133

Lara got a grip. 'Oh, but it *is*. I've been waiting years for this.'

'So, you arranged all this so that you could rant at me. I think that's very sad.'

Lara stared coldly at the woman she had allowed to become a monster to her. Jennifer was like broken glass: sparkly and vicious, but no longer harmful once you had the measure of it. Flesh and blood in front of Lara now, she was small and flawed.

'Oh, no,' said Lara deftly, all innocence. 'This had nothing to do with it. I wanted to do you a favour – I wanted to warn you . . .'

A sigh.

'You know *Reflections* does a poll every year.'

'Of course I do. Everyone knows that.'

'Well, I thought you ought to hear it from someone face to face as a matter of courtesy – you've been voted Worst Dressed Woman on TV,' said Lara. 'And Most Synthetic.'

The atmosphere froze across the table.

'That's a . . . new category,' said Lara.

It was a first vindictive lie. It gave Lara quite a kick.

Believe you are capable of overcoming any obstacles in life . . .

The following morning after a remarkably refreshing night's sleep, Lara turned over this piece of workshop wisdom in her mind as she stared into the depths of his wardrobe.

Maybe the time had come.

Maybe?

She should have done this weeks ago. Then maybe she wouldn't have got herself mixed up with the workshop. She shuddered at the thought, pulled herself up tall and strong, and then swung a fist at the rail. The suits on their hangers swayed as if to shrug her off.

She still could not understand why Will had not come

back for his clothes – nor why it had been so long before she had taken decisive action. She had tested her nerve by hauling the few pieces to Jo at the market, and found that she could not bear to rid herself of him completely.

It was different now.

So Lara reached in to the rail, and one by one she unhooked and pulled out the hangers which held Will's clothes. Deliberately she unfolded the trousers and rehung them beneath their jackets. Then she placed them on the picture rail, on the bed, and on the floor until the room was full of dark flattened headless men.

When this work was done she took some time to decide which he would be pleased to see again. Now and then rogue memories threatened her composure – how could she not remember what he had worn when he had taken her to the Ritz and told her he loved her, or what she had clung to when she forgave him, sobbing into its folds, for his first unexplained absence?

She beat such thoughts away.

Set your target and fulfil your journey . . .

Then she sat back on her heels in the middle of the room and gave her limp audience a snort of laughter. Bounding up, she skittered to the kitchen and returned a moment later with a bulb of garlic and a cakey jar of chilli powder.

The garlic was fresh and pungent. Peeling the first clove left a skunk's kiss on her fingers so she wiped them on the collar of a particularly good jacket which hung by the door. Then she reached into the trousers and rubbed the garlic on the silky lining of the crotch. She could feel its sticky moistness. After that small satisfaction, she grabbed the lapels of the jacket so it jumped off the hanger and gloried in the foul odour of chilli on underarm lining.

She started on the next, and the next. For a frenzied hour Lara was a witch stirring her brew.

Messages from Cass and Sandra and Colin squawked into her answering machine along with the others (although these were less and less) and she returned none of them.

Lara was not Annette or Al. She was profoundly uneasy about their stated objectives.

Lara was a nice person, and nice people did not change overnight into avenging furies. They sat at home and worried and tried to stop themselves falling apart.

She had made her gesture where Ella and Annie were concerned. She had faced down Jennifer. Now she had to find a proper way forward that worked for her.

This was simple but effective.

She was Cass, she was Sandra – but in her own way.

She was powerful in her fury.

In the bathroom Lara scooped up what remained to taunt her of his lotions and male unguents, congealing now in a dusty corner. She flung open the cabinet where her own preparations were kept, sending bottles over like skittles, scrabbling further into the dark store as they tumbled over the floor. She emerged with a tube of depilatory cream.

Then she squeezed it into a bottle of his designer shampoo and shook her potion in the air to mix it with a great cackle of glee.

Lara packed up her morning's work carefully in a tatty suitcase Will had left. Then for the first time in months she picked up the telephone and dialled his work number. It disconcerted her that her fingers found the digits so readily with not the slightest lapse of memory. They shook, but not with hesitation. If she got through to an answering machine, or someone who recognised her voice, what then?

The call was ringing.

She was riding too high. Too late she realised that she should have dialled 141 beforehand to make the call untraceable back to her.

She got away with it. She was on a roll.

An unfamiliar voice informed her, 'Narcissus. Lisa speaking.' And then, slightly peevishly, 'How *may* I help you?'

'I wonder whether you could,' said Lara. 'Help me, that is.'

A pause.

'I'm a friend of Janey's . . . Will's partner?'

She wasn't contradicted.

'This is rather awkward and I know it's a cheek to ring and ask you, but I couldn't think of any other way round this. You see, I've lost Janey's number which she gave me when she and Will moved in together, but I remembered the name of *his* work and found it in the book, so . . .'

Lara could sense the silence was charged with the words: Get on with it.

' . . . so I was wondering if you would be so kind as to—'

'We don't give out home numbers.'

'No, I know. This is awful of me, I know. Awful position to put you in. But you see, it's a bit of a long story. I live in the flat next door to Janey's old place and—'

The sigh of annoyance at the end of the line spurred Lara on. She was gambling recklessly. For all she knew, Will had simply moved in with Janey, wherever it was she lived.

'Well, I was wondering whether I could either leave a message which you can give to Will, or else you could perhaps . . . I dunno, it all seems an awful bother for you . . .'

'Look, I'm sorry, but—'

'You see, let me explain. I have this *enormous* bouquet of flowers that's arrived for Janey at the wrong address. The delivery man left them on my doorstep, you know

137

what they're like, get everyone to rally round and do their work for them. So here I am with this simply *huge* bunch of roses and lilies and all sorts of things, and I need to send it on. And then I remembered Will and the name of the company. So if I send them over to you, then *you* could . . .' Lara stopped, breathless.

The girl really didn't want to get involved.

'122B Albertine Steet,' she said. 'SW10.'

'Thanks,' said Lara and hung up.

In the taxi on the way there, Lara felt she had never seen so clearly. The streets were sharp the other side of the window. At her feet the suitcase full of Will's possessions attested to her determination. There was something positively primeval about her joy on this journey.

Or was that the occasional whiff of garlic and chilli? It seemed awfully strong now that every suit was impregnated.

On the flip-up seats opposite were advertisements for a conference centre at Heathrow and a dubious slimming centre. His and hers, was the implication. Outside, Lara saw Hyde Park pass in a green blur, then the great battlements of Knightsbridge shops. The driver was going the long way round – taking her for a visitor, with her inane smile and foreign-smelling bags.

She tapped on the window and gave him short shrift.

It seemed it was only a few sharp turns later and they were there. The taxi pulled up outside a fine house numbered 122 on a black door. Lara climbed out, leaving the baggage for the driver, and considered Albertine Street.

It was a tree-lined collection of white-painted houses. A highly desirable location, with the scent of overseas money. Will *had* gone up in the world.

Lara felt less impressed, though, when the bell for 122B turned out to be down some steps at the side. He was still below pavement level, then. She rang the bell, full of purpose.

A woman came to the door.

Lara gave her a professional appraisal. She was not so different from Lara – a similar height and size. She was younger perhaps, and her hair was blonder, cut in a good Kensington bob. Pretty, definitely. Complexion, excellent. Clothes, good. Shoes, none.

'Hello,' she said, taking in Lara and the suitcase.

'Janey?'

'Yes.'

'I've brought this for Will,' said Lara evenly. She nodded towards the luggage still on the pavement; she wasn't going to hump it down those narrow steps.

Then curiosity claimed the moment. Or did she want to unsettle the woman, to pay her back?

'I don't suppose you know who I am,' said Lara.

'Of course I do.'

'Oh?'

'You're Lara.'

That took her aback.

Janey answered the unspoken question. 'I kind of wondered whether you would come. And then ... I've seen you before.'

'Oh?' This time Lara imbued that with as much haughtiness as she could muster.

'I watched you once in Greece,' said Janey.

Lara was dumbstruck.

'He left you there, didn't he? He went off and left you alone in a strange town.'

The buried memory stirred as horribly as a corpse.

Lara felt herself swaying on the doorstep.

The Sunbathers

10 A Greek Idyll

All human form was there, thought Lara as she lay in the shade of a tree. Will, swimming in the sea, was far away from her, a speck in indigo way past the shallower turquoise water. Between them on the sand, in the surf, were bulging stomachs, jiggling breasts, grapefruit thighs, outbreaks of beach bottom and untoned women who wore their legs like crumpled trousers.

Inevitably Lara compared herself – and *them* – to the mythical ideal. Then she pulled herself up with a sharp annoyance. Give it a break. She was on holiday now.

The fierce July sun seared her body when she got up and walked down to the water.

Hot sand stung the soles of her feet.

Stoupa, the village where they were staying, was a buckle on the shoe of a Peloponnese headland. On one side of this land spit lay tavernas which dominated the bay and the main beach; this side was a wilder affair. Behind them rose scrubby blasted mountains. All along the coast, red and rust rocks tumbled and crumbled into the sea, speared by sentinel cypress trees.

There had been arguments, of course. Will would have preferred one of the other coastal resorts – somewhere with nightlife and beautiful blonde German women, she didn't doubt. For once, though, she had dug in her heels and prevailed. He had quietly given in to her with none of the petulance that would normally have flipped the decision. She chose not to ask why.

They had come away because of Janey.

Not that either of them intended to mention her.

'Have you forgotten what this is?' asked Lara conspiratorially, over their fourth Greek feta cheese salad in as many days.

'The safe option?' replied Will, considering the beachside taverna. There were puddles of sandy sludge on the concrete floor. Lightning bolts of sunshine through a canopy of vines made leopards of their faces and those of other sleepy lunchers.

Lara was momentarily nonplussed.

'Foodwise,' he said.

'Oh . . . yeah. I wasn't thinking quite so specifically, actually . . .'

'Oh?' Will barely paused in the efficient fork action of his refuelling.

Lara wondered whether this was the moment. Then he looked up and smiled.

'Three holidays, you said. Remember?' she chanced.

'Uuhh . . .?'

'Three summer holidays together, and a couple were . . . you know . . . linked for all time.' That wasn't what he had said, of course. The word was 'married'. Only she wasn't going to be the one to say it.

'Caro's wedding,' said Will. 'I remember.'

Lara paused, meaningfully.

'Is this really three – the third one?'

'Four.' As usual, Lara more than covered herself.

A summer cloud passed over his beautiful sea-green eyes. 'Well . . .'

When he said nothing more, she promptly gently with a little laugh that rang fake: 'We met at Caro's wedding on July the – in July . . . and went away first that September.'

'Those couple of days in Positano.'

'A week in Positano.'

'Then, the year after we went to St Lucia, remember?'

'I thought that was a freebee from the magazine.'

'It was two weeks' sumptuous pampering and romance and balmy nights, as *I* recall,' said Lara. 'I wasn't aware that accounting procedures made a difference to the theory.'

He only shrugged at that.

'Then the next year . . . we were in the Maldives.'

'Did I pay?'

'Business was good,' confirmed Lara.

'That was ages ago.'

'We didn't have a holiday last year.'

'No . . . so we didn't.'

'Four years, four holidays,' said Lara. She popped an olive in her mouth, strove for a kooky expression and gave him a pregnant grin.

'Sometimes . . .' said Will, moving his lips towards hers with a teasing smile.

They kissed lightly.

'Sometimes?'

'Sometimes, Lara, you are the most silly and logical person.'

'Both at once?'

'Yeah.'

'Is that not good?'

'Good, bad . . . indifferent. Why the constant ordering and organisation of life? All this *categorisation*.'

'Does that annoy you?'

He smiled not at all, then said, 'Since you ask, yes.'

Whenever anyone – usually Annie – asked her why she stayed with Will, Lara would answer, 'Because he hangs the moon for me.'

The response had become glib.

When they were introduced at Caro's wedding, she had already seen him across the room, had manoeuvred her way across the thronged reception to give herself every chance. Even now, he was imprinted on her imagination across jewel colours and morning suits in that grand chamber at the Athenaeum. He was in profile, head dipped in conversation with a pretty red-haired girl, his own sandy-blond hair flopping over darker sideburns. There was something in his ease of manner which drew her, the way he stood, althetic looking with one hand in a pocket, and then flipped his head back, but not too far, to laugh.

If you made the running, Lara found on the rare occasions she had done so, you always made more of an investment.

And this time, more than any, she had made it.

He was a friend of the bridegroom. Not an especially close friend; they had shared a flat in North London with others for some months after leaving university.

Even now, years later, she was faintly surprised when she considered his head and found that his hair was sludgy mid-brown. In her mind, he was always blond.

It didn't take long to see how self-absorbed he was, either – what else could you expect of a man who ran a video production company called Narcissus?

'Why Narcissus?' she'd asked guilelessly over a newly topped-up glass of wedding champagne.

'The image,' said Will, with a smile she would come to know well, 'of beautiful youth staring enraptured by its own reflection.'

'Youth . . . collective.'

'Exactly.'

'So . . . Narcissus is like . . . the target audience.'

'That's right.'

'Interesting,' said Lara.

So it was.

It must have taken a good twenty minutes for him to get round to asking, 'So . . . what about you?'

Although naturally, it was only much later that she realised.

As it was, they were swept up together in the surge as the wedding guests poured down the stairs and out of the club portals to Pall Mall to see off the happy couple. Caro, resplendent in going-away Starzewski as befitted a writer on *Reflections* magazine, subverted her bridal beam for a second to target Lara with a wicked grin. She made as if to throw the lily bouquet, but there were more deserving friends who needed the superstitious fillip, as they both knew.

By that time Will had asked if he could take her to dinner.

Lara's reply was writ large in her own grin.

Two days later, he called. A week to the day, Lara was staring at a menu without seeing a word in a restaurant half-way down the King's Road, then eating without really tasting and listening without hearing, exactly.

'I've had one or two serious relationships,' he said.

His voice was deep, with an actor's well-modulated self-awareness.

'Nothing that lasted longer than about a year.'

His eyes, across the table, catching a shaft of savage lighting, were the greeny-blue of travel-brochure lagoons.

'*You* tell *me* why not . . . perhaps I'm hard to be with . . .'

His hands were lightly tanned, like a yachtsman's. She saw them, expert, on ropes and strings, guiding and tying.

No, at the time she heard but did not listen to what he said although the words registered clearly in her head. But with the passing of the months and years, she did hear them. His words became louder and louder, as neediness and then self-doubt fretted at the volume control.

'I don't *get* attached,' he told her, in the same tone as someone might say, 'I don't get winter colds'.

147

Of course she did take note of that, and the challenge in the upturned twist of his lips.

It occurred to Lara now, that she had picked up those gauntlet words and had been running with them ever since.

Was that why she had not mentioned the note since the first (and last) time she had confronted him with it? She had found it in a pocket of one of his jackets, signed in fat loopy handwriting, 'Janey'. Thanking him for a great time, hoping they would do it again, some time, soon.

It was more than Lara had bargained for when she was mucking out his suit for the dry cleaner's.

She had no clue what *it* was. It might have been lunch. It might have been dinner. It might have been . . . She had stopped herself there. When she confronted Will, he said it was just one of those things.

'Revenge is the finest achievement,' asserted Will with his customary self-assurance. They were sunbathing on the beach, again, after lunch. Roasting flesh on the bone. He propped himself up on one elbow and stared out to sea. 'Blood is the ultimate proof of passion.'

He had this idea, he told her, that would be the breakthrough.

'What is it?' she enthused.

'I can't tell you that. It is still forming. I have this strong *idea* of tragedy and passion, good and evil, myth and monster . . . but I haven't decided yet how I will use it.'

'Oh,' said Lara. She went back to her book under the trees.

'You see things in black and white,' he said later, when his body was reddened bronze from another long swim. He had a good body. He looked after himself, although he was never so keen on workouts that his muscles rose above the vaguely sporty. Droplets of salt water glinted like diamonds in his hair. 'Is it possible to live in black and white?'

She looked up, then pulled down her sunglasses. 'It gets a bit colourless sometimes.'

He didn't laugh.

Lara looked grave. 'It's hard. Damn hard.'

'I'm being serious.'

It wasn't that much of a tease. 'So am I,' said Lara.

Shrieks and laughter from the beach seemed to reach them from a long way away. A ten-strong group of local youths had a volley-ball game going. Children churned and splashed in the surf. Only the vicious pit-pot from wooden bats as others played sand tennis intensified. Across her vision trooped fully equipped families, mothers labouring under straw hats like donkeys, saddled with all the paraphernalia of paradise: Lilos, umbrellas, bags, towels and six-foot blow-up dinosaurs and sharks.

'How do you see me, Will?'

He considered a moment. 'I don't see you, exactly,' he said in the tone which he used to tell her he would not be playing this game. 'I hear you. La-ra. You're the song of the sirens.'

'Luring men to their doom from the rocks?' She wasn't sure of the connotations there.

'Among other things,' he said.

She opened her mouth to press him for an explanation, but saw that he was no longer thinking of her. He was watching two lithe dark-haired girls as they patrolled the shore with the self-conscious exhibitionism of the newly knowledgeable.

She should have known, then.

Will's ideal woman probably did not exist. Or so he had told her right at the start.

Probably. How many sleepless nights across the dark world had been induced by that treacherous word?

149

With an immense effort, Lara concentrated on the heat and the blue sky and the ragged trees and the muffled pump of reggae music from the beach bar. She would not – *must* not – let her thoughts stray too far down that road.

They had come here to get away from all that.

Janey's unknown image was a coiled snake deep in her guts.

The Taverna Aphrodite grew out of the harbour wall at the far end of the small bay. From the tables on its deck, the ring of sand below gave the impression of a perfect corn-meal semicircle. Behind the beach were a few cracked trees and a half-hearted single-track concrete road used as a promenade. When the sun set in mauves and washed-out cyclamen over the headland, it was a cue for the strollers to move out of the bars and into the restaurants.

The manager bore a marked resemblance to a Minoan on a fresco. With his carved dark beard and straight nose, he had a face from which one should have been seeking news of distant adventurers rather than ordering souvlaki.

She would have said as much to Will, but his thoughts were clearly elsewhere.

The classical face he was studying belonged to a girl who emerged from the empty cavern of the inside dining-room. She carried a tray jauntily – she could not have been more than seventeen.

How old was Janey?

What was she like?

When did it start?

Why did it start?

Are you telling the truth when you say that it's all over now?

'What are you going to have?' Lara asked, to suppress her demons.

Lately Lara had been caught by disconcerting intimations that she was being tripped up by time. It wasn't only the way she was always three months ahead of the normal world at work, preparing the summer pages of the magazine in blustery April, and Christmas spreads while September burned. The three-holiday thing was undoubtedly part of it. Her parents had recently celebrated their thirty-fifth wedding anniversary with sherry and kisses of complementary dryness (never a divorce in the Noe family). She was now the age her mother had been when she gave birth to her, and that had been leaving it late, very late.

Time was kinder to women now, but not indefinitely. Women's expectations had changed, but only up to a point – ideally, a point of their own choosing. Then the great career could be shelved, and the next stage of womanhood explored: the destiny of motherhood awaited.

Lara used to wonder what a child of her own would look like, should she choose to have one. Recently, though, the passing months had brought not wondering but a feeling that gnawed at her under her ribs, that she should not leave it too late to find out.

Lately Lara had come to realise that although she might exist in it, she did not often live in the present.

She worried about the future, fears which might encompass the possibility of being unable to get to an appointment on time and the great imponderables of decades to come. And she reran the past, constantly rewinding and searching among the video tapes of her memories for clues and explanations.

Now, waiting for Will to return his attention, Lara looked down at her hands and saw that her fingernails were ripped ragged and she couldn't remember doing that.

'What does she say to you?' she asked.

He looked pained. 'Sorry?'

Lara nodded towards the young waitress. Her body was a voluptuous stem in jeans and a tight black T-shirt; her face strong and straight between curves and curls of long black hair. 'What do you think when you look at her?'

'Aesthetically?'

'That could come into it.'

Silence and a shrug.

'*I* was thinking,' said Lara, 'that she was what the ancients had in mind when they came up with Aphrodite, or Psyche . . . or someone . . .'

'How very generous.'

'Not at all.'

He was still appraising the girl. She had felt their stares now, and smiled coyly. She unloaded her tray, then hurried over. 'Can I to help you?' she asked. She pulled a little notepad and pencil from her pocket.

Her cinnamon skin was offset by beautifully soft brown eyes.

Will ordered casually. But Lara recognised all the signs.

'Women have always been up against the same problem,' she said when the waitress left them.

He narrowed his eyes warily.

'The ideal woman,' said Lara. 'All those impossible myths – beauty and magic. It's not so different to what you were talking about earlier, on the beach.'

He drummed his fingers.

'It was all about striving for ideals and attainment. In myth, the only way a mortal can escape punishment is to live in fear of not being good enough. You realise, we have had thousands of years of never coming up to scratch . . .'

'We?'

'Women,' said Lara.

'Sometimes . . .' said Will.

'Sometimes what?'

'Sometimes, Lara, you sound just like your bloody magazine.'

The heavy pink sun slipped away from them then, as she gazed beyond their table. The headland was in silhouette and a sudden wind made leaves slap all around.

Back at their apartment the next day, when she was toasted and drowsy from another afternoon at the beach, Will told her he was taking his camera around the headland. He wanted to capture the red earth and the tumble of the Hellenic landscape. He sounded like a brochure.

She watched his tanned calves from the bed as he moved away from her, and she waved him off. Not that she believed him for a moment.

The soles of his shoes skittered on the sandy stone path outside the apartment, and then were gone. The only sound outside was the constant sawing of the cicadas.

Lara put her head down on the crisp white pillow, and closed her eyes and mind.

Hours later she was disorientated to wake alone. Outside on the balcony where she half-expected to find Will strung out between two chairs drinking a beer, the only sign of life was her swimsuit, hanging limp and exhausted on the rungs of the drying rack.

According to the fly-blown mirror inside, Lara was a woman with a blotchy red patch down one side of her face where she had slept, and a nose the colour and texture of a ripening strawberry. Putting all other thoughts aside, she set to repairing the damage.

It was almost dark by the time she walked slowly down the dusty path to the harbour. There was no hesitation about where to go first.

And she was right.

'Oh . . . hi,' said Will, when he noticed her – which took him a while.

He was standing by the telephone at the taverna where Aphrodite served.

'Are we eating here again tonight?'

'We could do,' said Will.

'Or we could not,' said Lara.

'Whatever.'

They drank their beers and left.

11   Myth and Monster

They had tired of the beach, on that they were agreed.
Possibly not only the beach, although that issue was not
addressed.

'I'd like to drive inland, see some of the classical sites
– Mycenae, Corinth, perhaps. As we're here,' said Will.
'We could stay at a hotel for a night or two.'

'Sounds good,' said Lara brightly.

They hired a car, a new white economy model, and drove
east across the mountainous fingerbones of the Peloponnese. The roads were strung across the surprisingly
verdant countryside. The route wound up and down hills,
uncrowded, then was choked with dusty buses and cars
and motorcycles in small towns which seethed like pressure cookers in the valleys.

Fouled up in a one-way system in one of the larger,
more unpleasant ones, Lara watched Will's hands clenching on the steering-wheel. She suggested they park and
go in search of a cold beer, but he insisted they press on.

So they steered along new roads cut through highlands
of reddish rock, and when they saw the coast again it
was a spectacular vista miles below them. Their route
twisted and turned down, and the sight, again, of the
indigo sea seemed palpably to ease the tension.

On arrival in the crumbling port of Nafplion late that

155

afternoon, they found an air-conditioned hotel in a side street. In the room they were shown the wooden shutters were closed and the darkness was edged with a refrigerated chill. They took it and were given a large key which fitted only loosely in the lock.

In the town's main square, the paving stones were as slippery as glass. A byzantine church was wedged oddly in one corner, as if muscling in on the smooth secular lines of more modern lives. Above its mammary domes soared the craggy seat of the Palamıdi fortress.

Lara walked with Will over the satiny marble flagstones, knowing now that these were no less slippery than the togetherness she was trying to keep hold of. They did not hold hands.

They walked the harbour promenade with the throng, eyes set ahead or on the island fortress on the water. Then they found a table at a restaurant on the quay, ordered tepid food and ate it knowing they had made a bad choice. They talked about nothing of consequence.

Lara tried; he blocked her out. It's me, she wanted to shout, I'm the one who should be upset with you! So why am I the one making all the sodding effort?

But the red sun slipped down somewhere beyond the sea, and still she said nothing. She might even have smiled softly.

In bed that night, sex was as urgent and snatching and wet as a rescue at sea.

Detached, somewhere beyond the physical efforts of their slithering limbs, there was only the sharpness and soreness and desperation of two people clinging to the wreckage.

The following morning, in the laser path of the sun on the sheets, she woke floating on sweat, and chilled by the air-conditioning. Will lay in the recovery position.

He rose as soon as he woke.

'It's early,' murmured Lara. She pulled herself up a little. The clock showed half past seven.

'I thought you wanted to go to Mycenae. I thought that was why we had come.'

'Oh . . . yeah, of course. Great.'

'We have to get there early or we might as well not bother. Place will be overrun by ten.'

'Give me five minutes,' said Lara, bounding towards the shower.

They said little over breakfast. Down in the hotel bar the tables were laid with plastic covers and rolls and honey. They waved away aggressive wasps and flies, and drank bitter black coffee. Then they walked in silence to the hire car parked outside in the street and set off. Out of town, on strange industrial flatlands, new lidos were under construction, each painted in Day-Glo colours and manic with cinematic murals. At first, Lara thought they were discotheques – and maybe they were, at night. 'Splash Club', read a sign on one, 'Electra' blazoned another.

'Are you looking out for the road?' Will interrupted her thoughts.

She rustled the map on her knees. 'Er . . . should be off to the right any time now . . .'

The first row of the day was averted as they turned off on the road to Mycenae, while the sun was still tissue-paper hazy over the mountains.

He took an age to set up a photograph of the Lion Gate, fussing before the sinister blackened stone. The lions, for all their fame, were headless.

'Get out of it . . . silly cow!' he snapped.

Lara, hanging behind, lost in the high walls and the backdrop of mountains and plain that must barely have changed since they were seen by three-thousand-year-old eyes, started.

A German tourist responded in kind in her native tongue, and lingered all the longer in the entrance way.

In Lara's current mood, it required almost too much concentration to rebuild the lost city in her mind from the rubble and scrub. Fissured rocks were filled into shape with hardened slaps of cement.

They were picking over the ruins, that was all she knew. No matter how they might pretend, past tensions had made deep cracks.

What was it that Will had once told her? (Not that the subject had been raised lately . . .) 'The state of marriage,' he had said, 'is like a beseiged city. Everyone outside is clamouring to get in, while those inside are praying for rescue.'

'I don't see it like that,' she had replied quietly.

But she had known better than to pursue it.

And only then did Lara wonder about the ancients, who had seen this very plain, this chasm, this vast mountainous stronghold, and who had battled to defend these ruins, and had loved and lost.

They clambered past the Grave Circle and up the slippery stones of the citadel. She was almost there, mentally, while she stood on the site of the palace once soaked with the blood of betrayal, patricide, infanticide and treacherous cannibalism when—

'Fuck,' said Will.

She followed his gaze wordlessly.

The first of a long line of tourist coaches was grinding up the plain towards them.

Bit by bit, stone by stone, the lost city of her childhood imagination was being reduced to heat-baked rubble. She struggled on, trying to keep up with Will, clutching hat to head with one hand. She was losing her foothold; here too the stones were glass smooth, polished by the soles of thousands of foreign shoes.

She stopped, panting to capture a moment of magic, but there was none. There was the pounding of blood in her head, and a prickle of sweat on the back of her neck. There was dust and rock and scrub, and the arid plain over which the invading army of the tourist coaches thundered. Up ahead, Will marched on without looking back.

She slowed her pace.

When she caught up with him, they were in what appeared to be a square stone enclave. In one side was what she took to be a prison window complete with rusted iron bars. A group of young people sat there, smoking. Other, older, visitors poked around in the sand and stone; she recognised the intent as they squinted and searched, casting around for a spur for the imagination.

Will was staring into the mouth of a cave, at the steps leading down into its blackness. His hands in his pockets, he started down, then realised she was there.

'Secret cistern,' he said flatly.

She shook her head. 'What's that?'

'Hiding place.'

Still the spark failed to ignite. 'Oh.'

'I'm going down,' he said, and turned. 'Coming?'

'Excuse me . . . There are some one hundred steps which make a steep dank passage down to an underground spring . . . and long sheer drops into the water should you miss your footing . . .'

The English voice cut in and they both turned.

Under a khaki canvas sun-hat was a pimply youth wearing cheap mirror shades on a peeling nose. He waved a guidebook at them, but seemed embarrassed now by his unprompted intervention. He cleared his throat.

' "Vital for holding out against an enemy during long sieges should they have breached the citadel," ' he quoted from this tome. ' "It is recommended that this should not be attempted without the aid of a powerful torch." '

Will narrowed his eyes. Needlessly, he tossed off a short

retort before continuing his way, unilluminated, down the dark descent. Lara stayed where she was.

She mouthed an apology as the youth loped off.

He glanced back, but only when the coast was clear. 'Prick,' he mouthed in return.

'You didn't have to be so rude,' said Lara later.

'I am not a tourist. I am travelling,' said Will. They were back in Nafplion, and he was beginning to labour the point. They ascended the stairs to the first floor of the archeological museum.

'You are the man who said, "I want to explore my place in the universe."' Lara attempted a tease.

'God . . . I must have been feeling low.'

'It was last week.'

'*Was* it?'

'Uh-huh.'

'God . . .'

The place was full of gods, in fact. As they walked on through the cavernous rooms of minor finds at Mycenae, the gods gargoyled in icon form and shook snakes at their latter-day observers. Lara wondered – briefly, then more subversively – how many Will would recognise.

They were all women: the mother goddess in all her forms.

Will's awkwardness – she hestitated to call it unkindness – seemed to have seeped into her bones.

'So . . . you traveller . . . where to next?'

'I've been thinking about that,' said Will. 'I'm going to hire a motorcycle.'

She tried to look enthusiastic, then gave up. 'I thought you said Greek roads were death runs and the drivers the most unaware of safety you'd ever come across.'

'Well . . .'

'I'm not sure. No one's wearing crash helmets. I really

don't think I want to get on the back of a motor bike . . . Couldn't we just—'

'I meant, by myself.'

'Sorry?'

'I want to take off. By myself. Just me.'

'Ah.' She took a breath, to control her reaction, to stop the hurt exploding into words.

'Yeah . . . I thought I might take off to Corinth . . . somewhere . . .'

Still she said nothing, battened down. A coiled terra-cotta snake was poised to strike from behind a glass panel.

'I think . . . it's the *road*, that feeling of being on the road that I need. Maybe I shouldn't expect you to understand.'

Down another of time's snakes, Lara was walking along a suburban street in South London, returning from school. She would have been ten or eleven years old. She could still feel the sudden stab of excited terror. What would happen if she kept on walking, past the door where the number 39 was painted on the porch? Where would she go, what would she do, who would she be? She heard the whistle from the commuter railway on the embankment behind the houses. Then she turned into the driveway as if she too had been a train on tracks. As if her life were being lived by someone else.

'Oh, I understand,' said Lara.

'Good.'

'Fine.'

It wasn't, of course.

If everything were to come right, Lara rationalised, then Will had to believe that he had made it come about. She had let him go with good grace. That didn't stop her from howling to the wind on the Palamidi, alone in Nafplion.

For every one of the thousand steps up to the fortress

161

which glowered over the town, she had caught her breath with a doubt or a curse. Now, high above the town, flying – or so she could imagine – over the entire peninsula, she gave vent to her rage, her face contorted into that of a cracked terracotta goddess of Mycenae.

The site, she read with a scorch of furious irony, was instrumental in the control of the Peloponnese during the War of Independence.

She took a seat on the terrace of the bar.

For a long time she stared into space.

She had come to Greece intending to get a clearer picture of where she was going with Will. She had decided before they had set foot on the plane that Janey was an aberration. She was not going to ask him for a firm commitment, exactly, only whether he might see what they had ending – eventually – in marriage.

Surely that wasn't asking too much?

She needed to know, one way or the other. For if not . . .

She had no intention of talking babies.

Lara loved him, that was the trouble – and she knew that she should never push Will too far. Or was it rather that she was too frightened of disappointment to dare?

When you loved someone, you were always insecure – weren't you?

When she came back into herself, she felt as hard and as vulnerable under the sun as the ice in her drink.

A mental image of Will on his hired motorcycle (he couldn't *wait*), roaring down roads fringed with red rock and oleander, tugged at her equilibrium like a child at his mother's skirt. She dispersed it with a determined draught of Amstel beer.

Once, she remembered with a surprisingly physical stab of pain, the carefree figure on the bike had been her.

When she was nineteen she had travelled to Greece with her two friends, Liv and Mary. On arrival in Crete they dumped their fabric bags on the quayside at Heraklion and leaped around with heady freedom.

It was impossible not to think of them.

By which she meant herself, of course, once upon a time. Now it felt like a haunting.

Lara was never alone, she had come to realise. She carried these faces, these echoes, these bright pictures of the past in her head; they never loosened their grip on her. They travelled with her, in other words, long after their owners had drifted on and away.

We knew nothing, thought Lara, lost now in her long-ago summer, except what we would be. We would dare to live because we were newly released; we would dare to look and taste and try with no obligation; we who had always lived in sunny uplands were poised to discover the delights of the forbidden shadows. We dared, and yet we were safe in our wariness. *We* would not descend too far, nor fly too close to the sun.

Lara looked around, but intercepted no one's gaze.

Somehow, in the time that had elapsed since she was on the brink of becoming her adult self, she had become invisible.

Then, she and Liv and Mary had all been so strong and so sure that life was a straight path to certain reward – if only one was honest and kind and worked hard enough.

By the time Lara came to Greece for the first time, that summer, her father had worked his way up. He was no longer an ordinary administrator, he was a bank manager; they lived in a prosperous small town in Kent. Lara's father balanced the books in life as in office. He was a meticulous man. Lara had been surprised at the age of twelve or so when she had looked up the word 'meticulous' in the big dictionary and discovered that it contained an element of fear in its root, a fear of making mistakes. The more she thought about that, over the years, the more it rang true.

It was a word which appeared regularly on Lara's school reports.

Sometimes it seemed that Lara herself had hardly changed at all.

The wind rifled through the open pages of the guidebook on the table in front of her. The fortress prison behind her had the stumps of crumbled iron bars at its windows.

Lara, gripped by sudden stark truths, felt fear as a slow dance which turned her around within the clutch of bony hands.

The more she thought about it, the clearer her course of action seemed to be. That night she spent an hour preparing herself. She was making a solo debut. She rubbed expensive scent into her body, took great care over her make-up and hair, and dressed confidently.

When she went out alone into the dusk, she felt she meant it. She had not been abandoned, she had chosen to do this. She might not have been nineteen again, but she was in her mind. She held her head up as she joined the crowds strolling around the narrow streets, browsing through jewellery shops and contemplating taverna menus.

Down by the harbour she noticed for the first time a tang in the air as the sea slapped against the grey wall and exhaled the smells of the day.

She stood, taking in great breaths of something which felt very much like freedom. Then, after a while, she turned back towards the maze of pedestrianised roads.

In one, she found a sandstone entrance hung with travel plans and tariffs. Possibilities, in other words. There were coach trips and boat trips which would take her anywhere she wanted. Why, she could disappear without trace should she decide to. When she came back to what had been her place in the world she could *be*

someone different. She was on her way in when she
realised that the hire car was parked outside the hotel,
its keys were in her bag and the map was in the glove
compartment.

Down another thoroughfare there were restaurant
tables set out the length of the street on one side under
crumbling stone balconies and cracked façades from
which sprouted tenacious climbing plants. She found a
homely establishment and made for the smallest table.
There, she sipped wine and ate a simple salad with a
sense of relief.

Maybe being alone wasn't so bad after all.

When Will joined her, in her thoughts, he could not
touch this new feeling of oneness with her surroundings,
far less disrupt it.

She made her own plans.

There was an ancient amphitheatre; for as long as she
could remember she had wanted to see the place where
a whisper could carry to the furthest vantage place in
the gods, and a coin could be dropped on a spot on the
stage and the sound of it hitting the ground would be
heard on the top tier high above. Why not?

Tomorrow she would go – alone – to Epıdauros.

Resolved on action, she slept dreamlessly.

When she woke, the shutters of the hotel room
admitted distorted slats of white light. The cyclops eye of
the clock said it was seven o'clock. Lara blinked
towards the window with a vague sense of disbelief. Then
patted the empty expanse of bed next to her. Had Will
really not returned last night?

To staunch the ebb of the previous night's confidence,
she climbed into her clothes and went down for a deter-
minedly hearty breakfast, willing her limbs into
looseness.

Finally, outside in the car, she folded the map and

started the engine with the single-mindedness of a woman with a mission. It hiccuped once or twice as she got to know the clutch, but she kept it going.

Harmony of mind and body. The words popped up from her subconscious and swirled around her mind. Rather less smoothly, she coaxed the car around a tricky roundabout blocked by a lorry – and then cursed as she saw she had missed the turning east to Epidauros.

Once more she drove round the town's one-way system. Harmony of mind and body. *Sure.*

The engine gasped again as she set its course once more towards Epidauros.

She did not make it.

By the time she had coaxed the car into a roadside garage, the needle of its temperature gauge was on critical and there were wisps of steam rising from the edge of the bonnet lid. Lara felt embarrassed, stupid, incompetent . . . and alone, for all her brave resolutions.

Was *this* how she was doomed to be?

On the garage forecourt she grimaced furiously at what she had to do. It had come to this. She braced herself to ask, 'Do . . . you speak English?'

The reply was a maybe–maybe not shrug from a handsome young mechanic in oily overalls. Lara ducked down to feel under the passenger side of the car, but surfaced shaking her head. She pointed to the bonnet. 'I'm sorry . . . I can't find . . . how to open . . .'

The youth furrowed his forehead.

Oh great, thought Lara. 'Too hot . . . the engine is too hot . . .' she ventured hopelessly. What price now the international language of the motor car? She got out of the car.

'You have a problem?'

She spun round to see a man had left his car behind her, and that she was blocking his way to the petrol pumps. He looked impatient – the door of his sleek saloon was left open – but this did not register in his voice.

'I – I'm sorry. I'll get this out of the way,' she said with a dignity she did not feel and with which alone it would prove difficult to push a car on her own.

'What is your problem?' he asked again.

Relieved, she told him. A rapid-fire exchange of Greek followed, during which the mechanic nodded vigorously. Her protector turned to Lara.

'Come,' he said.

His name was Nicos, although he did not introduce himself until they were sitting at a cafe table in the main square back at Nafplion. For her part, she had allowed him to show her to his car and drive away without a qualm.

'Lara,' she said simply and smiled.

He was not good looking. He was only a little taller than her, with a long bony face, a prominent nose and full lips. He was not much tanned and there were strands of wiry grey in his unruly dark hair. Perhaps he was a little older than she was; perhaps a lot. He wore old blue jeans and a button-down American shirt; on his left wrist was a gold watch.

'You live here?' she asked. It was a fair assumption, given his obvious aquaintance with the boy at the garage.

'I come from this town. I do not live here for many years.'

'Ah.'

He offered her a cigarette, which she declined. 'I don't.' He lit one for himself and his liquid brown eyes were melancholic through the first curls of smoke. There seemed no race to establish a conversation. He considered her a moment, his expression unreadable, then took another drag on the Marlboro.

Lara sipped at a tiny sweet coffee, and sometimes met his gaze and sometimes not.

'You are English?'

'Yes.'

'I lived in London for a while.'

'Oh?'

'I was studying.' He did not elaborate.

'Where do you live now?'

'In Brussels. I work for the Commission.'

'The EC?'

He tutted gently. 'EU.'

She couldn't help smiling. 'They . . . *you* keep changing it.'

He paused to consider this. 'Perhaps this is true.'

They drank in silence for a while, yet the silences with this man were unalarming.

'I was going to Epıdauros,' she said at last. 'I wanted to see the amphitheatre.'

'It is beautiful, although perhaps too many people in summer like this.'

'Even so . . .'

'You are alone here, travelling?'

'I don't know,' she answered truthfully.

Nicos looked intently at her.

'I came here with my . . . friend, but he has gone somewhere by himself. I don't know where he is.'

'When did he go?'

'Yesterday morning.'

'And so you are going to Epıdauros. Of course.' He laughed.

'Why . . . of course?'

'It is a sanctuary, is it not? Dedicated to Asklepios.' It all seemed to make sense to him.

She shook her head.

'Asklepios . . . the god of healing. The place where

dreams can be cured ... no, can *make* the cure. That is what the ancient Greeks believed.'

'I only knew about the theatre. Where Sophocles first saw his plays performed.'

'Ah, yes, but he was a priest. To watch a play was a ... cure. A *catharsis?*'

She nodded. 'Like a therapy?'

'That is the word.'

Lara smiled widely now she remembered where she had read it. 'Harmony in mind and body.'

'Naturally,' said Nicos.

What was it about this man that made her feel so calm? Was it the way he had assumed control so smoothly? The way he was so still when he sat? When he moved, it was slowly and deliberately. He did not stare around him; he smoked and drank and spoke with a sense of peace and purpose, she decided.

Or was it simply that they had no history together?

'Your car will take some time,' he said. 'And I would like to make love to you.' These were statements and he did not smile.

She took the pace from him. Languidly she consulted her watch and saw it was almost midday. She was not herself now. She was acting a part – although not that much when she replied, 'I am a good woman, I would like you to understand that.'

The spaniel eyes across the table were bright with amusement. 'I am sure you are very good.'

She deflected that. 'I am not in the habit of meeting a stranger in the morning and becoming his lover by the afternoon.'

He seemed to know what she would say next.

'However ... by the evening I may think very differently about the matter.'

'Who can tell?' he shrugged.

'Indeed.' She got up to go.

'Where shall I meet you this evening?' he asked, rising to his feet. 'For your change of heart.'

She was light and free. She considered him for a moment and said, 'You may come to the Hotel Ares at eight o'clock this evening.'

There was a ghost of a smile at the corners of his mouth. 'I shall take you out to dinner?'

'What else?'

'Indeed,' he parroted her.

She wore the flimsy dress she had brought to play out the same scene with Will.

Nicos kissed her hand when she appeared in the hotel reception. 'Beautiful,' he said, and she allowed herself to believe him.

Outside was the white hire car.

'It is fixed,' said Nicos.

She thanked him.

They strolled past all the restaurants and bars she had come to recognise, apparently aimlessly for some time. Conversation ebbed and flowed as they walked with no sense of urgency. They were part of the human tide which filled the streets. Eventually, when it was quite dark, they turned up an alley of steps. At the top was another square quite unlike those where the tourists and students congregated. He led her towards a wide, peeling portico in one corner where a laden orange tree grew up the pastelled sandstone building.

Nicos was greeted warmly by the proprietor.

They sat. She hardly remembered now what they said; it did not seem important, either then or now. She felt released from the tyranny of words, the minute examination of what they might be made to mean if they were polished and turned to catch the right light.

Whatever her desires were – for a different Will, for any other man – they were flotsam and jetsam on a dark tide. So she did the only thing she could. She had another drink.

Food arrived and they ate.

'I watch you,' said Nicos unambiguously, when they had finished. He meant it in a purely lascivious sense.

'Wolf,' said Lara pleasantly.

He lit a cigarette without offering one to her, and exhaled.

'No, before. When you get in your car to drive through Nafplion. I had to watch you to see if you would meet someone.'

'Just my luck, then. I met you.'

'Very very good luck.'

Nicos moved closer. 'I want to ... watch you now,' he said. 'In the way that you wanted.' Slyly his eyes unbuttoned her shirt. Then he called for the bill.

When he stood and held out a hand for her to go with him, she did so. It was what she had intended all along.

'We could have a brandy,' said Lara. 'Back at my hotel.'

He accepted with a chivalrous nod.

As if in a dream, she waited as he pressed settlement of the bill on the proprietor, then followed him out into the square. The sweet sharp fragrance of the orange tree filled all her senses.

Then she was sucked into a stranger's embrace.

She made him into what she wanted and needed.

It was all down to Will, the fact that she was all wrong.

No ... *that* was wrong, spun her thoughts. What had been wrong was having Will and wrapping him in hope and illusion.

This time – for perhaps the first time – she knew exactly what she was doing.

She clung on to Nicos, real Nicos, encircled by arms of iron, making it happen.

There was a sweet tang of foreignness in his neck. She

shivered as his hand traced the line of her spine to its base.

He licked her lips. 'I knew that it would be like this, with you,' he whispered.

They walked – who knew where? – until they were outside the Hotel Ares. In the lobby, they sat at a small table and rode the tension.

They drank Metaxa. Nicos smoked. Lara let the alcohol pull her down gently towards uncaring until—

There was a thunderbolt from the night above. Actually, a hand hammered down on the table.

'What the *fuck*, Lara!'

A glass smashed on the stone-flagged floor. Olives bounced and rolled across the white cloth. She watched them quite dispassionately.

Only then did she raise her eyes to Will. He was blazing, manic. He was *alight* with anger.

'I'm so sorry,' she said to Nicos.

The Greek was inscrutable.

Will was a man possessed. 'I've been waiting for you for two hours! They said you had gone out! Have you been at it in *my* room, Lara?'

She was so calm, she scared herself.

'You're coming with me. *Now*!' screamed Will.

With sideways glance Lara saw Nicos wave away the barman as if for a moment's grace.

She sat stock still for a moment, looking down, until Will grabbed at her hand. She snatched it back.

'I'm so sorry,' she said again to the Greek as she stood up to leave.

There it was. She had been on the edge of a life that might have been, even if only for a night. She had been there, and she had drawn back. She could have gone with the Greek, but she had not. She would live her night, of course, but only in her dreams – which were not dreams but imagination so strong that it produced all the physical symptoms of fight and flight.

She hated herself. Why could she not hate *him*?

Lara did not ask Will where his travels had taken him, and he did not volunteer the information. There were deep creased shadows under his eyes, burned in now by the relentless sun. Judging from appearances, he might not even have slept the previous night.

This impression was reinforced by his intention, as it transpired, to lead her back to the hotel room not for furious argument and retribution, but to sleep.

He crashed immediately.

She closed her eyes beside him, alert to every sound. Should she slip out from the sheet, dress and go silently? Would she find the Greek where she had left him – and what would his reaction be?

Her heart pounded; her mind was a maze of indecision.

For a long time she lay, clenching her eyes shut against her instincts, and did what she had done all her hemmed-in life. She was bold and brave and devil-may-care, but only in the sanctity of her own ecstatic inventions.

Will gave a slumbrous snort.

Nicos, risk free yet real as could be, kissed her heroically.

12   Falling to Earth

At the end of the Mani peninsula was the entrance to
Hades. Lara knew that already, of course. She had
already been to hell and back in the past couple of days.

As they drove away from Nafplion, Lara felt in her
pocket for the precious paper which bore Nicos's family
name and the house where his family lived. It was
nothing; it proved the existence of a tiny, untaken possibility. She gripped it like a talisman, feeling the sweat
from her palm seep into its crispness.

The sun was an interrogation lamp as they drove over
the mountains. Neither spoke. At the side of the road,
strange sentinel plants grew in the rubble. Like hollyhocks after the blooms have fallen, their sun-seared
stems were unsheathed swords waving at the passing
vehicles.

She had not wanted to come to the caves. He had prevailed, though, and she walked as if she were not there
towards a concreted entrance. There they waited, as cold
vapours reached their bare arms from the dank entrance.
Lara observed her goosebumps dispassionately until their
turn came to be shown down.

Darkness, globe lights, and drips.

Lara, wedged into a wooden boat low on the black
water, leaned in still further as the cold clammy swell of
a stalagmite loomed at her.

Now, out of her body, incapable of feeling, she was floating through an exotic decaying boudoir. The electric lights which floated on the underground lake illuminated four hundred million years of drips, and made them into grotesque pillars, statues and drapery.

For the first time in five days there was a hint of complicity in Will's voice.

'It's very phallic,' he said.

It was entirely indicative of her state of mind, Lara supposed, that she interpreted the same formations as bloodied entrails. Rust red in places from some leaking iron deposits, the stalactites drooped towards the water as malignant udders, festering polyps from the walls of some cold, diseased womb.

They pressed across the dark stream, pushed still further into the caves by the boatman's wooden paddle. Now and then he pushed too hard against one dark wall and the boat scraped and shuddered against the other, and then another grotesque underground chamber would open up for them.

Now the scene, lit by her imagination, was of melting candles, banks and banks of them, and mouldy wedding cakes and crumbling temples. Ruined fairy cities, newly discovered, slid into the dancing black sea. In the corner of one hall, there were piles of forgotten bones; from the ceiling of another hung the fringes of a thousand witches' shawls.

When Will unexpectedly reached for her hand, his had the same cool clamminess of the walls which pressed in on them.

'Don't look back,' he whispered.

Of course she did.

They were back at the taverna at Stoupa that evening. Darkness fell leaving lights hung like stalactites across the water of the bay. Lara stared into them, tracking the

175

liquid pathways back to the ring of tavernas above the beach.

'Earth to Lara,' said Will.

She remained obstinately somewhere out there.

The stalactites glowed white and fizzy lemon and tangerine, shifting and recomposing on the ripples of a weak tide.

There was a railing in front of their table at the Taverna Aphrodite, between the diners and the drop into the sea. Above them was a canvas canopy arrangement where other establishments had trees or luxuriant vines. And lashed to the upright supports at the front of the deck, Lara noticed for the first time, were bunches of clear plastic sheeting.

'It does rain, even here,' Will intercepted her thoughts.

'Hmm?'

'The sheeting. They draw them. Like curtains.'

'Curtains,' said Lara, and began to laugh.

To Lara, they looked like nothing more than the kind of protective covering used for the most expensive dresses. So big and bunchy, they could have contained wedding dresses. But they were empty. Nothing to wear.

Unable to reply, she laughed some more.

His stony face fractured but he could not understand.

His vagrant heart could never put down roots with one love. Lara knew that now. No, she had known that for a long time. Only now had she admitted it.

Across the table, a mile away from her, Will's forehead was smooth and blank once more. She did not look at him directly, but past him. Lara studied a young man beyond, who was alone at a table, fidgeting and tense in his baggy cotton clothes. One knee bobbed up and down compulsively as he played with the cutlery and the bottles of oil and vinegar laid out for him. Had his girlfriend abandoned him? Had he come alone?

She barely spoke to Will. It would have required too

much effort and deception to put aside the raging hurt to talk and smile. So she drew a curtain across him.

The girl at the taverna was acting in a strangely similar way. The way her silky cheek turned when she put down his plate of food, the toss of her hair, her reluctance to meet his, or even Lara's eyes . . .

The shadows grew longer. Out on the horizon, the sea was an immensity of darkness.

They picked over the ruin they both recognised together.

'Is it the end?'

'Is it?' he asked in reply.

But still she could not give up. Some myths still remained.

'I forgive you,' she said.

Of course she did.

When their charter flight landed at Gatwick two days later, her tan was peeling and she had already begun to fictionalise events. If anyone asked, they had had a wonderful time.

By the time she was back on the twenty-second floor of the tower by the Thames, she was rationalising the tensions within her by writing an article for the magazine about the stresses involved in taking holidays. It was titled 'Trouble in Paradise'.

Holidays *were* stressful, especially when women tried to use them as a cure-all for the everyday ups and downs of a long-term relationship. There was too much expectation. A package deal only guaranteed the flights, the transfers and the accommodation – and *that* not always to complete satisfaction. A holiday only gave you the world in the brochure.

And if you wanted a holiday romance, you should make it with someone new.

No false hopes, wrote Lara, you should use the time away to get to know yourself again, and what is possible for you.

Know Thyself, said the Delphic oracle. But the problem was that Lara had strived for so long to be the ideal woman – for her mother, for Will, for the world – that perhaps she had become someone else altogether now.

The Moonbathers
II

13   The Total Eclipse

On the day there was a total eclipse of the sun over Asia,
interpretations differed wildly. Some said it was a portent
of certain doom and disaster; others claimed it could only
mean good fortune. In darkest Pimlico that day Lara
decided that it was a new beginning.

Farewell, Will and Janey.

So long, Ella and everyone else.

Goodbye, workshop. *Especially* the workshop.

Lara had had her spell of madness, but now it had
passed. She had come face to face with Janey and yet she
was still living and breathing. She knew now that Janey
had not been left far behind in England when she and
Will were in Greece. She had been with them all the time,
not only emotionally, but physically too – staying with
friends in a villa along the coast from Nafpion. Will had
been able to telephone her there and then, in travelling
mood, had hired a motorcycle and gone to her. Now Lara
came to think of it, the Greek holiday had been his idea
in the first place.

All this she turned over in her mind quite dispassionately now, surprising herself in the process.

This was the worst, and already it was distant and
obscure. She was here, still herself.

Better than that, even. She was at large and on the loose.

Sure, there were experiences she drew the line at –
like eating jellied eels or developing a passionate appreci-
ation of rap music – but these didn't amount to much.

She bought a pair of rollerblades and decided she would
enjoy terrorising the denizens of Kensington on their
sacred patch of Hyde Park.

She went swimming and signed on for scuba-diving
lessons at the Queen Mum sports centre on the Vauxhall
Bridge Road.

She went by herself to West End matinees, and once
to hear Rossini from a standing space in the gods at
Covent Garden.

She did not baulk at grazing her way round the super-
market, popping a grape into her mouth here, a cherry
tomato there.

It occurred to her that if this was the timid beginning
of her search for courage and self-knowledge and her
place in the world – then she ought to be setting her sights
rather further afield. What would she do, where would
she go when she *had* the guts?

She had no idea.

Until she thought: That is it!

She would pack her bags, go to Heathrow ... and
simply stand in front of a departure board until she had
decided. Then she would march up to the right airline
desk, slap her credit card on the counter and buy a ticket
there and then.

It might be San Francisco, or Bermuda, or Sydney,
or Kinshasa ... on second thoughts, not Kinshasa. But
wherever it was, she would be strong and sure and her
own woman.

She fetched her atlas. Poring over the intricate maps,
she let herself go.

Surfing this wave of optimism, she opened the bank statement which she had tossed unread on the kitchen dresser some time ago.

Amazingly, her luck held. Lara could scarcely believe it.

If Ella the editor was a card-carrying harridan – and Lara had known *that* for longer than she had cared to admit – then her tenacity once her claws were in was an example to all her awestruck acolytes.

She had Lara, and she did not intend to let her go.

Incredible as it seemed, in Lara's new topsy-turvy life that translated as a salary in the bank. Lara scrutinised her Barclays statement and the dates and could find no other explanation.

Topsy-turvy was one thing, but this was quite another. Surely she wasn't going to be obliged to start liking the woman?

In the mean time, Lara thought she might as well take advantage.

She went out again and returned with a half-kilo box of Belgian chocolates and a bottle of Gordon's.

Later that day, though, there was thick cloud and confirmation for Lara that, for all Ella's sunny side up, she was still wielding the power. Lara, if the editor had her way, was in the grip of greater forces than ever before. Ella was now *concerned* about her, and Annie had been dispatched to the eye of the storm. Or rather, to Lara's flat – which came to much the same thing given that Lara rarely tidied up when she was feeling happy and in control.

'Lara . . . we've all been so worried about you!' stressed Annie one more time. 'We've given up calling and leaving messages on the answering machine. You've never once returned my calls.' This indisputable fact was accompanied by a pout indicating hurt and bafflement.

Annie was standing, immaculate in beige and untouchable as a phantom, in front of the mantelpiece in Lara's jumble of a sitting-room. The expensive clothes and cosmetics she wore for the task positively enhanced her concern and incomprehension – and the gulf, as Lara saw it now, between rationality and madness.

'Ella keeps on: Where's Lara, when are you coming back, are you OK...? I had to come.'

'I'm fine.'

She *was*, in point of fact. And the devil was still bubbling under, so she asked, 'How's Ella?'

Annie pulled a face. 'Not that great. She looks *terrible*.'

'Oh?'

'Word is... she and Skelton have split up. *Major disaster*.'

'Much weeping and wailing?' asked Lara.

'Much.'

'Oh, dear. I *am* sorry. Now...' Lara waited, unsure what Annie expected.

Annie appraised the shambles. Light momentarily caught the lenses of her glasses, freezing them strangely as though in a sudden blast of polar wind on her face. She seemed to notice then that there were muddy footprints leading from the back door, through the kitchen, to the sofa via the television. 'It's just that... Lara, have you been burgled?'

'I haven't been paranoid about clearing up,' said Lara with a shrug.

'Ah. It's very... funky. And you're smoking.'

Lara exhaled showily.

'You hate cigarette smoke!'

'You get used to it,' Lara assured her. 'So... how's the lovely clever glamorous world of *Reflections*?'

'It doesn't sound as if you want to know...'

'No, well...'

'So what have you been—?'

'No, let's talk about you,' said Lara brightly. 'I can see

184

things are happening in your life. You've undergone a dramatic change of hairstyle.'

'Lara . . . stop this.'

'Oh, I *am*, don't you worry. I'm getting on with my life on my own terms.'

Annie leaned forward sympathetically. 'Still no known cure, then?' She *knew*, her shoulders implied.

'I'm sorry?'

The voice was lowered. 'For Will.'

'Annie, this has nothing to do with Will. Absolutely nothing. And if only people would realise that—'

'Lara, what *is* all this with you? I thought we were friends . . .' The sincerity in Annie's eyes was magnified now by the metal-rimmed glasses.

Lara felt herself thaw a little. But she anchored her gaze to the rug and said nothing.

'What have you been doing with yourself?' Annie tried again.

'This and that.'

'Right. In the sense of . . .?'

'In the sense of not doing anything I don't want to do, or that I think is perfectly pointless.'

'You *are* down.'

'Not yet,' said Lara. 'Not at all.'

'I'm sorry?'

'Never mind.'

A hand went to soft beige hip. Annie assumed the aura of a fictional sleuth at the end of a book. 'So . . . Ella was right.'

'Oh, come on, let's not give her the satisfaction.'

'You're on gardening leave,' asserted Annie.

'Eh?'

'Before you can take up your new job.'

'Well . . .' Lara supposed that was a fair description.

'Where are you going to? Glossy, or one of the newspaper supplements? You know Ella was just about to give you a pay rise.'

'Annie . . .'

'Not *Vogue* – tell me you haven't gone to *Vogue*! Ella will *absolutely* flip! You know how she is about loyalty—'

Lara gave an acid laugh.

'—about other people knowing what she's like.' This was delivered with another attempt at empathy. 'She *knew* you'd take it like this!'

'Now just a minute – take *what* like this?'

'Well, being passed over, you know . . . for the job . . .'

Lara had wondered how long it would take to get round to that. 'Oh, let's not—'

'I know . . . I *know* it was St Lucia. *I* would have been pissed off if I'd been shafted like that,' admitted Annie.

So this was . . . *what*? Yet another indignity, and she hadn't even known about it. How much else was to come out? Lara shrugged. 'Was I?'

'Well . . . I – of course the trip was yours by right, everyone knew that . . . but then Tigi happened to be there when Raff Longlon was at Le Caprice, and so . . . you know . . .'

'I really have no idea what you're talking about,' said Lara coolly. 'Nor do I give a toss.'

'I don't believe that.'

'I've met someone,' said Lara at last. 'I've met quite a few people as a matter of fact, who have opened my eyes to what is what.'

'So you're still only talking then.'

'As yet.'

'Look . . . don't do anything rash.'

'Why not? Doesn't everyone else?'

Annie strutted an awkward pace or two.

'I've met a man,' said Lara, feeling her spirits rise. 'A rather unlikely one.'

'We're not talking about work now?'

Lara shook her head.

'I *knew* there was something. Well?'

'Well what?'

A sigh. 'What's he like?' She was trying to understand, to do her best. Lara knew that.

'Oh,' said Lara, deadpan. 'Don't think I'm jumping to conclusions when I say that he's an axe-wielding psychopath.'

Annie laughed, relieved. 'Well, that's all right then.'

Lara found she was mildly offended at that. 'I'm serious. He also has this thing about saris.'

'*Thing?*'

'He likes to tie women up with them. Until they're all wrapped up and can't move – and then he gives you a shock.'

Annie gave her an old-fashioned look. 'Strange . . .'

'Do you think so?' asked Lara. 'When you get to know him, you discover it's one of his more endearing and harmless activities.'

That did it for Annie. 'My God, Lara! What's happened to you? It took you weeks to sleep with Will for the first time, and you were mad for him!'

'Did I really tell you that?' asked Lara. 'I must have thought you were a friend.'

Annie acted as if she hadn't heard. 'Lara . . . something has happened, hasn't it!'

'Yes,' said Lara. 'It's to do with growing out of the need to please, to be striving continuously to be good enough, to do the right thing . . .'

'I *do* see where you're coming from.'

'I know you do,' said Lara smoothly.

'Only . . . it's not as bad as you're making out. Really.' The attempt at reassurance was as misguided as it was futile.

Annie did not stay long enough for the conversation to reach the point at which Lara would have to tell her she was wasting her time, and that they had both clearly and mutually mistaken workplace pleasantries for friendship, but she must have seen it coming.

Lara's former colleague went soon after.

14   Up, Up and Away

One morning the sun was so bright and the spring birds on the garden wall were squabbling so sweetly that Lara even wondered about children. Could she ever have a child on her own? She turned the notion over in her mind as if she were handling an explosive device. Other women did it.

But there was no point in pretending. She would never do it, not deliberately. It went too far against the grain.

So she made another list of places to go, and plays to see, and people to interview if she ever felt up to some gentle freelancing again. Then a list of lists.

Why did she compile all these lists? Was it for lack of someone to talk to, or to pretend they could keep her life from slipping into chaos?

She had no answers beyond making more toast.

If Lara had decided to opt out of her previous world, there was one snag: the world wouldn't let her go. The telephone rang incessantly. But now, weeks and weeks after she had left them wondering where she was and what she was doing, it was rarely one of her friends. Fi and Mary and Bea and Sue had retired hurt, waiting for her to make the next move. Liv had not called from Tokyo – she would have understood the enormity of Lara's transformation, would have laughed fit to burst at her exploits – but then Lara had still not replied to her letter.

For others however, it seemed, like the old advice about how to snare a lover, as though she had made herself an object of desire by being unavailable.

In modern parlance: Treat 'em mean, keep 'em keen.

That was her first thought, at any rate.

As the messages piled up she realised that it wasn't her the callers wanted, but what she could do for them.

So she made yet another list.

Jennifer. She was spitting, then pleading, full of dread at the ramifications of being named *Reflections'* Worst Dressed Woman on Television, not to mention Most Synthetic. She was calling Lara as doggedly as she had once been dismissive.

Christy. This was the sister of an old college friend who attempted periodically to play Lara's sympathies in order to trade up from freelance hacking to a magazine staff job. She wouldn't give up either.

Matt. A male sub-editor at *Reflections* who'd always found Lara malleable, and whom she'd been fool enough to ask round for dinner a couple of times to make up numbers.

Jens. Lara had met him at a party years ago when he was newly arrived from Denmark, knowing no one. He had stayed in touch; she had kept him in dinner-party food and new acquaintances. It went without saying that she had never got further inside the flat he eventually acquired in Clapham than seeing the estate agent's details.

Sarah. She was another who never managed to invite her back in return. Their friendship had floundered lately on the realisation.

Stephen. He was a PR for whom she had done so many

favours that there was now some pique and unpleasant-
ness if she failed him.

What it boiled down to was this: They wanted to know
when Lara was going to put food in their stomachs and
influential people in their path.

Inevitably, some of them caught her as soon as she
decided it was safe to go back to answering the telephone.
The conversations progressed along remarkably similar
lines.

'Well ... yes, I have been very busy ... I *am* very busy,
so ...'

'We *must* get together! It's been too long.'

'We-ell ... I suppose—'

'*Great!* When?'

'I'm not sure, I—'

'It would have to be a weekend. And that's always
better anyway because then we can all kick back and
have a real session, can't we.'

'You see, I've—'

'So much better to be able to have a *real* talk. Your
suppers are ace for that. Don't know what it is you do,
but you've always had the knack ...'

'I'm not ...'

Bloody say no!

It was never enough.

'Tell you what,' Lara would concede. 'I'll see what I can
do.'

The call from Stephen the PR interrupted the third
peanut-butter sandwich of a self-indulgence session. The
public-relations man was on a high-octane high. He
launched (and how practised he was at that) into an
update of his own life and times with barely a pause to
greet her.

' ... so there we are ... it's all booked: the great concert, the great venue, the *fabulous* party . . . and five hundred gilded invitations with one fatal misprint: *An Evening with Tuna Turner* . . . I mean, can you *imagine*?'

Lara found she could, all too easily. She tuned in and out of the monologue – for all its relevance it seemed to her to come from another planet. When he finished his spiel, it transpired that he had an event in mind for her.

He had it all planned.

'A balloon trip?' repeated Lara.

'I knew you'd love it. It will be fabulous,' he assured her.

'I'm scared of heights.'

'But you'll *love* this!'

'And if I don't?'

'Then you can write about it anyway. Look, sweetie, it's *perfect* for your little column: not too far from London . . .'

'Stephen, the last time you said that I ended up knee-deep in mud—'

'Townie!'

'—in deepest Gloucestershire. The "Metropolis" column, Stephen. City? Urban life?'

'You'll *love* this,' he reverted to his theme.

Lara sighed. 'I hate press trips.'

Silence.

'OK. I'll tell you what. I couldn't do this for everyone, but it's a new account and I think I can arrange it.'

'What?'

'Forget the other journos. You can have it to yourself. Invite some mates. Then you can do a larger piece about your own private party in the sky. Right up your street, eh?'

Lara was about to tell him where to get off, to tell him that she was no longer working for *Reflections* even . . . when an idea began to take hold.

*

There was no shortage of freeloaders eager to climb aboard.

Jennifer, Christy, Matt, Jens and Sarah – and Stephen himself, of course. The others had been only too pleased – not to say relieved – to hear from her, especially when she went through the guest list. Why, there was someone for everyone!

'Let's have a picnic,' she suggested to each one in turn. They all thought that was a wonderful idea.

'Bring something with you that we can eat outside, and we'll share and share alike,' instructed Lara.

'I don't suppose you're intending to make that wonderful thing you do with sweet onions and sun-dried tomatoes?' asked Sarah.

Jens was keen on her famous cheesecake.

Matt adored her chicken stuffed with cashews.

'The one I gave you the recipe for?' countered Lara.

'Mmm . . .'

'Perhaps you could make it then?'

'Well . . . I could . . . but it would never be a nice as when you do it. Best cook I know! You've got that touch . . .'

Yeah . . . the soft touch.

The ballooning centre was in Kent. They would take off from a hilltop above one of the most romantic moated castles in the country. The setting was outrageously beautiful. The views would be stunning.

Lara suggested that if she sent out detailed maps, then they could all meet there.

'Are you driving down?' Jens was the first to ask.

'My car's been stolen.'

'Oh no! But haven't the insurance company come up with a replacement for you while everything's sorted out?'

'Not mine.'

'Bummer,' said Jens.

'Don't you have a car?' asked Lara.

'I do ... yeah ... but I thought it would be cool if we, you know, went there together. We would have a few drinks ... mellow out ... I kinda thought it would be easier.'

Easier for whom, exactly? Lara wondered.

There was much the same conversation, all too predictably, with Sarah.

The appointed day found Lara and a bulging rucksack on a Network South-east train to Sevenoaks with Sarah, Jens, Matt and Christy. Stephen had gone ahead and Jennifer preferred not to travel on public transport.

Lara could barely bring herself to look at them, and when she did she saw them with new eyes, these people who belonged to the life she had abandoned. They were hardly more than ciphers.

Sarah was over made-up, showing her age in the pouches developing around her set mouth. At college she had been a big bubbly blonde; now those bubbles had turned sour – she would be blowzy soon enough.

Christy she hardly knew. She was a tall thin dark girl who was – ludicrously – wearing finest kid loafers and pale suede trousers for the expedition.

Matt was a goatee beard.

Jens was a silly grin and a ponytail, six foot two up.

None of them was carrying a hamper, or any kind of bag which promised a lavish spread.

Thirty miles south of London they alighted. Lara left them to phone the ballooning centre to tell Stephen they would soon be there. When she returned they were sitting in a row waiting for her to organise their onward transit. She commandeered two minicabs and they set off.

It was party time!

Lara was not surprised to see Stephen was empty-handed too when they arrived at their destination. He was a dapper little man who did not carry anything larger than a Psion organiser. And she would have been positively shocked if Jennifer had made any kind of effort.

The introductions were made in a cobbled courtyard. On three sides squatted farm buildings now converted to storage units and garages for the Land Rovers emblazoned with the Grand Balloon Company logo.

'I thought we could walk half-way up the hill where we'll take off,' said Stephen, 'and eat the picnic there.'

They all agreed readily – so long as it wasn't too far. The walk, Lara noticed, was the first opportunity for strategic getting-to-know-yous: Jennifer, subtly dramatic in a minimalist trouser suit, opened her offensive on Matt the man from *Reflections* with a blood-curdling smile; Jens buttonholed Stephen; Christy latched on to Lara with a run-down of her most recent features ideas.

When they reached a snug hollow between two ancient oaks, the spot was pronounced ideal. They all looked to Lara, so she motioned them to make themselves comfortable. Then she shrugged off her rucksack and set it down. All eyes were upon it.

Lara unfastened the buckle and pulled out the entire bulk in the form of a checked travelling rug. 'Did anyone want to share my blanket?' she asked.

Still they all looked expectantly at Lara. So she reached deep into her bag. 'I've brought some cherry tomatoes,' she said. 'Everyone likes those.'

And . . .? demanded hungry expressions.

She let them wait. 'Has anyone thought to bring some bread?' asked Lara.

Jens produced a bottle of cheap white wine from the pocket inside his jacket but no glasses or corkscrew.

Christy had some dips from Sainsbury's but nothing to dunk into them.

Sarah contributed two plastic packs of strawberries.

Matt came up with one slice of delicatessen pate.

195

Stephen dived into his black jacket and emerged with a bottle of champagne but the problem of glasses remained.

There was a disappointed silence. Disappointed in *Lara*, that was clear.

'You said you were making a picnic,' frowned Jennifer.

'No,' said Lara. 'I said, "Let's have a picnic" – that's what I *said*. You all presumed. I thought someone might treat *me* for a change, given that you were all so keen to see me.'

There was still no reply, so she stifled a giggle by tossing a cherry tomato into her mouth. She was enjoying this.

The bad grace which characterised the group as they sat down for a hillside lunch lasted until the bottle of champagne had been passed from mouth to mouth, and Stephen went down the hill again and found that, after all, he did have another in his car. That was seized on, and went some way to salvaging the occasion.

Below them, a mile away, the crenellated stone castle was fairy size. Birds wheeled in the sky. Flocks of sheep made white clouds on other green hillsides.

Lara alone ate with relish. She rolled cherry tomatoes in sour-cream dip and licked her fingers. She felt every bubble of Veuve Clicquot prickle her tongue; she felt the blades of grass under her and the light breeze on her face.

Conversation was still fissured with awkwardness. For once, Lara did nothing to cement the cracks.

She tuned in and out of the voices around her. So it *was* possible, after all. After years of being the person who looked after guests and made the effort at parties, she could be as rude as she wanted.

Stephen and Jennifer had failed to see eye to eye over the timing of the trip. In fact, he was not nearly as impressed by her presence as he might have been. But she, ever the pragmatist, had quickly focused on the need to recruit Matt – or rather his influence over the *Reflections* Best List – to her cause. When she began her charm offensive on him, however, this quickly degenerated into mutual antagonism. In no time they were at odds over restaurants.

'I bet you like going to the Caprice,' he sniped.

'What's wrong with the Caprice?'

'Oh, pul-ease . . .'

Meanwhile Christy had noticed how inexorably Jens disposed of other people's food with no visible sign of enjoyment, and was clearly irritated to see Sarah now offering him the strawberries.

They had struck up a pointless repartee Lara had heard before about the impossibility of judging the culture of the cinema against the theatre and keeping up with the diverse artistic life of the capital.

'The last film I saw was that one with Arnold Schwarzenegger,' said Jens.

'I don't think that counts.'

It was obvious Christy had no desire to hear about Stephen's latest launch triumph, but she was having to.

Jennifer was getting nowhere. She and Matt had quickly decoded each other's personality through their stated preferences in urban eating and shopping, and found they were incompatible.

'What a silly, fake little world you inhabit,' she snarled at Matt.

He was unabashed. 'Me black kettle, you pot, darling.'

They all droned on as they did the last time they had sat round Lara's dinner table, showing no signs of realising that the party was over.

And Lara sat and ate and wiggled her toes luxuriously and melted some more into the furry green hillside. There was a delicious aroma in the air – the faint whiff of a bit of a stink.

It seemed she might have a talent for trouble, after all.

'What do *you* think, Lara?'

Six faces had turned on her for reassurance or rescue.

She had no idea what they wanted to know but she let them wait anyway.

'What?'

'Shall we go sooner rather than later?' Stephen pressed her.

'Sooner,' said Lara decisively.

'Have you told the photographer where to meet us?'

'Photographer?'

'You *have* got a photographer?'

'No,' said Lara.

That went down about as well as the picnic.

There were two balloons. The party clambered up the rest of the hill to the pitch where they were to take off. It was a busy scene: two Land Rovers were parked, and men in jeans were checking the equipment and knotting guy ropes.

The balloon baskets lay on their sides, held down by thick cables. Behind them stretched out ripples of silky material, one daub of blue and one of red, spilling out on the hill like paint from giant pots. Lara tried to imagine what it would be like to stand inside one of these baskets, swaying in the wind with the roar of the flame taking them higher over the the patchwork fields.

The wicker of the baskets hardly looked strong enough to hold them.

'The rise and rise of the Grand Balloon Company,' joked Stephen, for the owner's benefit.

Blasts from the burners were beginning to fill the great flapping domes. The silk danced on the ground as the heat was directed in.

'We are all allowing ourselves to go a long way up on a lot of hot air,' said Lara pointedly.

There were no steps into the baskets: boarding entailed hurdling over the top. The others climbed in before her: Jennifer, Jens and Stephen in one with their pilot; Christy, Matt and Sarah in the other with theirs.

Lara stared at them all as they jostled for the best spaces and then waited.

'Now you,' said Stephen. 'Take your pick.'

'Hurry up!' called one of the pilots. 'The wind's up!'

Sure enough, the balloons had begun to pull at the guy ropes. The men had unfastened some in readiness to cast off.

Lara shook her head.

'Come on, Lara!'

'I'm not coming.'

'What? Of course you're coming! Look, there's plenty of room!'

'No, I'm not coming.'

Stephen smiled, but through exasperation. 'Lara, you are coming because this trip has been arranged for you and you are writing about it.'

She stood her ground. 'I'll write about it anyway, I don't care. Or Matt can write about it.'

Matt began to remonstrate but then fell silent.

'If we want to catch the wind . . .' said their pilot.

'Oh, come on, Lara,' called Sarah.

'Yeah, come on,' added Matt.

'If you're not coming, you can look after all the bags,' said Jennifer. 'It's far too tight a squeeze in here. In fact, maybe I won't come either . . . if you could just let me out—'

'You stay there,' ordered Stephen, angry now. 'She can take the bags.' He began to haul them out, handing them to Lara like a punishment.

*

The balloons rose.

Lara watched them go, the bags and mean detritus from the failed picnic at her feet. She watched the flight hands pull up metal jacks from the ground and jump back into their Land Rovers. Refusing the offer of a lift back, she stayed stock still on the hill until the billowing orbs had floated off with their baskets of scowling passengers.

She was left alone, and she had never felt happier. The wind whipped through her hair. She couldn't remember a party she had enjoyed so much! She danced around all their baggage until she was dizzy.

After the long dull haul of playing by the rules, giving full rein to her anger and imagination was proving such fun. She liked herself so much more for standing up to these people.

She kicked one of the bags. Then she spread both arms like a child playing at aeroplanes and let her legs run her down the slope. Away she went, faster and faster, not caring if she stumbled or fell.

She was free!

15   Into the Blue

It was soon after this that Lara hit on her own solution. Perhaps it was due to the pricks of memory (and how many of them there were when she came to consider her former colleagues) that Annie's visit, and seeing Matt and Stephen, had released like nettle rash. She could never go back to *Reflections*. What she remembered most vividly when she thought of the tower by the Thames was the oddly elasticated lift up to their floor.

Whatever transformation had occurred – and who knew, maybe it was even the effects of the oriental eclipse? – Lara made a decision which released her. And once she had done so, she began to enjoy herself, or as much as a woman could do who had steeled herself to face the fear.

When the appointed day came, she woke falling, with a jolt. Then Lara gathered herself. In the previous weeks she had taken her first tentative steps; and now this really was the morning of her giant leap.

She did not eat breakfast.

She was positively gleeful as she grabbed her jacket and slammed the door behind her. She set off to the river, through Dolphin Square and towards Battersea feeling light and free as her feet sprang her towards her appointment.

201

She was making decisions.

She was filled with a sense of purpose and symbolism.

Maybe her true spirit was breaking out at last.

Even the Thames was making an effort for the occasion, like a sullen old dowager decked out with all the family diamonds. From the point on the Embankment where Lara stopped to get her bearings, the dull grey water drew every sparkle to be had from the sun.

Lara shaded her eyes with one hand, then set her course upriver. She felt not a tremor of trepidation. And what was more surprising was that the confident feeling – the feeling that this was absolutely the *right* thing to do – held even as she walked up to the site and waved to the figures clustered around the base of their steel tower.

'You came!' said one man who detached himself from the group and came towards her. His grin was huge beneath his yellow hard hat. So was the antipodean accent when he said, 'Hi. I'm Greg.'

Lara smiled. 'Hi, Greg.'

'You spoke to Chris on the phone, right?'

Lara nodded.

'I'll be taking you through your paces today. You feeling good?'

She was overawed by the thought that this was the man to whom she was preparing to entrust herself. Perhaps she needed a little more time. Or perhaps she was just mesmerised by him, by his height, by his broad shoulders. And it was not possible to overlook the shape of those strong thighs even through battered jeans.

'Ah ... Australian?' she croaked, stalling for time.

'New Zilland.'

'Ah. That's good. I mean ... I read somewhere that's where all this started.' She gestured up and around them.

'Sure did,' said Greg. He had very white, very even

teeth against a Marlboro Man complexion. 'You ready to fly?'

Lara nodded, willing her legs to be strong. They were shivering beneath her jeans.

'Right, then, let's get you ready. Go through the safety precautions. Get you prepared for the big moment.'

An hour later she stood taller than tall over the city. Greg checked the ropes and harness for one final time. He tugged forcefully at her as if he were securing a child.

'Feeling OK?' he asked.

Lara turned round on the platform at the very top of the steel tower. It jutted over the grey water. Battersea Power Station was an upended table to one side.

She was terrified. 'I suppose . . .'

It went through her head that she had never before tried suicide as an answer, and this was surely the nearest thing to leaping to certain death.

The wind up here was much stronger than she had supposed. It whipped her hair into a maenad's, stung her cheeks.

The drop was dizzying. Far, far below, the choppy surface of the river seemed to pull her down into her own fear. She could not do this. This was madness.

'Second thoughts?' he asked.

And third and fourth. 'No,' she said.

'You're going?'

If she turned back now . . .

She nodded. No turning back.

Greg had started to count down. Then, 'GO!!'

Lara launched herself backwards into the unknown. Head first she plunged down so fast that there were no doubts, no certainties and no cares.

'Aaaaagh, AAAARRRRGGGGHHHH!!!'

Then, when the end was not only in sight but rushing in her ears and cold in her nostrils, and the grey water was coming up to claim her for ever – the bungee rope janked her back from the abyss.

She soared upwards by her ankles. Everything was sky.

Then she plummeted down again to the water, loose as a puppet.

Six or seven more times she yo-yoed, screaming.

And she knew for certain that the *Reflections* experience riding the lift up to the twenty-second floor all those years had been nothing like the real thing.

After the jump, Greg pumped her hand by way of congratulations. 'Hey! You did great!'

She was still fighting for breath, but nodded euphorically.

'Was that good?'

She was still nodding when the bungee man said: 'Do you think you could keep a drink down?'

She didn't know about that. Not immediately, anyway. 'One night soon, then.'

More nodding, when words would not come. There was a fist in her chest, but it was clenched in a power salute. She had done it.

'I'll call you then?'

'Do,' gasped Lara. Why not?

She drifted back to Eccleston Square, oblivious to the roar of the streets, noticing only leaves and blades of green life that would not be suffocated by the city's plains of concrete.

Things would be different now. She had jumped, and she had landed in a new city, where her nerves no longer sharpened the sounds of traffic and made her scan the pavements and kerbs for imaginary dangers. One where she was no longer held back by fear, in other words.

She stopped off at the travel agent's and collected shiny brochures for the Americas and Australasia and the

Indian Ocean. Then she detoured to the market stalls in Tachbrook Street to buy sharp apples and wave at Jo between her flapping clothes.

For the first time in a long while, she felt whole.

For the first time *ever*, she was not going to fret about tomorrow.

She did not come properly down again to earth until she was back at the flat. The telephone rang. Lara decided to answer.

'Guess what?' It was Cass.

'I hate it when people say that.'

'I'm going to tell you anyway.'

'I guessed as much,' sighed Lara. Impatiently, she wound the telephone cord around her fingers. That had been another of her decisions: sever the ties with Cass and Sandra. They had become cumbersome, somehow, with their crazy schemes; their ponderous dedication to a lost cause was a burden on her own flight. Lara, alone, was light and set to run.

'Sandra . . .' said Cass, spinning it out, 'Sandra has taken action. Drastic action.'

Lara waited, willing animosity into the electronic silence.

'Sandra . . . has bought . . . a motor bike!'

'Well,' Lara found it hard to summon up the requisite amazement, 'good for her.'

'Is that all you can say? A sodding great black *hog* . . . makes a noise like Concorde landing . . . with Sand on board doing a ton up into the rectory at St Leonard's!'

Lara chuckled despite herself. 'I like it.'

'That's not all,' warned Cass.

'Oh?'

'Not at all. She used the cash raised at the church bazaar on Saturday! Seems they asked her to bank it – three thousand odd quid – and so off goes Sand in the direction of the Nat West . . . and she comes back with an old Harley Davidson. *And . . .*'

'And?'

'She seems to have the bloke to go with it.'

'What do you mean, bloke? She's in with the local bikers already?'

Cass sighed. 'A man mountain. You should *see* the tattoos . . .'

'Oh, my God.'

'Her husband's reaction was along the same lines . . . only *he* meant it.'

They laughed, a little guiltily.

'Do you want to meet somewhere?' Cass asked this with a tinge of urgency which reminded Lara uncomfortably of a TV film she had once seen in which fellow alcoholics drew on each other's resources.

'The thing is, Cass . . .'

'Or I could come round to you?'

'Um, you know . . . I'm really not feeling too good. Bit of an upset . . .'

Cass was all solicitude. Not that she was letting excuses deflect her.

'Headache,' said Lara, emphatically. 'Bad, bad headache.'

It had come to something when she was having to use that old chestnut.

But she knew she was doing the right thing. She didn't want anything to take the shine off her bright new day.

16   Scanning the Horizon

Lara was on for it. She was going to meet someone new and it looked as though Sunday would be the day. With something like her old verve for research she had gathered useful data and spread it all over the floor.

'Meet and Eat.' This was an organisation dedicated to dinner parties for single people. Lara considered the ramifications of that one. She had been doing a bit too much eating lately. There were times when having her appetite was like living with a swarm of locusts. What if it ran away with her at a crucial moment, when disappointment set in, say? There would be nothing left of the table, not a fruity centre-piece unravaged, not a crumb remaining on the plate of the eligible dentist from Northwood on her left and the Fulham architect to her right . . . Meet and Eat was not her first choice.

There were dating agencies for discerning professionals – for professional singles, even. What were they? People with degrees in Independence and an MBA in Being Very Picky? In any case, the joining fees made her reel.

There were lower-key clubs which ran events for the unattached.

There were specialist gatherings for single mah-jong players and potholers, sailing enthusiasts and wine buffs.

There were any number of advertisements offering a selective and caring introduction service As Seen on TV.

Lara sighed. The more she read about in-depth profiles and rigorous interview procedures, the more she went off the idea. It was the sheer *commitment* involved that was so off-putting. She would have to ease herself into this: she needed a more casual approach.

She discounted answering a personal ad straight away. She had no desire to put herself up for such instant rejection if she wrote and no reply came. Besides, that would take too long.

Not that she wanted Cupid, with his plump little buttocks and dodgy aim. She did not particularly want to find a new relationship. All the signs were that she had had quite enough of one of those. But, as she examined her motives, she concluded that she would do this because she needed to prove something to herself.

That she was still an attractive and lovable person, perhaps?

She did not want to start all over again with someone else; only to know that it was possible.

Over a new packet of chocolate biscuits she came to the conclusion that the most promising ideas came from a page ripped from one of the Sunday newspapers. 'Tried and tested,' it assured her. 'The best places in London for singles to meet.' That was more like it. Direct and reassuring, without the need for great amounts of cash and planning.

Pencil in hand, she studied the list given.

Some suggestions were impractical: walking a dog or rollerblading in Hyde Park, for example, due to lack of dog or skill on rollerblades. Despite a great deal of determination, she had discovered that much about her brave new persona. There were bruises all over her legs.

Some were discarded straight away: hanging out at Harvey Nichols's Fifth Floor bar got a thick black line. Was it the 'younger women, older men' tag, or all that Harvey Nicks had meant in her former life?

She was left with the Tate gallery ('for thoughtful types in their thirties, especially on Sundays') and Sunday brunch at the V&A cafe ('intelligent eligibles reading papers and clever books').

Lara had always felt self-conscious about eating on her own, or even drinking a cup of coffee, come to that.

The Tate it would have to be. She could walk there.

Or was it the word 'thoughtful' which was the clincher?

On her way through strangely quiet Sunday afternoon streets, wearing her black urban commando look yet again, Lara made one more mental list: No Go Areas.

No goatee beards.

No razored baldies.

No rough diamonds.

No sandals with socks.

No polyester trousers.

No jeans with ironed creases.

After all, she thought, clothes maketh man as well as woman. Then she laughed aloud at herself, and her inane supposition that she would meet anyone at all.

The high light atrium of the Tate always reminded Lara of a railway station. It was not so much the lovely space as the way the crowds gathered in it: here, bustling and purposeful; there, meandering, waiting, seeking directions.

And of course, hoping to meet someone.

There was a special exhibition of Braque on loan from the Musee d'Orsay in Paris – a place, funnily enough, which *was* once a grand railway station – but Lara decided to give that a miss. Mentally she added to her list: No one who thinks nicotine-stained collages are a patch on Picasso.

She went with the flow into the main rooms.

Usually when she visited one of the great art galleries of the world, she came to marvel at the sheer brilliance of the works on show, never ceasing to notice how the originals glowed with a size and detail unseen in reproduction. This time, however, her critical faculties were anywhere but concentrated on the inanimate.

She hadn't looked around this brazenly since she was about eighteen.

There were plenty of youngish people. Mostly they were tourists and couples. A flock of Japanese schoolgirls bobbed past a Matisse. It was a while before Lara saw anyone remotely feasible.

When he did materialise by the side of a Whistler, he was conventionally tall and dark, and not that far off the handsome mark. He had a high forehead – no, his hair was receding – and a lanky walk. He was carrying a paperback copy of a novel by Primo Levi, and his denim shirt and chinos weren't bad at all.

Lara prepared herself. She would do this . . . She *would*!

Lara began her advance – she may even have been smiling – when another woman took him by the arm and led him off. She was small with a friendly face; they laughed together when she made a quip Lara could not hear. Why was it that her appearance immediately made him seem all the more attractive?

After an hour wandering the treasure-lined rooms, Lara saw that there were plenty of men on their own, as the article had promised, but most of them were in their early twenties, and studied the paintings intently. Clearly they were not interested in an older woman in black.

Self-conscious suddenly, and unwilling to embark yet on another circuit of the gallery, Lara sat down to pretend to view Millais's *Ophelia*.

This was obviously the way it worked.

Minutes later she felt someone sit next to her.

'Lovely, isn't she?' said a voice.

Lara turned to see she was sharing a seat with a centre parting and whiskery chin. Large grey eyes blinked at her, and a mouth twitched. He was young – but not that young. The overall effect was of a friendly river-bank animal in some anthropomorphic tale.

Lara left it too long to say anything. She opened her mouth – but then moved off abruptly. Feeling herself very young again, she swallowed a giggle. As Lara's granny might have said, 'I know he can't help his looks, but he could stop in.'

Her steps quickened on the polished floor.

The second time round she stopped in front of the dusky lanterns of *Carnation, Lily, Lily, Rose*. She was immersed in the blue-greens of Singer Sargent's garden with his joyous English girls when it happened.

'Luctisonant.' It cut across her thoughts.

She jumped slightly.

The voice moved in on her. It came from thickish lips on a pleasant, if fairly ordinary face. 'That's the word which comes to mind,' it said. 'Luctisonant.'

Lara smiled quizzically.

'It's the light . . . for me, anyway,' said the man. He was standing at her side in front of the painting now, taller than her, with round steel-rimmed glasses under dark wavy hair. He looked nice enough, nothing special. His jeans were stone washed but reassuringly unironed.

'Lucti—?' said Lara.

'—sonant. Means kind of sad and . . . crepuscular.'

'Ah.' That wasn't quite how she saw it. 'You mean,' she

indicated the little girls in their Victorian smocks 'a kind of retrospective sadness for us now, for a time that's gone?'

He frowned. His forehead furrowed deeply. Above his glasses on either side of his nose two creases formed like quotation marks. Then he smiled. 'Maybe that's it.'

Maybe it was.

They shared their views for what they were worth on several other paintings in the room and then he offered to buy her a cup of coffee.

She accepted.

Across the table in the tearoom she discovered that his name was Stephen. Not Steve.

'I've never been a Steve,' he said, and she could imagine that somehow. He was probably older than she was, or that may have been the pedantry with which he chose his words. He was most precise.

He put three sugars in his coffee.

He told her he was a council officer in the housing department.

Lara told him as little as she could about herself.

He countered by telling her about the changes he had faced in public-sector housing since September 1986. He admitted his worries about the dawn of the millennium on the council's computer system.

There were no lightning strikes and thunderclaps, just the damp drizzle of a conversation with someone who was turning out to be dull as ditch-water.

Neither of them mentioned a relationship, current or previous. Lara tried to imagine him with a woman – what kind of woman would come up and lead him away with a private joke? – but did not succeed. His conversation was proceeding with a series of ponderous enquiries.

She deflected an opener concerning her views on public

transport. She was beginning to feel that she was submitting to an in-depth vetting interview after all.

He raised bold questions about her likes, dislikes and preferred route to Wembley. Lara told him that she didn't have much cause to go there. She drank her coffee and let herself off the hook by deciding that this was warm-up session – she was practising the art of conversation with a new man in a new situation. Or would it always be like this?

And what *did* she enjoy doing with her free time?

Conversation began to stutter.

Stephen was not her type but neither was he an unpleasant man. He was trying too hard. Soon he was gamely telling her how much he felt out of his depth being single again after so long.

Lara deliberately failed to pick up on that.

'It's life, but not as we know it,' he lamented. 'There's a green bookshop in Camden that's supposed to be a useful place to start a conversation,' he told her. 'But the women almost all had very short hair and rather cross looks about them. I can't say I'll be going back.' Then, when he mentioned getting a dog to walk in Hyde Park she realised what he was saying.

Oh no . . .

Her fears were confirmed when he added, 'Have you tried the Sunday brunch at the V&A yet? I've heard it's very good.'

He must have read the same *Sunday Times* article.

She was cool. 'Good . . . for the food?'

'Well . . . that as well, probably.'

When he scratched the dregs of sugar in the bottom of his cup it was the sound of a barrel being scraped.

'So . . .' he began (did he imagine that some accord had been reached?), 'would you care to go to the theatre, perhaps, one evening?'

'It's very kind of you to ask,' said Lara, 'but this time

tomorrow I shall very nearly have arrived back home in North Yorkshire.'

So she had lied.

When she got home and looked up 'luctisonant' in the *Shorter Oxford Dictionary* it wasn't there.

17 Ups and Downs

If life were ever to return to normal – and Lara had decided, inevitably, that this would have to be the case – then it was largely her heart-stopping, *idiotic* elasticated jump to certain death over the Thames that had done the trick.

Or rather, the man who had pushed her.

As good as his word, he had called her.

Greg the bungee-jump instructor asked her if she would like to meet him in a homely wine bar and she found she would. She went, and she drank some wine and ate some food. It wasn't a big deal, but it was the most fun she'd had in a while.

Greg was a free spirit. He told her that he came from a homestead some way outside Auckland, but he was capable of impassioned eulogies on his native country without constant reference to its undoubted superiority to present surroundings. He was laid back without being horizontal. He was intelligent without, apparently, needing to impress his qualifications on anyone, let alone a prospective employer. He alluded once to a degree course – in dentistry? – but he had not offered details and she had not asked.

He agreed with Lara's theory that the good rarely won, but had never been surprised or infuriated that this was, unequivocably, the way of the world. For he had long ago come to the conclusion that in order for rage and frustration to be stoked, there had first to be an acceptance that the rat race was worth running.

'So you never had a moment,' she asked him, 'when you felt as though you had tried all along to do the honest best you could – to be good enough – and then realised that everyone else was up to every trick in the book? Daring to be bad enough, in other words?'

He considered this for a moment. '*Every*one else?'

She spread a palm to concede the point.

'Perhaps,' he replied, 'it was not that others were bad, but that they were scared to be themselves.'

She had to think about that one for a while.

He seemed to be one of those rare souls who were happy existing in the absolute present. In fact, when Lara came to think about it, this was probably a prerequisite for a career involving vertigo-inducing heights and a very large rubber band.

In the well-balanced drop-out (drop-down) stakes, Greg was gold-medal standard.

In all ways, he was the antithesis of the men she had always chosen. And what did *that* say about her life so far?

In short, with Greg she felt her life was back on track. She saw him again, and then once more. She *felt* normal for the first time in a long while. He called her when he said he would; they went to normal places. They sauntered out to a local pub and drank lagers. They went to the cinema where, having braced herself for his choice of the Stallone movie, she amazed herself by laughing when she was supposed to.

Greg, it seemed, was heaven sent.

And purely by the by, he had a *great* body.

It had been two weeks since her giant leap. They celebrated in watery fashion, by a small boat across the Serpentine in Hyde Park one murky afternoon.

He heaved on the oars, pitting his back against the wind. Above a vast sheepskin coat, his face was square and weathered: an outdoor man, no question.

She suspected – no, she *knew* – that she was not the only woman who had leaped from his tower by the Thames and then into his arms, but that was precisely what made him so attractive. The only strings were on the bungee jump.

They rowed round in a circle. It occurred to Lara that she knew very little about this big man, and that that was a supremely good thing. For years and stultifying years she had only ever considered seeing men who came from the safe social circles of existing friends. Introductions at drinks parties in SW6. Ludicrous dinners in taffeta in Battersea. Crowded seat-hopping restaurant dinner parties. Tried and tested meetings for the exuberantly desperate. Never before had she leaped into the unknown. But here she was, with this man, giving him a chance.

No . . . giving *herself* a chance.

She tried to explain a little of this to him.

'You can't take life too seriously. It's absurd,' he said, still pulling smoothly and strongly.

'I know that now,' she said.

'It's possible to enjoy not liking people. They don't have to make you angry.'

'That's a harder one.'

'Tell me about this prick Will, with that in mind.'

She laughed. 'It seems I may already have influenced your view.'

'Not for the reason you think.'

'Well . . . he was arrogant, shallow, narcissistic, often drunk . . . and it went downhill from there really.'

There was a sardonic twist in the corner of his mouth.

'Guys like that can be maniacal in their determination to show off their talents.'

'You don't know how *great* it is, what a *relief* it is, to cut out all the bullshit. To meet someone . . . different.'

Obviously he didn't see himself as different. He went on rowing as her thoughts slipped overboard into the dank choppiness all around them: the wind-blown watery remnants of London dust, the particles of old exhausted lives which had settled into this cold grey soup.

'It's true what they say about like finding like. You end up mostly with friends who have the same interests, and background, and aspirations. And then – suddenly – it's great to meet someone who *doesn't* have the same record collection as you.'

He gave this a moment. 'You mean – you don't have any Lightning Seeds?'

Encouraged, she told him a little about the workshop.

'I got this press release at the office,' she said. 'It was for this workshop which helped people who felt they had been walked all over because they were just too nice. And it kind of played on my mind . . . so I went. I was going to write a piece about it, you know.'

'What was it like?'

'I met some crazy people . . .'

He laughed lightly.

'You had to laugh,' Lara assured him. 'There they all were, getting into a stew about how awful other people were and what they could do about it.'

'And what could they do about it?'

'They talked about getting their self-esteem back, sharing their worst moments . . . and they ate a lot of wholemeal rolls.'

'And then?'

'They talked some more and tried some weirder therapies. One of them went berserk with his wife's

clothes and teapots and stuff and made the local paper.
That went down a storm with the others.'

'And then?'

An expressive shrug.

They laughed companionably.

'You know,' he said, although there was no way that she
could have known, 'it's my birthday today.'

'Well,' said Lara, 'happy birthday then. Are you doing
anything special later?'

'I might be,' he grinned.

'I've never even asked how old you are.'

'Twenty-six.'

'Ah.' She was light-headed with the cold, or there again
it could have been the intensity of his dark blue-grey
eyes.

'Now I know you're a woman of proven journalistic
skill.' He dared her, always, with that amused stare.
'Always get the age in.'

She laughed with a strange relief.

'You're a game girl, Lara,' he said.

Girl? 'What happened to "sophisticated older woman"?'
she teased through chattering teeth.

He cocked his head with a grin. 'Older?'

'Sophisticated.'

'Well, one more thing . . .'

'Hmmm . . . I did think anyway that maybe . . . this
evening . . . we could kick back at my place, I could cook
some dinner maybe . . . and then . . .' The more she
thought about it – which had already been quite a bit –
the better it sounded. 'Now that it's your birthday as
well . . .'

He leaned down to kiss her and as their lips touched,
and then their tongues, the effect had the same thrilling
effect on her insides as the bungee jump.

Lara let herself fall with a sense of senseless excitement.

She would have been happy for him to wait for her at the flat, but he insisted on coming to the supermarket with her. 'I like this,' he said, loading up a wire basket. 'It's kind of companionable.'

He tossed in a ready-washed salad and they had a brief moment of dissent over chicken versus lamb. They picked up some wine and chocolate pudding and cream for if the mood took them.

It was all so easy.

It wasn't any harder to cook and eat and fall into bed.

Sex that night was as simple and satisfying as newly baked bread and fresh butter. Only with the erotic charge of pure self-indulgence. His body was ridged and hard. She felt she had never been with anyone so pure.

She lay tingling and sated for a long time after, and thought with contempt of Will's self-serving gratifications, of Colin's octopus clutches.

No, she was definitely better off with Greg. If she was going to be part of Real Life with all its ups and downs, then let it be with a simple man. What goes up, must come down. If any man lived that philosophy, it was Greg.

With Greg, it would be the easiest option in the world to make love, not plans.

She told Greg, drip by drip, about the job situation. Best of all, he seemed to understand. It didn't seem too much of a surprise to him that a normal person could only stomach so much air-kissing and retro chic and four-teen-year-old girls made up to look thirty, let alone take it seriously.

'So what are you going to do?' he asked her one day as they were walking hand in hand one afternoon along the Embankment.

'Collect an armful of old wire, drag in a burned-out car and throw red paint over it ... and become a world-renowned modern artist?' The previous day they had been to see an exhibition of outlandish modern devices masquerading as art in the form of dead animals and bodily functions. It had stirred quite a few unresolved frustrations.

He did laugh, but then said, 'Seriously.'

'I hate to tell you, but those people *are* serious.'

They pondered on that for a while as they walked on by the river, in a Chelsea direction. Through the thick, speckled trunks of the trees on the Embankment she could make out now and then the top of the bungee crane. She hadn't realised until today how far she had walked that morning when she set out into the blue to make her dizzying leap; she had been focused only on the destination. What she was sure of was that she had come a long way since.

'It's coming down tomorrow,' said Greg, latching on to her line of vision.

'The crane?' Her symbol?

He nodded. 'It was only ever a temporary home, while work was stopped on the site there. The local council didn't want to waste the pretty boards.'

That made sense, she supposed. The backdrop of the sights of London, the peculiarly balloon-like dome of St Paul's and the jolly beefeater, which encased the building behind, was being dismantled. She saw it now as they came round a bend that one never noticed unless on foot. It was only amid the shifting perspectives as the road snaked upstream against the river that all sorts of things became clear, she thought now.

'Where's it going to, then?'

'Somewhere downriver. Isle of Dogs?'

'Not so scenic,' she said.

'We'll see. Go with the flow.'

She laughed, mostly because that was what she liked best about him.

Later, though, when they were drinking wine and waiting for a pizza to be delivered, he asked her straight, 'And where are *you* going, Lara? What are you going to do about a job?'

It was a valid question – all the more so because it came from him.

'I *have* been thinking about it.'

'What have you been thinking?' He wasn't nagging; he was straightforward.

'Well, I'm doing all right, you know, for money and stuff, at the moment . . . They seem to think that I'm on some kind of leave from the magazine – my salary and everything, I mean . . .'

'Are you going to go back?'

'No.' She was certain of that.

For once, he did not let her off the hook. 'Then the money won't be there soon and you'll have to find another job. You need to do something, everybody does—'

'But I'm the kind of person who needs to most of all?'

'You don't need me to tell you.'

She had already told him more than enough. Of course he was right.

'What are you going to do?' he asked again.

She answered that, for the moment, by leaning over to undo a button on his shirt.

The next morning the brave new Lara got up and peered into the depths of her wardrobe. Then she did what anyone else in her position would have done: she went to the telephone, promised the impossible and called in a favour.

The glorious black Armani trouser suit and white shirt were hers for the asking.

A courier arrived on her doorstep before lunch-time bearing a large cream box marked 'Lara Noe, *Reflections*'.

Why had she never done it before?

Then she went to the files under her word processor and found the telephone number and address on an advertisement she'd cut from an old copy of *UK Press Gazette*. The time had come to contact the Media Exchange – a job agency by any other name.

It sounded rather less promising when she called to make the appointment but she was set now on her course.

The day after, Lara put on the white shirt and black Armani trouser suit.

The agency was located in a dingy alley around the back of Regent Street, so that the prospective media person marched optimistically along the gracious concave sweep of the famous thoroughfare and then dropped left into far less enticing prospects. Lara had some difficulty in deciding whether the grubby brass plate which announced the offices of Media Exchange in a down-at-heel doorway in Black Dog Passage was her destination or not.

She rang the bell, hardly caring. It gave a squawk–splutter, and the door buzzed open straight away. Lara climbed a dingy staircase on a well-worn stained carpet because there was nowhere else to go. At the first landing was a battered fire door, much scuffed under a glass window, which she pushed open when she saw a girl sitting at a desk the other side.

'Excuse me . . . have I come to the right place for the Media Exchange?' There was not even a scrappy sign by which to confirm this.

The girl nodded.

'Lara Noe. I'm due to see Paula Martin at ten thirty.'

'Take a seat, please.'

For an outfit which claimed to operate under the mantle

of the communications industry, there was a decided lack of chat.

Lara sighed inwardly and took the chair indicated, saving her admiration for the perfect ovoid stamped in the green fabric and foam by a cigarette burn. The only other sign of life was a dusty yucca plant which was struggling to survive in one corner.

Later than billed, Paula Martin appeared at another door and asked Lara to follow her into an office of starkly contrasting style and sleekness. She slithered behind an impressive black desk and assessed Lara, fingers steepled together. Lara did the same.

With her luxuriantly wavy dark hair worn past her shoulders and extravagantly streaked in gold and red, her eyes lavishly outlined in black, and her broad white smile, Paula was a summer holiday brochure made flesh. Across the desk, unseasonably tanned in her flamenco-red jacket, she shimmered in living – but curiously less than lifelike – colour.

Lara's subversive chip went into overdrive immediately. Do not adjust your sets . . .

'So – Lara – tell me why you are here.'

I'm wondering that myself . . .

She got a grip. 'I've worked for *Reflections* magazine for the past four years, nearly, and—' There must have been lots of other reasons, but it actually started with a bad clothes day . . .

Paula's face was all cosmetics.

'—it got to the point when it was time for a change,' said Lara, as brightly as she could manage.

'What kind of change do you have in mind?'

Behind Paula there was a large poster of a David Hockney in brilliant blues and greens. In contrast to the muted exterior, sitting opposite this was like waking up unexpectedly in California at midday.

Dunno, well . . . anything really . . .

Lara opened her mouth to come up with something a little more convincing.

'Only, don't say television,' said Paula. 'Everyone wants television, and it is very, very rare that those kind of jobs come up.'

'I wasn't really—'

'Everyone thinks they can walk in here, and by next Tuesday they'll be the next Esther or Ricki Lake or Jennifer Gould.'

'I don't—'

Paula was nodding vigorously. 'You do know that it takes a hell of a lot more than will and determination to get where they are.'

'Better than most, I can assure you.'

'Why do you think we make this place look so . . . unlikely?'

Because you are smug, self-satisfied pillocks who've obviously never managed to get yourselves a decent job, let alone anyone else?

'Because otherwise we'd have more no-hopers crowding outside than at the open auditions for *Fame*, that's why.'

Lara crossed her arms.

'Now . . .' Paula dragged a well-manicured red talon down the CV that she had taken from Lara without acknowledgement. 'Degree?'

'Sussex University. English and European Literature.'

The other woman pulled a tight expression which told her it hardly mattered, let alone the details.

'How's your typing? You're a bit on the old side for reception work.'

Lara swallowed that. 'As good as anyone's – anyone who has been working on a top national glossy as a writer, that is.'

'Hmm,' purred the other woman, missing all the inflection in Lara's voice. 'How do you feel about telesales?'

'I beg your pardon?'

'That's where most of the vacancies are. Once you accept that you'll be working on commission and you give it your all, the rewards can be very satisfying.' She burned browner than ever, and emitted a hundred-watt smile.

So that was it. Like everything else, the Media Exchange was too good to be true.

Paula tapped a pencil on the desk, then gave her a direct look. 'Unless . . .'

'Unless?'

'How relaxed are you?'

A pause. 'Meaning what, exactly . . .?'

'About going back to secretarial.'

Lara crossed her Armani-clad legs and played it disingenuously. 'Is that all I could expect at this stage?'

'We-ell . . .'

'That's what you have to come to terms with really, isn't it? Accepting the way it is,' said Lara after a moment's consideration.

'I'm glad you see it like that. People can be very unrealistic in their expectations.'

Lara acknowledged as much.

A sifting of papers on the desk was followed by the wide smile of a woman who was about to clinch a fat commission. 'Tell you what,' said Paula Martin, 'why don't you take these and have a look at them.' She handed over a couple of sheets. 'Then you can do a speed test for me. What are you used to?'

Lara took them without a downward glance. 'Word processing? Windows.'

'Windows *what*?'

'Er . . . 95?'

That seemed to be good enough. Lara allowed herself to be led into another room, in which were standing a desk, a chair and a computer terminal. It was a cell with no natural light.

'The point is, of course, that we place you – and yes, it *is* secretarial – but that is only the beginning. It's—'

Don't say it's the foot in the door, prayed Lara.

'—the foot in the door. You learn what it's all about and after that, it's up to you to move into the slot you want.'

It was timeless advice, Lara knew that. It might even have been good advice.

Paula told her to start right away and then exited.

Lara was left face to face with the word processor and the list of tasks designed to show off her skills. Very deliberately, she sat on the chair and rested her hands on the keyboard. Above her a strip light fizzed.

She found the switch and pressed the machine into life.

Then she sat and stared at the screen.

Of course she had known that it would probably come to this. She had no illusions; she wasn't stupid. She had not come here expecting to secure an interview for the editorship of a magazine, or even a features editor's job. She knew that those jobs simply weren't up for grabs through an agency like this. Sure, they might be advertised in the *Guardian* on a Monday, or in the trade press, but only to satisfy legal requirements or if there were no obvious candidates lined up through the grapevine. Lara knew all this.

For a long time she sat and stared at the screen, hypnotised by its electric nothingness.

Then she simply switched it off again.

She stood up and went to find Paula.

'Finished already?' She was rewarded by an encouraging smile.

'No,' said Lara. 'I'm not doing it.'

There was a stunned pause. The smile changed to a sneer which implied that Lara would never make it with that attitude.

Which was exactly what Lara needed.

'It's not the starting again at the bottom and working

up that worries me,' said Lara. 'But the problem is that I just don't want to go up any of the ladders on offer any longer.'

Outside on the street once more, she threw her bag in the air and caught it playfully. It was a gesture to convince herself that it had not been a wasted morning. She knew that, deep down.

For what was certain was that the old Lara would have sat at that desk and taken the test – perhaps even been mortified that she had made mistakes, or misunderstood some part of the task, and scared that she had not been speedy enough.

As it was, she was no closer to getting a job – but equally she was not about to agree to one that she did not want and she was more certain than ever that that was progress.

She *had* achieved something. When she allowed herself to, she felt *great*.

Bit by bit, Lara was beginning to feel that she had crossed an ocean. Or a watershed of some description at least. Being London, it was probably some damp Victorian sewer, clammy and slimy, deep under the foundations of the street, but that was the city for you.

Did she feel different?

She no longer cared what she wore in the mornings, although evenings were trickier. During the day, she dug out old clothes for the garden, more particularly ones that would leave Colin cold, should he arrive unexpectedly. For Greg, on the other hand, she contemplated all sorts of outdoorsy turn-ons. Was it actually possible to buy a stone-washed denim basque?

She went along to Liberty while she was in the area, just to see.

Greg wasn't fooled for a moment when she told him that

she was glad she'd gone, but he got the general point about the importance of finding out what she *didn't* want.

Raindrops smacked against the kitchen window-pane. The wet slapping sound reminded her – well, actually she would rather not be reminded of Colin's mouth on hers. She hurried to fill the kettle and set it boiling to make some tea.

Although that did make her wonder whether the same theory could be applied to her misadventure with Colin and that evening when ... She stopped herself right there.

Greg had started to nuzzle her neck.

18   Cause and Effect

She arrived when Lara was on a roll.

Lara had spent the night before clubbing with Greg and his friends. Did they *know* she was thirty-four? She hadn't felt it. Then, positively buzzing with happy exhaustion, she passed the afternoon in the local library assessing her chances of turning a great idea into reality. Had she hit at last on what she should have done all along, which was to accept her need for there to be a right and wrong, and try to implement the rules? In the end she did it – she sent off for details of how to get into law school.

When the doorbell rang she was performing brain surgery on half a cauliflower (she was even eating properly again).

In Lara's mind, if she had paused to think about her, Cass would have been cooking up a storm at home in some North London kitchen, the television alternately lulling and making monsters of the four children.

Telephone bulletins from the Cass and Sandra front had continued long after it was plain – or so Lara thought – that she had ceased to show any interest. Lara was evolving her own course of action now which had nothing to do with a couple of workshop Rottweilers who had gnawed through their leashes.

Yet the calls had persisted. No sooner would Lara feel

that rudeness and disinterest had paid off at last, than the telephone would shrill and a dispatch from Crouch End would assail the answering machine. She never lifted the receiver; she never called back.

It was a tribute, in its way, to the dogged creed instilled in the recovering TN sufferer: Do not take no for an answer.

On Lara's doorstep, Cass – suddenly larger than life, leaning her finger on the bell – was a woman who had travelled far in the intervening weeks. She was transmitting all the jangled nerve signals of a Great Escapee. She had the wind in her hanks of red hair, and mud on the unflattering leggings which bagged around her great thighs. Gaily painted wooden parrots dangled from her ears.

Lara swallowed her surprise. 'Cass! . . .' She didn't want to say it but, face to face, politeness tripped her up: 'Come in.'

Cass panted. 'I was hoping you'd say that.'

A sisterly friend-in-need shrug sprang instinctively to Lara's shoulders. Inside the flat, standing by the kitchen window, Cass looked around jerkily.

'I could murder,' she said with feeling, 'a drink.'

So they had one.

'I haven't spoken to you since . . . the *incident*, have I?' asked Cass gnomically. The parrots jiggled either side of her moon face.

'Mmm . . .?'

'The incident . . . with Sandra and the church-flower rota and the grease monkey . . .?'

Lara hadn't heard that one but she knew she was about to.

'Almighty row . . . so to speak.'

Cass told the tale, which seemed to involved several good ladies of the parish, a quantity of Dutch tulips which had been destined for the altar and a motorcycle mechanic.

'Cass, this ... *shocking* people tactic ... are you sure there isn't supposed to be more to it than that?'

The woman ignored her. 'Amazing, isn't it! And it turns out old Sandra is a natural ...'

'So it seems.'

'Once she got over all her inhibitions. Quite an example to us all, I say, eh?'

'Well, you know, I think I may be over all that, Cass.'

But the other woman was not to be deflected from the telling of the tale. 'You know Sand was always in the choir at St Leonard's?'

'Mmm.'

'She's got a great voice, I'll give her that, a real belter. Anyway, get this. She's still singing, only at the Railway Tavern in the Seven Sisters Road. She's lead vocals with this band—'

'A band ...'

'Maximum Offence. That's what they call themselves.'

'That's ... direct.'

'It's what they call a thrash metal group, apparently.'

'Oh, for God's sake.'

'No, that was the choir,' Cass pointed out.

'So is all this with the man mountain, the biker?'

'His name's the Grunt, and he may have long tatty hair and a prominent facial scar from a knife wound, but he's a beautiful person when you get to know him, apparently.'

'Right.'

'You could sound a bit more interested. I mean, this is *wonderful*, isn't it?'

Lara hesitated fractionally before replying with a question of her own. 'Cass ... why are you telling me all this?'

'What do you mean?'

'Why do you keep calling me? Haven't you noticed that I never ring you?' It sounded brutal, she knew.

A pause. 'I thought we got on. That you liked us . . . That we had something in common.'

Another pause yawned. It hardly deterred Cass.

Like it or not, Lara had become party to the cosmic transformation of Cass's previously banal life. This, to Cass's chagrin, was taking a little longer than that of her previous best friend Sandra, and the intervention of more complex technology.

'I've been thinking about getting a job,' continued Cass. 'I went to this place, right, where they log all your personal details in a computer, and then they run their programme – and it tells you what you should do.'

'So what did it say?'

'It came up with – well – debt collector, and dog handler.'

'What *did* you tell them to put into this computer?'

'Never mind that,' said Cass.

'So what are you going to do then?' asked Lara without enthusiasm.

The other woman's voice struck a sinister note. 'I have decided to stop compromising. If Sandra can do it, so can we . . .'

Raw visions of a thrash metal group named Maximum Offence and their newly unleashed lead singer filled her head. 'Cass, leave me out of this.'

'Nothing and no one's going to stop me.'

'Fine.'

'I mean, if *Sandra* . . .' It was a graceless admission of motive.

'So, what now? Now that you're armed with the vital information that you and debt collectors are compatible.'

'Well, there you have it,' said Cass. 'I reckoned that if I could do that, I could do other things as well.'

Lara doubted that anything could be that straight-forward.

'So . . . guess what? I've got a job,' said Cass.

Maybe it could. 'That was quick. Doing what?'

'I dunno.'

'Ah.'

'By which I mean that I don't know yet what it will entail.'

'But you have found something.'

'Al has offered me a job. He was at the workshop last night – you should have come, by the way. We covered blaming others as they would blame us, and hiding the traces of revenge. Really quite inspirational.'

'Hang on. Al? I thought you and he were . . . having a thing . . . Quiet Al the accountant?'

'That's the one. And we are.'

'And . . . you're going to work for him as well but you don't know exactly what this job consists of?'

'Isn't it exciting?' whooped Cass.

They had another drink as the awkwardness of the unexpected visit lingered – although Cass was beginning to look perilously comfortable on the sofa. She kept looking around the sitting-room as if appraising it but without passing comment.

'We gave up the poisoning,' she said conversationally.

'I'm sorry?'

'The poisoning. Sandra and me . . . the extra bit of seasoning in *their* food.' She gave Lara a sidelong look.

'You – what? But I thought . . . I thought that was all just a joke!'

'Joke? Depends on your sense of humour, I suppose.'

'You and Sandra – you *were* actually putting weed-killer in their food?!'

'Among other things.'

Lara swallowed.

'You don't have to look at me like that. We never managed it, did we? Properly, I mean.'

'Well, no . . .' Lara clenched her hands. She wanted Cass out of her flat, now.

Cass, though, was impervious to the signs. She blew her nose on a pink tissue and stuffed it up one sleeve. She followed Lara into the kitchen when Lara cleared their glasses, then returned to her seat.

'I have a body I don't know what to do with,' said Cass. Her butterball thighs were spread once more on the sofa cushions.

Lara was all empathy. Here, at last, was a scenario she knew well. She could deal with this topic and then show Cass the door. 'Me, too. Or I used to feel like that. When I let these things rule my life. I don't any more.'

Her visitor stared grimly.

'There was a woman on one of those American talk shows,' Lara went on. 'God knows why I was watching, but there you are. And she said – get this! – "There's a lot of fat people are filled with tears. And the fat is just the tears they haven't cried yet!" Can you believe it?'

Cass stared as if trying to imagine. Politely.

'Oh God, I didn't mean you were fat. I—'

Cass's face was a mask.

Lara jabbered on with what she hoped was companionable encouragement. 'I got rid of it – the body thing – by refusing to think about it.'

'But . . . apart from that?'

'All the usual ways: exercise, eating one bar of chocolate rather than six, other interests.'

'Other interests?'

'Hobbies,' said Lara. 'To take your mind off food. Or even if it was on your mind, if you were at the gym, you know, you couldn't actually be stuffing your face and thumping along on the running machine at the same time. Physically impossible.'

Cass didn't look convinced. 'Bodies tend to stick with you.'

'Well, yes. Absolutely right,' grinned Lara, recognising the admirable shorthand between women.

They both laughed, but Cass's expression was unreadable. 'This other body we're talking about . . .' she said after a pause. 'It's not *mine.*'

'But that's such a common reaction, Cass, you wouldn't believe. If you've always been slim before, and then you're not – it's a self-esteem thing. Women feel they are not the person they were before—'

'No,' said Cass emphatically, her mouth hard. 'You did it, didn't you, with your ritual?'

'My ritual?'

'Got rid of your body.'

'My *symbolic* body.'

'It's the same, only it's not my body. It's *hers* . . .'

'What, you mean—?'

'In the boot of my car. Outside.'

It took a while to assimilate this.

'You've come here with it?'

'Yes,' said Cass.

Lara had to ask. 'Anybody we know?'

Cass frowned. 'I need your help, Lara.'

'Sure.' She wanted to deal with her quickly. 'Whatever.'

'I need to get rid of her, you see. She's been there since last night.'

Lara humoured her. 'Hadn't you better check?'

Cass answered that with the oddest look.

'I'll have a squint at your garden now, if I may,' said Cass after another drink. Lara had given in.

Lara was caught unawares. 'My *garden?*'

'I've heard all about it.'

'Er . . . if you want, but it is dark outside.'

'Colin told me you haven't finished your beds yet.'

'Did he now,' murmured Lara, even as Cass was attacking the lock on the back door to let herself out.

'We talk, you know,' said Cass. She exited into the night.

Lara remained standing inside, wondering, as a draught of cold air from the open door coiled around her legs.

Cass clomped back inside after several minutes.

'Hold on,' she said, businesslike. 'Don't go away.'

Lara's knees buckled at the command.

'Where are you going now?' she called as the older woman bellied towards the front door wearing a shark's grinning snarl on her determined face. Her night skin, under the dimmed lights, was whipped up and pitted like the wind on the surface of a lake. Purpose sealed it tight.

'*Cass!* What are you doing?'

'To investigate ... the surroundings,' came the reply from the hallway.

'What for?'

The woman gave her an intense look, as if wondering whether Lara had been paying any attention. 'For my ritual,' she said.

'Your *what*?'

'You heard.'

'Cass ... *Cass!*'

But she was off.

For twenty minutes Lara paced and tossed back another gin and hardly-any-tonic – and wished she had never mentioned her ritual to Cass and Sandra. Then she decided that this evening was part of an elaborate game, a fantasy adventure invented by a sad woman who needed only the attention, who had given more than she had ever taken, a woman who felt her time had come and now would not stop until she had made her point.

From the street outside Lara could hear the rush as a car passed, and once the disconcerting tick of a black cab drawing up, then a heavy metal door slamming. She held her breath for the denouement, but nothing came. There were no footsteps, no caller appearing. Why should she have presumed it was anything to do with her?

Paranoid . . . I'm becoming paranoid . . .

She flew to the door when the bell rang, overriding the main buzzer with a death-or-glory dive into the communal entrance. Cass's face loomed at her in the harsh electric light.

'There you are . . .'

The other woman beamed, wordlessly, as she strode across the threshold. The fall of her feet was a heavy heartbeat. Then Lara noticed, with a lurch of the stomach.

'Cass . . . why are you carrying a *spade*?'

Cass widened her eyes, as if trying to communicate telepathically. In the end she succeeded.

Lara shook her head, as much in disbelief as to transmit a 'No way' back across the thought waves.

There was a charged silence.

'You're not going to . . .' It was a weak protest, Lara knew.

An emphatic nod.

'Cass . . . it was my ritual. It won't work for anyone else. You need to find your own way.' And when this met blankness on the round white face, 'I don't want your effigy of whoever it is. I don't want you churning up my garden in the middle of the night!'

'You're going to help me, Lara.'

'No, I am not. *No*, Cass. No.'

At least – and Lara clung to this – the word she needed was coming out of her mouth.

Not that it did the slightest good.

'There *is* no happy ever after, Cass. In the fairy-tales, that's the biggest lie of them all. And even in the best and most magical of them, there's always a price to be paid no matter how good the soul or how pure the motives.' Lara was babbling, she knew. 'You have to find your *own* way to be happy, not dependent on other people.

If I've learned nothing else in the past few months, I've learned that.'

They were standing in the line of parked cars in the street, peering into the cavernous boot of Cass's old white rust-bucket of a car. Lara decided to stick with Cass this time, to make sure this idea was nipped in the bud. She wished Cass would go home.

By the feeble light in the boot Lara could see something. There was definitely the shape of a woman there, shrouded in used Sainsbury's bags.

Lara turned away. She was doing nothing to encourage Cass.

'Look!' commanded Cass.

Lara did. The shape in the car boot was horribly real. It gave Lara the creeps. It was almost like a *real* woman, doing a good impression of sleep, but an awkwardness about her position gave the lie to that.

Cass pulled back some of the covering. Under the tiny light a glimpse of the head seemed absurdly lifelike.

Lara felt sick.

'You have nothing to do with her . . . it's perfect,' said Cass. She rearranged the plastic bags until the horror was once more sublimated into the heart-warming appearance of a week's provisions from a reputable super-market. She tweaked the corner of a cloth tool bag to cover a stray foot, and looked up proudly, as if pronouncing herself satisfied with the taking of an opportunity.

The woman was unstoppable.

Passion and revenge, thought Lara.

Cass – unheeding of any pleas – went off again after another stiff drink. Lara went inside and sat alone in the dark sitting-room, wondering why she wasn't doing more to prevent this madwoman from destroying her garden. She could call the police. But what would they do? She had invited Cass in, and she had to deal with the consequences. Cass needed help, she decided. She was cracking up. She had to be.

Mud was smeared over Cass's black sweat-suit top when she returned this time. It had oozed under her feet and hardened into a caked frill around her desert boots. Lara watched dispassionately as the brown crumbs fell on her floor, some stubbled with grass. The woman smelt of physical labour. Matter of fact, she washed her hands at Lara's sink, leaving worms of earth trickling down the white sides. They were not much cleaner when she dried them on a tea-towel.

'I've buried her,' said Cass, with a great drunken smile.

So Lara found herself – once more – humouring Cass, wondering all the while what the hell she was doing. 'So . . . where did you put her then?' she asked. She began to make some sobering black coffee.

'I had a look around. The main garden in the square would have been good, but it's a bit exposed. Too many houses looking over.'

'I was going to say, earlier . . . this is a very built-up kind of area to be any good for your . . . purposes.'

'Besides, it's locked.'

'The main garden – you tried it?'

'Of course. In the interests of investigating every possibility.' This came out slurred.

Lara had sudden inspiration. 'Cass . . . she's the Fury, isn't she?'

'You *do* understand – I knew you would!'

'She's Al's wife. Because you need to feel—'

'*Was*,' Cass corrected her sanguinely.

'Was?'

'I said I had a body, didn't I?'

'Not a real body, though . . .' Lara had to believe that.

Cass nodded vigorously. 'A dead body.'

At that Lara's heart was a crazed animal in her ribcage. 'But . . . Al's wife isn't *dead*.'

'Well, it all began that night. Al's big night.'

'I don't understand,' said Lara, although she had a dreadful feeling she did.

'What do you mean it all began on Al's big night?' Lara trawled her memory of the story. 'The police went round to Al's after the disturbance. She was there then . . .'

'And she said nothing,' prompted Cass.

Oh no.

'Because . . . she wasn't . . .?'

'She was *there*. Only so was I,' said Cass.

Lara's mind raced down blind alleys. It was left to Cass to supply the triumphant last detail.

'We told them *I* was Veronica.'

Somehow Lara didn't believe a word of it.

'So,' said Lara, after a conspirational mock-heroic pause, 'where did you bury her?'

'In the garden, at the back.' Cass motioned vaguely behind her.

It took a moment for Lara to assimilate this. 'The garden *here*? *My* garden?'

A stunned silence, broken only by noisy slurps of tea.

'You can't have done.'

'What do you mean?'

'You can't have got in. I was here.' A flood of absurd relief surged through her.

'Were you?'

Lara, at last, was able to nod sympathetically.

'There wasn't a light on here.'

'I was in the sitting-room.'

'Well, that explains it then.'

'Oh?'

'You wouldn't have seen me. Which is good, because I did think I might have made too much noise.'

'I didn't hear anything.'

'That's a relief.'

'Cass . . . have you thought about . . . *talking* to someone about all this . . . someone other than me and Annette, I mean? There are other people who could help, you know.'

She looked puzzled and a little hurt. 'I wouldn't have asked anyone else.'

'No . . . That wasn't what—'

'There was a moment when I thought there was someone out there – not you – but it was all right.'

'Sorry?'

'There was a noise, after I got over the wall. It wasn't easy, not with *her* as well.'

'The wall?'

Cass stared at her as if she couldn't give credence to this continuing stupidity. She frowned more and jerked a soiled thumb over her shoulder. 'Out there. In the garden.'

'No, Cass. Let's get this straight. You have not been in my garden.'

But Cass was nodding emphatically. 'I *told* you. The bed was even ready.'

'Bed?'

'Lovely deep hole. Colin told me what you'd been doing . . . in the garden. Saved me a lot of trouble, that did.'

Lara slumped at the table. 'It's real, then?'

'Real? Of course it's real.'

So that was that then. Madness.

'Look at these grazes. They're real.' Cass thrust out plump forearms; they were scored with scratches and the pebble-dash of stripped skin and bruising. 'There was that fence to get over, too.'

'Fence . . .'

An exasperated exhalation. 'By the garages. The back path between these gardens and the ones which go with the houses in the next road.'

Words, Lara felt, were failing her. Perhaps a nice Gothic scream might be in order? She tried. No sound came out, just as in the bad dreams she had had since she had been living alone in the flat.

Again she found no more than a whisper. 'No . . . this is ridiculous. Joke over, Cass. Go home.'

'I *could* have just done it and not told you. But I thought we were in this together. I thought you would help.'

'Cass . . . we're not in anything together.'

'We are now.'

Outside the window the darkness was dense like a mink coat. Lara bit a finger. The woman was crazed. Clearly a different approach was needed. 'So . . . how long have you had . . . um . . . Veronica?'

'A day or so,' said Cass.

'Oh.'

'We kept her in a wardrobe in the boxroom upstairs for ages. But in the end, it wasn't terribly practical. She was still making a lot of noise, you know.'

'And . . .' Lara was frightened now. She was probing the extent of the insanity here.

'It *was* an accident.'

'Thank God,' said Lara. The words were out before Lara knew what she was saying. What she meant was that this was a relief in one sense. It seemed to make a difference that Cass and Al were not claiming to have murdered the woman. Not that she believed for one moment that there was a woman.

'I know,' said Cass. 'That's why I came to you.'

'No . . .' said Lara, and tried to explain.

She did not get far.

'Tell you what,' said Cass. 'I'll show you.'

Out in the dark garden, Lara switched on her torch. The light caught the wall at the end so that it seemed to rear suddenly. Quickly she directed the beam down where Cass indicated. There was indeed a heap of freshly churned soil towards the back of the bed under the hawthorn.

Lara kicked at the earth with a foot.

'Go on . . . push it all back if you want . . .'

'I've seen enough.'

They went inside.

'There's nothing we can do about *her* now,' said Cass.

'Well, I don't know about that.'

'Besides . . . she's gone now.'

Lara raised her eyes in supplication.

'She's not a woman,' said Cass. 'She's just a body now. And unless you want to dig the whole thing up again, and make more mess, and risk attracting attention all over again . . . Like I said, it was touch and go out there for a while.'

Lara closed her fist and beat it against her head. Her temples pounded. 'Shut up. Shut *up*! Go home. Leave me alone!'

19   Moonshine Moment

The next morning Lara soaked in a hot bath. She let the steam burrow into every pore and tried to put away the thought that this might not be the sense in which she was up to her neck in hot water.

The surreal night-time episode with Cass was nothing more than the fantasy of a deranged drunken woman, she decided firmly.

She had not put anything in Lara's garden. She had gone now, and taken whatever it was with her.

When she padded into the kitchen in her bathrobe, everything was tidy and in place apart from half a cauliflower on the chopping board and mud by the back door. On the table were her notes on the City University and the law courses on offer.

Lara fixed herself a double-strength coffee and tried to concentrate on what this great leap forward would entail. She could not.

Her eyes kept taking a wander up the garden path.

She loaded the washing machine and swept crumbs – and the cauliflower – from the kitchen work surfaces. She made a brave stab at tidying the sitting-room. She had some more coffee.

It was hopeless. She gave in.

Lara dressed with furious hands, pulling on whatever was lying on the bedroom floor, and opened the back door.

She picked up a trowel, and poked around the nearest flower-beds. The ceanothus she had planted with Colin was bright blue with fuzzy little balls of blossom, and she fingered these. But this was just for show.

Gradually she made her way to the end of the garden, to the place by the hawthorn. The bush caught on her clothes with spiteful snatches. She bent over the soil. It was dark and crumbly.

She began to work it over.

She had to do this; there was nothing worse than not being sure.

She dug deeper.

Then she wished she hadn't.

Lara had worms under her skin: slimy, earth-filled, burrowing worms.

Yet still she did not call the police. She half-dialled the number, then she replaced the receiver.

In years to come she would see this for what it was: the moment when, against all that had been in her nature, she did not do what was expected of her.

It was a moment when lightning should have struck, and the world tilted on its axis. Nothing came. The birds in the trees around did not stop squabbling, the hands of the clock did not stop, the same muffled sounds came from the city beyond her garden.

But in this moment, Lara was not herself.

She hesitated and then she went inside. She foraged in the cupboard over the hot-water cylinder in the bathroom, and pulled out a towel and her costume.

Then she went swimming.

After fifty lengths of the pool – she swam blindly up and down with only numbers in her head – she called Annette from outside the changing-rooms.

Annette was not the easiest woman with whom to initiate

a heart-to-heart, let alone a frank and fearless exchange of views. Too many years of finding her own centre and freeing the inner child had taken their toll. Annette could expound her rash, vile theories but it was becoming gut-wrenchingly clear to Lara that she was all talk. The snap decision so crucial to the outcome of the present emergency was not, Lara felt instinctively, Annette's basket.

But Lara, attached to a lost and desperate cause, had little choice but to throw herself on the mercy of its instigator. It smacked of desperation, but there again, she *was* desperate.

She was fending off disaster with every hour. She was giddy in this protean landscape of evil which surrounded what had once been her sanctuary, at least for the short two months since Will had left. But now, twenty-four hours after Cass had blundered in with her foul cargo, Lara looked out of her back door and saw panic in the patterns of the crazy-paving stones she and Colin had laid. Inside her garden walls, she knew, were tell-tale fingerprints and human whorls and secret trails. And the gods of mayhem and muddle looked down.

Lara looked wantonly at the gin bottle.

'There *are* natural alternatives, Lara,' said Annette. She sat bolt upright on the chair by the fireplace. Her scatter-gun delivery of platitudes in the very jaws of disaster had reduced Lara to a state of near-murderous intent. Which had absolutely not been the intention when she had called the woman and begged her to come at once.

Annette had resisted vigorously, as Lara expected she would. Now here was a woman who knew how to say no.

In the end Lara drew on her own interpretation of the workshop dogma; she resorted to blackmail. The Quiet Al affair, Lara intimated, would be the undoing of Annette's nascent media profile when the story behind it was revealed to a hungry press. Once her methods were revealed there would be ridicule. There would be no more appearances in magazines and no more nice people willing to part with five hundred pounds.

So here was Annette sitting straight and sanctimonious at the scene of the crime, looking for all the world as if she were a parking meter ticking up the charges for doing nothing.

This was the woman who had told them there was no good or evil, that there could be no judgements. And here she was, doing that number again.

Lara could take no more. 'This is what I am trying to tell you. They came, and they heard the word . . . and they are on the loose! And now we must face the consequences!'

The group leader fixed a guru's smile across the plump down of her cheeks. 'Uh-huh, let me see . . . perhaps we could try some—'

'*No!* Listen to me, Annette. This is for real, can you understand that? This is not some faked-up ritual the woman is playing at! *I* thought it was all fantasy, but it's not.'

Annette's stare was now a death ray. 'When you are under pressure, tense, stressed—'

'I know how it feels, thank you.'

'Confrontational, aggressive—'

'Annette. Get to the point.'

Annette went on, unabashed. 'If you make the time and space to delve . . .'

Any more of this and she would delve into Annette's inner whatevers – with a sharp knife. Lara paced over to the gin and unscrewed the top defiantly.

'This is not working for you, Lara.'

'Oh, you noticed . . .'

Annette geared up to try again but Lara raised a palm at her, calming herself down. 'I think we need to pare down the situation here, don't you? Let us see what we have here. A woman who attended your workshop, urged on by your ritual theory, has dumped a body on me. A dead body.'

'So now it's my fault. I think you should see that you are making a judgement on that, Lara.'

'I think we should delve deep within ourselves, Annette,' spat Lara, 'and see that it's a predicament.'

They gave this some moments of respectful silence.

'Would you at least come outside and take a look at what is in my garden?' said Lara, more calmly than she felt.

Annette allowed herself to be led to the back door.

Even so, Annette would not give up. 'OK, so the problem we have here is that you may not be at the stage in your personal development when TN can be of optimum benefit—'

'Shut up,' said Lara.

She didn't, of course. 'So you wish you'd taken a class in car maintenance, or cookery—'

'Cass and Sandra tried that, or didn't you know about the foundation course in attempted poisoning? They were still on that tack when I met them the first day at the workshop. At that stage, though, they were too half-hearted about it to get further than provoke stomach upsets with dodgy moussaka. As for me—'

'You can still learn from this, *grow* from this, Lara.'

'Please don't imagine,' said Lara loadedly, 'that I would not far rather be fiddling around with a tarragon quiche at this precise moment.'

They walked out into the darkness. The yard was lit in patches with the pumpkin lantern light of a few neighbouring windows. Their soles scratched and crunched across stones and scattered soil.

Lara led the way. 'Annette . . . has anything like this ever happened before?'

DEBORAH LAWRENSON

The other woman considered for a second. 'No . . . I can't say it has. This group has been unusually *responsive* . . . I mean I've had a few mishaps before—'

'Oh, I reckon we could call this a mishap, don't you!'

'—but usually more in the leaving-home-and-spouse-and-children sense. More taking themselves off, really. Not actually . . . disposing of other people . . . although I doubt very much this is what has happened. In my experience . . . talking it over can produce a rational strategy for dealing with violent emotions. It is always unwise to become overwrought . . .'

The woman would not give up.

Then they came to the mound. Or rather Lara stopped and looked down slowly, and Annette did the same.

'Under here?'

Lara nodded. 'Can you smell anything?'

There was a long pause, during which several deep breaths could be heard in the blackness. Cold night air curled around Lara's lungs and a leafy bitterness lodged in her nostrils. She switched on her torch to check their exact bearings, then placed it, light down, on the earth. With a foot she kicked into the soil.

It was still there, far closer to the surface than in her worst imaginings. Adrenalin fireworks exploded inside her as she reached down for the torch. For a second, it illuminated one waxy smudged hand.

Annette's reaction was immediate and alarming. She gasped, then seemed to regress to the earnest pop-eyed child she must once have been. It was a long time before she whispered to the damp darkness, 'Lara, are you there . . .?'

'Yes.'

'Do you . . . remember . . .?'

'Remember what?'

'Hear no evil, see no evil, speak no evil . . .?'

250

'Well,' said Lara. 'I think it's a bit late for that, don't you?'

Lara was shaking and sick as she pushed earth over the hand once more. Then she stood and turned her back on the mound and the grisly certainty that this was beyond a nightmare. Behind her there was a sigh and a thud. She looked back over her shoulder but Annette had disappeared.

Lara lowered her sights.

The architect of their downfall was lying flat out on the ground.

'And thank you for your great support,' cursed Lara.

She scrabbled about a little more but without any particular aim. She prodded Annette to rouse her from the faint. Then she went to the corner where she kept the watering can. It was heavy with rainwater and she hauled it over to the recumbent Annette. Her violet-rimmed glasses gleamed silver in the moonlight, and then globules of water exploded over their shine and over her white face, like mercury from a shattered thermometer.

There was no sound from Annette. No gasp or splutter came.

But the window of an upstairs flat raked up.

Lara thought fast, all sense of absurdity annulled.

'We're fine . . . we're moonbathing,' she told the woman at the window.

Or she said something similar. She said something quite ridiculous. Quite what she ventured was lost in the giddiness of foul play and terror.

And that aspect of the night was not yet over. Not by a long stroke.

Lara went back inside, her legs carrying her as if they were wading through deep ocean currents. It was pure instinct, self-preservation. She was fleeing from the scene. Or perhaps she was fetching a wet sponge with which to revive her latest unconscious visitor. Either way, she was stopped in her tracks.

Cass was in her kitchen. Large as life.

The last person she wanted to see. The *only* person she wanted to see.

'I let myself in,' said Cass. She was a trespasser of some proven ability, after all.

Lara stood there, feet nailed to the floor by fear. Panic and guilt seized her. She had come in from the garden – why had she come in? She had come . . . to find a bottle of brandy . . . to call a doctor . . . to call the Samaritans . . . to call the police . . .

No . . . not the police.

'Sorry if I startled you,' said Cass cheerfully. 'I'm on my own,' she added as she noted Lara's frantic casting around.

'I'm not!'

Cass continued grinning. 'It's a party then.'

'At least . . . I hope I'm not. I don't want . . . although I better had be on my own . . . now.' The words caught in her throat, on her tongue, like lethal angler's bait.

'Ah-hah! Colin's here.'

'No!'

'Who then?' asked Cass, as if prompting a social simpleton.

Lara's thoughts were a whirlpool. 'No one!'

'But you just said . . .'

This was too much. 'What have you *done*, Cass?!'

But Cass had noticed the bottle of Gordon's, and held up a stray tumbler for permission. Lara was too weak to resist joining her.

'Cass . . . you do remember . . . the other night, don't you?'

'I . . . *might*. Why?'

Lara was losing it. 'You came round the other night. With your car.'

'Oh, God, yes.'

'So you do remember.'

'It was pretty lethal of me.'

'We need to talk about this.'

'I know . . . I should never have been driving. I was way over the limit. Don't lecture me – I've still got the hangover. It was fun though, wasn't it?'

'*Fun?*'

'Well . . . to be honest, the whole evening's a blank. I know I spent the day with the old man's credit card, then went round to Al's, and ended up here. But after that – nothing. How did I get home? I tell you I haven't got that pissed since, well, since the last time I got that pissed. Which is quite a lot these days. Talking of which . . .' a pause for gulping gave way to a broad grin on Cass's mouth, ' . . . who have you got here then?'

Lara gulped too. The neat alcohol hit fast. 'Annette,' she croaked.

'Oh.' Surprise and the absolute resolution not to be surprised battled on Cass's face until a brave nonchalance won through. 'I didn't know you were . . . that you and she were, you know—'

'Cass, she came round here because I needed to sort some things out. Get some things *straight*. Although she was no help with the *dead woman* in the *garden*, let me tell you.'

Surely that was enough.

It did not seem to be. Of course not. Cass wanted precision. Explanations. Details. The whole shooting match.

Lara had to supply it.

Cass was remarkably cool as her own part in the drama emerged.

'You do remember now?' prompted Lara.

'It's beginning to come back to me. Where is Annette now, then?'

'She's in the garden.'

'Bit cold, this time of night . . .'

'She collapsed. Just like that. I didn't do a thing. One moment she was behind me, and the next . . .' The dam which held back chaos and disorder threatened to burst. She was shaking. She may even have been screaming – someone was. She prayed it was Annette.

'Calm down. *Calm down*, Lara! Is she still there?'

'As far as I know . . .'

'Come on, then,' said Cass, and led the way out again.

The group leader lay, curiously sarcophagus-like, where she had fallen. Cass pulled down the sleeves of her sweater, buried her hands deep in the wool, and clouted Annette's face, first one side and then the other, with muffled thumps.

'Where did you learn to do that?'

'On *Columbo*.'

'What was it supposed to do?' asked Lara, attempting to feel for the woman's pulse.

Cass pushed her away roughly. 'How do I know?'

'And you have that scheming look on your face, the one that worries me . . .'

'Lara . . . you're killing me. Just get off my back.'

Now that was a novel way of looking at the situation.

'We should call the police. We *must* call an ambulance. Two wrongs do not make a right,' said Lara feebly.

'Maybe not,' conceded Cass. 'Would three do it, do you think?'

They jumped as the doorbell rang like an urgent grunt.

'Who the fuck is that?' snarled Cass.

'How do I know?'

'You're not going to answer that?'

'Yes, Cass, I am.'

Cass consulted her luminous Swatch. 'It's gone midnight. It might be . . . a homicidal maniac!'

'Cass, *you* are the homicidal maniac.'

By seemingly mutual consent they left Annette where she lay. The look on her face left them in no doubt that the group leader would soon have more than enough to say about this turn of events. They did not relish the prospect.

There was urgent pounding on the door by the time Lara reached it. Cass was right on her tail.

Wild eyed, Lara spun round to Cass for immoral support as she reached out to the latch. But Cass was unconcerned now.

Preternaturally calm, Cass gave her a Lady Macbeth look. She was in her element, cursed Lara. 'Go on. Open the door. I'm here.'

'How – how did whoever it is now get in through the main door?' cried Lara.

'I may have left it on the latch.'

'You *what*?'

'Open it!'

Lara put her hand up to the catch. Her heart could have powered the national grid as she opened the door slowly.

Through a tiny gap, she saw a figure in gleaming black. She took in the leathers, the bicep tattoo, the ebony lipstick and nails as the witch lifted one hand in macabre greeting.

Lara felt faint herself. She sensed rather than saw the combat boot wedge open the door.

Only Cass was equal to words.

'Ah, Sandra,' she said. 'Lovely but lethal.'

Sandra gave a parody of a snarl, and stuck up one finger.

'The bitch is back,' announced Sandra, striding into the room. 'Dressed to kill.'

'You as well!' thundered Lara. 'All of you. Leave me alone, can't you!' All they needed now was Quiet Al with his own brand of grim relaxation and perhaps, for good measure, Colin with a roll of coffin silk.

Yet Sandra and her apprentice Cass stood their ground. If only they had been as resolute when it came to taking control of their lives long before it had come to this. Or to Lara's front door. Again.

They marched down the passage into the sitting-room and gave each other daring why-not? looks. They were clearly not going to go.

'I am going to be forty,' said Sandra by way of introduction to her purpose. 'It's a turning point.' She heft a litre bottle of Jack Daniels on to the dresser where the glasses were in view, but started on Lara's gin first.

'See,' said Cass to Lara. 'I told you it was a party.'

Lara felt faint again. 'I don't believe this . . .'

'Sorry if I'm late. Due to what has been impaired judgement after a gut-load of Tennants Extra, I passed out with the goat.'

'The goat,' repeated Lara incredulously.

'Yeah.'

'Right . . . so you're subverting the young farmers of Tottenham Hale now – or perhaps they got to you first?'

Sandra sneered her disdain. 'The Goat. He's the bassist in the band.'

'Ah . . . of course.'

'Same difference,' sniffed Cass.

'And what about Al?' asked Sandra.

Lara would have asked the same question, only for a different reason.

'Veronica has left him,' said Cass, cheerfully enough. 'She might even be missing.'

If Sandra made anything of this odd expression of the

circumstances, then she showed nothing. The Sandra in front of them now was a broad beaming tattooed woman, unrecognisable from the person Lara had first seen at the Islington workshop. She picked at a scab on her forearm and Lara looked away.

'Missing?' ventured Lara incredulously.

'Ummm,' affirmed Cass. 'Although the vast majority of missing people turn up again, sometimes after spending years away . . .'

'And . . . does Al expect Veronica to turn up soon?'

'Oh, no.'

'No,' said Lara. 'I feared not. Cass, do you *realise* what you have done?'

An aggressive pause. 'I haven't done anything,' said Cass slowly. 'It was an accident. I only wanted to help.'

So that was the tactic.

'Yes, but . . . why did you have to . . . deal with it the way you did – by bringing her round here?'

'I did it for Al.'

'But still—'

'Only when all the pieces of the jigsaw come together, can you see the true picture,' aphorised Cass.

'So what did happen exactly, to Veronica?'

'I don't know. I wasn't there. I think she hit her head.'

'There seems to be so much of this kind of thing going on. The more you look, the more you see. No wonder the police are corrupt,' butted in Sandra, nonsensically, still scraping at her scab. 'Tip of the iceberg, if you ask me,' she concluded.

Whatever it was they were all suffering, Lara began to wonder how long a defence plea of temporary insanity would hold up. Awake, she was in the bad dream in which her teeth wobbled and split and fell out.

'So . . .' asked Sandra aggressively. 'What's cookin' here?'

Lara watched helplessly while the Cass explained the

257

situation, as balefully as a weak patient watching the whispered consultations of white-coated doctors in the corner of a hospital room. Then they left her. She heard them out in the kitchen, and switched off her senses.

Alone in the sitting-room, chilled by the draught from the open back door, Lara heard one o'clock toll in the tower of a church two streets away. She looked at the telephone and was too weak to move.

Annette would be fine. She had arrived at the scene of the crime and faced up to her responsibilities – shocking as they were – and then she had experienced an unpleasant, if entirely natural physical reaction. She had fainted, and she would come round. Any moment now she would come lumbering, white faced and gritty with mud, through the back door.

Still Lara sat, numbed.

The moon travelled on, over the roofs of the white stucco houses around the square, while the mysteries of night and day and life and death unravelled and retangled. Cass and Sandra returned alone.

'Er . . . this business with Annette,' said Cass. 'She doesn't seem to be there. We did have a look-see.'

'What?'

'Lucky we came round when we did, eh?'

'What?'

'We could have buried her as well,' pointed out Cass.

So she did remember. 'Annette fainted. She was flat out,' said Lara.

'Yes.'

'Cass . . . I . . . She wasn't *dead*.'

'Ah,' said Sandra. 'We weren't sure about that.'

The other women were both flushed with exertion and excitement.

Lara tore out of the door and up the path to the spot where she had last seen Annette. There was nothing but the smell of earth newly turned in the night. She ran back.

'Where *is* she?' Lara demanded. She was sweating. Cold trickles of fear wormed their way down her back.

'We have found ourselves,' chorused Cass and Sandra across the bottles they had annexed. 'We have self-esteem.'

They had her drink too, Lara could not help noticing.

'We cannot control anyone else in our lives but ourselves,' recited Sandra.

'We are the creators of our lives, not the victims,' intoned Cass.

'*Where* is Annette?' shouted Lara.

Below the demented din came the answer. 'I'm here,' whispered a voice.

Annette was propped on the sofa with a half-pint of Jack Daniels. She seemed to be in a state of shock.

The other women were clearly delighted to see her. They hurled questions at her and related their triumphs large and small. The night wore on and they showed no sign of wanting to leave Lara's flat. On they rattled, taking Annette's few disjointed mumbles as the mysterious encouragements of a Dalai Lama.

'My head may be lost but my heart is loving it,' concluded Sandra triumphantly. She wobbled on her mud-caked shoes, slopping whisky into the boggy patches she had made on the floor. 'The question is, where do we go from here?'

Lara's throat burned. 'I think you should go, full stop.'

'A woman's work is never done,' said Cass. 'There is now the enticing prospect of that man in the newsagent's who has always been so rude to me.'

'That bastard who keeps complaining to the parish council that I don't do enough jumble sales, and the one who hates my dog barking,' mused Sandra. She drew a finger across her throat. 'And then there's the barn dance and church supper they've put me down to do.'

'What do you suggest?' asked Lara.

'A delicious and exotic beef madras?'

'I'll help,' said Cass.

From the looks on their faces they would cook up a storm.

'And you,' said Sandra, pointing a black-painted fingernail at Lara, 'are now a revolutionary. You are fighting the cause.'

'No. I have nothing to do with this. I left you all to it weeks ago.'

'Honesty, that is what this is about, Lara,' went on Sandra.

'Honesty . . .'

'Honesty to oneself,' echoed and elaborated Cass.

'Acting truthfully on your feelings,' said one.

'No more deception,' said the other.

'Gerrr . . . agh,' said Annette.

In that case, thought Lara, I'd like you all to leave. She did not say that, because Sandra had placed a murderous paw on her, Lara's, telephone and address book, the book that held her lifelines to the outside world, her hard-won contacts and her hard-won friends. Sandra was leafing through with a dangerous air of intent.

Venom rushed in Lara's arteries.

And she dared not rush over to grab back what was left of her former life.

'You're part of this now, Lara,' said Sandra, making clear her seriousness by cracking back the spine of the book, rubbing a wrist up and down the open page and dialling a number. She waited some moments, then put down the telephone. She grinned. 'No answer.'

'And anyway,' chimed in Cass, who was making free with a corkscrew on a bottle of red she had found in

Lara's cupboard, 'we may physically have acted alone, but the whole of society has helped us get this far.'

Annette groaned.

This notion appealed to Sandra, to the other woman's unconcealed delight. 'Yeah,' she said. 'It's everyone's fault, communal guilt. You all helped me pull the rope tight. Dare to be bad, and you will succeed!'

'I cannot believe I am hearing this,' sighed Lara, although she could believe it, and only too well, after all that had brought them to this point. She wondered whatever might come next in their pursuit of this very public therapy to confront their private turmoils.

'You see,' said Sandra, as if reading her mind, 'I have found a way. I am finally expressing myself.'

'Getting in touch with our roots . . .' echoed Cass, beaming broadly.

Arguably, that was what poor Veronica was doing, covered as she was out there with the dank loam and the thirsty curlicues of living plants, thought Lara. She thought better of saying so. 'There would have been other ways.'

'Everything happens for the best,' asserted Sandra cheerfully.

Lara did not dignify that with a reply either.

They went when the drink ran out, leaving her with the slumped form of Annette on the sofa. Lara had no idea of the time. She went to the cupboard in the hall and pulled out a spare blanket. She spread it over Annette, and crept to her own room. She was all played out and more than relieved when she heard the unmistakable sound of snoring.

Not that she was able to sleep herself.

20   Watching the Oracle

As the sun came up on the darkest night of her life, Lara
watched the light put a glow to the hem of the curtains.
She lay in bed aching with the knowledge that if she had
slept, it was for minutes rather than hours. She strained
for a sound from the sitting-room but heard nothing. All
that did was confirm how much her head hurt.

Thinking about the mad women and fermenting words
for Annette – Annette *had* to help her – made it ten times
worse.

So she crept into the sitting-room en route for the
kitchen and the drawer where she kept some painkillers.
There was no sound from the crumpled heap on the sofa.
It was only when Lara was on her way back to her bed
that she realised there was no crumpled Annette on the
sofa.

Aflame with frustration, Lara threw herself at the
bathroom door. It swung open to an empty space. She
spun round. She opened the door to the airing cupboard.
She called out.

Silence.

Annette had gone.

So nemesis descended once more. He, too, was becoming
a tiresome house guest.

Lara kicked a ball of screwed-up paper across the asphalt

path. Through the trees on the eastern flank of the Eccleston Square garden the sun promised that summer was almost upon the city.

Annette! she fulminated. How could she simply leave? Annette had started all this – surely she had some responsibility? But no, she had run when it suited her, when it all became too real and complicated to deal with. Lara was sure of one thing: she was not going to let Annette get away with this.

In Annette's position, would Lara have run? She thought about that carefully. No. She would not have run. She would not have been able to: she would have stayed to face the music because it was her nature to do so. *She* would not have disappeared and left other people to deal with a bad situation. But then ... She stopped, feeling logic bear down on her like a steamroller.

Was that not exactly why she *had* been left in this predicament?

The other women had worked that out for themselves: Lara would be the one to resolve the dilemma because she was the one who was so sure that there was right and wrong.

Lara considered this for a long time.

She had sat on a bench, numbed, but not with cold. She started to walk when a disreputable band of pigeons, battle scarred and mangy, started to fight in front of her. In their shrieks and squawks, she could hear the wheeling triumph of Cass and Sandra in their finest hour.

Resentment was a stone in her stomach.

Then at last she dared to think, no. She would not do what was expected of her.

In the flat morning light, the flowers thrust out of dull earth beds in fiesta colours. They glowed as forbidden jewels, and then brighter and deeper as Lara reached out in her mind and uprooted the hardier specimens for transplant. She would spread them over, dig them in, and they would cover the body . . .

Didn't a grave deserve a floral tribute?

Fresh air had done nothing but fan the flames of her dread. Or was this the beginning of insanity?

No, she told herself. She had been caught in a situation which was not of her making. Only three days ago she had been as sane as anyone! Surely that counted for something. There was a way out of the net.

Or was the game up already? Was it all too late, far too late already?

The truth was incredible. The woman was in *her* garden: what could Lara say or do now that would not leave her carrying the can while the guilty women escaped, protesting their innocence? She was not mad. But she might be soon if the questions in her head did not stop.

Why hadn't Lara gone to the police in the very first instance?

Because she didn't believe that Cass was serious.

Was that a viable explanation?

It was the truth.

Why didn't she dial 999 when she realised that Cass had not been joking?

Because she still didn't really believe it.

Yes, but when she *did*?

Because . . . because . . . because . . . for once in her life, she chose to break the rules. Because when every moral fibre she possessed was screaming: Call the police now, you can explain!, she stood back and thought that for once in her life she would stand outside the rules and see what happened.

After the weeks of fretful isolation, the feeling of unreality, the cauldron of self-reproaches, she had finally thrown off her well-worn overcoat of caution at the moment the situation became more terrible than she could ever have foreseen.

Those whom the gods wish to destroy they first make mad . . .

When she saw the figure moving towards her, her instinct was to hide. It was making steady progress on a collision course with her own.

If it was Cass or Sandra, she was ready to tell them all this, to make them take responsibility for their own actions, to tell Cass that she must go to the police and confess her part in the crime, to try to tell them that these were actions undertaken – no, not *undertaken* . . . carried out – while the balance of the mind was impaired.

But if this was Cass or Sandra, who knew what new disaster might not have been unleashed . . .

Lara slowed and braced herself.

It was a woman, and a familiar one.

'You're out early, dear.'

'Er . . . so are you.' It was the bluebell woman from weeks back.

She had pulled a brown wool hat deep down on her brow but the quizzical expression was unmistakable. 'Look as if you've seen a ghost, dear. Is everything all right?'

'Yes . . . of course . . . fine.'

The appraisal grew harder.

Lara snatched up her remaining resources like a naked woman taken unawares in the bathroom of a rooming house. 'You live in the square?' she asked valiantly.

'In the same house as you do.'

A pause. 'Do you?'

'Number 126. I'm Flat C.'

Lara's exhausted heart beat in her throat. It couldn't be. 'I . . . I was told that was rented by a . . . some flamboyant fortune-telling-show person . . .'

265

'How very flattering.'

'So you see . . .'

The woman gave her a once-over which would have stripped paint. 'I *am* Madame Isadora.'

'You're what?' asked Lara weakly.

'Madame Isadora. At times.'

'And at others?'

'I'm Dora. Dora Allbright. I changed the name. Couldn't see it in lights. But I'm Dora at the minute. Harmless old lady and nosy neighbour. Devotee of the Oracle.' The old woman hitched up her pointy chin and managed to look beady over the swell of her double chin.

'The oracle?'

'On the telly. The whatchamacallit . . . the teletext. I like to keep up with all the news.'

'Ah,' said Lara feebly. 'That's as Dora, I take it.'

The older woman narrowed beady blackbird eyes.

'I'm sorry, I . . .'

'Not a good idea, dear, to dismiss the power of what you do not understand,' said Dora stiffly.

'No . . .'

'We all have other lives, if we only could tune in to them.'

Lara felt she was stumbling towards more bleak revelations. She had to find out, and yet she did not want to know. The words came out as a jumble. 'And your life here? When you aren't being Madame Isadora?'

'My life here?' she answered. 'My life has been something of a white-knuckle ride, at times.'

She did not go on.

They sat in silence for some time until Dora Allbright creaked into movement beside her. 'I'll be seeing you, dear,' she said, and walked off with a pained hitch of one hip.

There was no answer when she tried to ring Cass, so

Lara looked up the telephone number for St Leonard's vicarage in Muswell Hill and dialled that.

A light male voice answered, but it sounded harassed. 'Reverend Barry Stubbs.'

'Ah, hello. I'm ... this is a friend of Sandra's. Is she there, please?' Why did she feel so awkward, and – yes – blasphemous?

'She's out,' said the Reverend Stubbs. There was a barely repressed hysteria in his rising tone, as if he was speaking of an escaped tiger on the loose.

'Ah,' said Lara. She thought it best not to enquire when he was expecting her back. 'I'll try again,' she said feebly.

The man of God said nothing to encourage that.

'Or ... perhaps ...'

He was as friendly as might be expected of a respectable man whose wife had recently been transformed into a punk princess. As far as Sandra was concerned, it was clearly far too late for keeping up appearances.

'She's gone out somewhere. Good day to you.'

There was no help there.

By now Lara's imagination was off the leash. Was it possible that Veronica had only been unconscious when Cass opened the car boot? Could Lara have done something to save her then, before it was too late? Why had she been so sure that Cass was not serious?

And then, tortured by imperfect recall, Lara found she could imagine vividly that she had heard a sigh from the heap. Or was that the wind in the trees?

What do you know, you charlatanous, curtain-twitching, meddlesome old bag?

Lara did not say this, naturally.

The thought seethed inside her – it had been fermenting for hours since their dawn encounter – that it was Dora/Madame Isadora who had appeared at the upstairs window at the worst moment when Annette was out flat in the dark garden.

What did you see, woman? What do you know, and what are you going to do about it? And why did it have to be *you*?

Lara's intended opening lacked nothing in conventional politesse. She climbed the stairs and knocked on the old woman's door, stepped back a pace and got ready with a neighbourly smile.

From the other side (although Lara did not presume on anything more metaphysical than a locked entrance here) came the sounds of a chain being slipped. There was a wheezy groan as a hefty bolt was shot back.

Seconds passed before the door creaked open and a round face floated up, like a balloon, in the crack from latch to eye level. The slack wide mouth quivered. 'Yes?'

'Hello, Mrs Allbright, it's me.' Lara held out a droopy bunch of pansies from her garden.

'Me?'

'Lara.'

A steely squint. 'So it is . . . so it is . . . hold on . . .' The door closed, the chain was released, and the door opened once again. 'Come in, dear. This *is* a nice surprise.'

Lara relaxed infinitesimally. The rigmarole said much for the success of safety campaigns for the elderly living alone, but hardly such great things for the woman's reputed powers of second sight. She followed her through into a crowded sitting-room where the older woman took the flowers.

'How lovely. From downstairs?'

Lara nodded.

'You have done well there, dear. Lovely, it is now. Quite a transformation, and you've worked so hard. I've been watching you, you know. I've seen what's been going on.' Was that gruesome grin really as maniacal as it seemed at that moment?

Or was that pure imagination?

'Now, what can I do for you, dear?' asked Mrs Allbright, surely disingenuously.

'I . . . I was wondering . . .' Lara stopped, feeling rather more genuinely awkward than she'd thought she would. 'This is rather embarrassing . . . but I was thinking . . . if you do, are involved in . . . *readings* . . . for people, you know, what might . . . happen to them, and it's just that . . .'

'You are at a crossroads.'

That was a fair interpretation. 'Um . . . yes, that does . . . um, sound about right,' Lara mumbled.

'No need to be shy, dear. We could all do with help to guide us at certain stages in life. I knew it this morning.'

Lara said nothing.

'You haven't been working lately, have you?' said the woman. That much should have been obvious, seethed Lara, especially to one who passed the day spying behind an upstairs curtain.

Dora Allbright settled her at a table covered by a plum velvet cloth. No cliche, it seemed, would lie unturned.

'Fancy-show type indeed,' sniffed the old woman.

'Flamboyant,' said Lara. 'I think I said flamboyant.'

After some minutes of raw contemplation, she said to Lara, 'The world comes to me, you know. For consultations.'

Lara had to ask. 'Do you – you know – get in touch with the recently dead?'

Dora assessed her. 'That depends how badly you want to hear from them, dear.'

'I mean, might they . . . *come through* . . . of their own accord?'

Another pause.

'Rare,' she said, at last.

It could have been an admission – but then again not.

'Might try to raise your spirits, dear.' That was a heart-stopper.

'Er, sorry?'

Dora poked a rutted finger at the empty cup of tea Lara found she was studying. 'A glass of something stronger?'

Why not? 'Ah, yes. Lovely. Thanks.'

'Drop of blood?'

Lara was losing it. 'S-sorry?'

The self-proclaimed clairvoyant produced a bottle of Bulgarian Bull's Blood wine. 'Your face!' she said, with a twitch of a smile. 'Now . . .' Dora handed over a large goblet. 'Here we go. Feeling Transylvanian . . .?'

Was she doing this on purpose?

'Don't start predicting,' said Lara firmly.

'Wouldn't dream of it. Although . . . give me your hand, dear.'

Madame Isadora examined the mysterious creases of the palm.

'Hmm . . .' she said, and then again.

'What?' asked Lara.

'Interesting. *Very.*'

'*What* is?'

The mystic cleared her throat. 'A parting of the ways, dear. A life choice. Right on target, too.' She stared deeply into Lara's eyes.

Lara defied her as long as she could.

'A crisis, even . . . any day now.'

'Hmm,' said Lara. 'Is that right?'

'Clear as night follows day, my love.'

'Nothing I can do about it then.'

'Well, now . . .' The older woman closed Lara's hand with hers. It was warm but not as much as Lara's burning cheeks. 'That's up to you, isn't it?'

As soon as she slammed her own door behind her, Lara hit the telephone.

She dialled all the numbers she had. Then she threw the wretched appliance at the wall in despair.

Not that she had seriously expected Annette to answer. But she knew for certain from the BT message on the workshop line that the crusade had been abandoned.

Lara would need every particle of guile she possessed to track down Annette now – before Annette went to the police herself and told them what she had seen in Lara's garden.

21 Dark Returns

The next day Lara received a crisp letter from the drama department of one of the television stations she had targeted. She was praised for her previous successes and invited to discuss her new screenplay with the head of development.

Perhaps, thought Lara, she ought to knock off something on the word processor so they actually had something to talk about. It could be the start of a brilliant bogus career.

It would have to wait, though. She ranged telephone, directories and a notepad around her on the floor where she sat cross-legged. First – *damn* her – she had to find Annette. Lara had spent a sleepless night going through the motions.

The workshop number was still unobtainable.

Lara left a message for the custodian of the hall in Islington, and estimated that the directory listed more than five hundred Taylors in the right part of London. She was contemplating how long it would take to call them all when the doorbell buzzed in space, a power-drill noise burning through her predicament.

Lara tried to ignore it.

One thing was sure: she was not allowing herself to take the rap for this when her only crime was that she had failed to see how seriously the workshop women had taken their vows of disobedience.

Another ring.

She padded out to answer it.

This time it was Colin she found framed on her doorstep, optimism and purpose lighting his face.

'I haven't seen you for a while,' he said. 'I've come to see whether you're all right, and whether you need any more help in the garden.' He held up a polystyrene tray of pink petunias. 'For you. I'll plant them out for you if you like.'

'Ah! Colin!'

'It was a choice between these and verbena. These give a better show, I think.'

'Um, the thing is, Colin . . .' She had assumed that their association (such as it had been) was over. How to put that to him?

'I'll get cracking then, shall I? No time like the present.'

She was rapidly realising that it was rash to assume anything where Colin was concerned. These days, despite appearances, he had all the iron conviction of an immovable force.

Like Cass and Sandra.

Which brought her back to Annette. What *had* she done to them all?

Uninvited, Colin made his own way down the hall. Of all of them, Colin was clearly the most harmless. Or rather she felt that she could handle him and his stalk-in-the-wind body. It was as non-threatening as his will to please.

Yet how much did she really know about him? The mayhem unleashed by Cass and Sandra hung over her like an awful warning. But then she thought – can it *get* any worse?

Maybe Colin knew where she could contact Annette.

*

DEBORAH LAWRENSON

She made him some coffee.

Colin waggled his size tens a little, as if flexing them to their task of settling down for good by her welcoming hearth, and said, 'I was wondering what you would think about me moving in.'

Lara opened her mouth but no sound emerged.

He gave her a what-about-it? leer over his mug.

Then they both waited, until a nannyish tone filled the expectant silence, taking them both by surprise. 'I *beg* your pardon?' came Lara's voice at last.

'I could move in. We could live together.'

'Colin, we haven't even *seen* each other for weeks! And anyway,' she grappled for a gentler way when she saw the look on his soft face, 'why would we want to do that?'

Even he was taken aback. 'Well, I thought that maybe ... we could ...' It was ineffectuality now that made his cheeks glow. And how could he sit so still when the squirming shame in his body could be felt so uncomfortably in hers? And how did one ever explain to a person who does not understand, that he does not understand?

'You said you might have to take a lodger, ages ago. And then I came round to thinking, well, if it was *me* ...' The wind died in his sails.

'Why, what difference would that make, Colin?' she asked cruelly.

'Questions,' he said. 'You always ask so many questions. Just think how much happier you'd be if you just got on with life.'

That was low. 'And what is that supposed to mean?'

He sighed right down to his boots, so that even his soles seemed to be sucked in. Lara got to her own feet and stood her ground, arms crossed, legs apart.

He sighed again, and she could feel his lungs collapsing – or maybe they were her own caving in. That worried her. Since when was this odd relationship empathetic?

'Colin, you may have misunderstood...' she began more gently. For, just in time, she had remembered. It wasn't every day one had to give bad news to a confessed axe man.

The pucker in his brow grew deeper. He looked so hurt – but at least it was a bloodless hurt. 'Don't,' she said, 'take this the wrong way.'

She could not help it. The idea of Colin moving in, making himself and his lengths of fabric at home, made her flesh crawl. In fact, her skin was creeping stealthily towards the door hoping for a lucky escape even as she spoke...

'Lara, I do lo—'

'Colin!' she interrupted desperately.

His mouth froze in a choirboy's O.

'I think that it would be a good idea if you...' Lara cast around for calming measures, '...had another cup of coffee.' Before you go; she willed the thought into the charged atmosphere of the room. The words prickled like static on her skin, but whether they reached him seemed doubtful.

'You don't have to make up your mind at once,' he called wanly to her retreating back as she went to boil the kettle again.

Lara forced herself to calm down with some more pleasant thoughts.

She wished Greg were here. Greg's lack of complexity. Greg's broad shoulders. Even his old sheepskin coat. The suntanned small of Greg's back. Greg's ... Greg, in other words. She would call him as soon as Colin had gone.

Perhaps together they could arrange a gentle let-down for Colin – from a great height.

When she dragged her mind back into the here and now, she was staring out at the damp garden. Dense grey puddles had formed which might have been potholed passages to the centre of the earth. All around was belladonna and henbane and poison ivy, but only in her mind. She shivered, and poured boiling water on to ground coffee.

Colin was a sad person. That was all. Nothing more to it than that.

She went back and told him no, firmly.

She was about to open her offensive on the Annette front when he got up and plodded past her, out into the garden.

The garden!

'No!' called Lara. 'No . . . It's fine . . . It's wet! You . . . stay in here, and talk to me . . .'

He came back, sadder than ever.

'Oh, Colin, I—'

'Don't say anything.'

So they didn't, until he told her, 'I don't feel well. I don't suppose . . . could I lie down for a minute or two?'

And with that, he took himself off into her crumpled untidy bedroom and did not re-emerge. Lara sat on the floor by the telephone, head in her hands.

She felt Colin's presence in the flat as a dull ache, a constant worry which she felt disinclined to probe further, all the time hoping the unease would slip away – rather like a nagging toothache in a spot which has caused trouble in the past.

When she heard a movement, she assumed it was him. She prepared herself to cut any display of sympathy and show him the door.

Then came the unmistakable sound of a key in the lock.

Lara shot into the narrow hall as the front door was pushed open. Through one carelessly gaping door was Colin, pink as a sausage in the roll of her duvet; through the other, thunderously, strode Will.

She reeled back, tugging the bedroom door closed. 'What the hell—?'

'Lara.'

For several appalling seconds each contemplated the other. It was clear he hadn't expected to find her in.

She noticed first how short he was. How short his legs were in the dirty jeans. All that seemed most familiar about him were the facets she had forgotten: the sunken cheeks; the way his stubble grew when he had not shaved for a couple of days; the way his eyes slid away from hers whenever she was speaking.

He stood four-square to her, a strangely familiar stranger.

'Why aren't you at work?' he demanded.

'What the *fuck*—?'

'I thought you would be at work. I let myself in.'

'You don't say.'

He was brazening out his mistiming; she retreated to clutch at the bedroom door. Any contribution from Colin – duvet wrapped, or in any other state – at this juncture would surely be unwise. Lara could only stand and stare.

'What do you want?' she asked finally.

Convention, as the circumstances demanded, might have stretched to the pretence of civilisation over yet another cup of unwanted coffee. Instead, she barked the only conversational gambit she had.

'Why?'

He did not answer.

She repeated it. 'Why have you come back here?'

'I need something.'

It was her turn to stare that down. How many times had she imagined what she would say to him if he came back now? All these last weeks, one question had remained constant. So she said, 'I need something – just

277

one thing from you. I want you to tell me what I did wrong.'

'Nothing.'

'Of course I did. Tell me what it was, that's all I want from you. Then you can go.'

'You were always trying to be so perfect,' said Will. 'You want to know what really bugged me about you, Lara? You never actually *did* anything. Your life was so bloody theoretical.'

If ever she had needed him to say the right thing, he came through for her then.

So it was time for some home truths, was it?

They were still standing in the sitting-room, and she began to tremble. She was too full of words which she needed to disgorge.

'Will, it was horrible, being with you,' said Lara.

She should have known he'd take that as the rhetoric of the wronged. He was actually grinning, with a hint of sneer. 'That wasn't what you said at the time.'

'I didn't know so at the time. It was only when I began to get my life back for myself, that I realised what an empty, draining existence it was.'

'Draining?' He imbued the word with an impression of every rancid smell and dankness and rat dropping his imagination could supply.

'Yes,' said Lara. 'Of my spirit, my self-confidence, my inner resources, my independence – do you need me to go on?'

Will scratched his head in a way calculated to suggest amiable bafflement. 'Bloody therapy,' he said. 'All women end up in bloody therapy. You can always tell. Yapping away together about their inner resources till you all sound the bloody same.'

'Oh,' said Lara. '*All* women – or all the women who ever get involved with *you*, are we talking about here? I wonder what that says?'

He seemed darker about the eyes, now she came to study him. Definitely pouchy under the eyes. His bags were packed there, at least. His lips, strangely for him, were cracked, his hair wilder, as well as darker, than it was in her mind. And if she were to be brutally frank, a visit to the dentist would not have gone amiss either. Strange. The Will she had known had vanished, and in his place was this unappealing husk. Or there again, was this what he had been all along?

'And I was too stupid to see it,' said Lara defiantly, out loud.

There was no reaction, in any case. He took in the room with an intensity that seemed not quite resentment, nor covetousness, and certainly not nostalgia. He was looking for something which may or may not have been there.

Then he set off while she was still working on the words to show she had seen through him. She was so detached that she observed him turn his back and go out of the room as if he was nothing more immediate, or indeed any more to do with her, than an image on the television screen or a photograph in a newspaper.

She came abruptly to her senses. 'Hey – where do you think you're going?' she gasped, starting after him down the corridor. He was heading for the bedroom.

The bedroom where, to the best – or should that be, the worst – of her knowledge, Colin lay. Perhaps, needled her wildest imaginings, by now he was even shackled to the bedstead with a length of shot silk and moaning in tender anticipation of whatever release might come his way . . .

'Will!' she cried.

He turned.

'Do you mind?' she shouted indignantly enough to make him stop, exasperated, in his tracks. 'This is *my* place now. You can't just turn up and start poking around wherever you feel like it!'

'I have *every* right to be here. If anyone wants to know, I live here.'

'Wha-at?' Later she would be furious she didn't ask him what the hell he meant by that. She was so taken aback she stared blankly.

'My stuff is here,' he stated.

'I got rid of your clothes,' she said. 'They looked quite picturesque, flapping on the rail on Jo's stall in Tachbrook Street. Like semaphore announcing the death of an era.'

There was barely a reaction. A mere flicker.

'So you see,' said Lara. 'I have become dangerously addicted to taking charge not only of what was left of you, but of my own destiny.'

There was a pause which went on fractionally too long. 'We'll see about that,' was all he said.

Then he pushed open the bedroom door.

Lara held her breath. She stood outside with her eyes clenched shut, as she closed herself off from every wounding consequence which was sure to ensue.

Nothing came.

Will pulled back after the tiniest glimpse and closed the door. Had he not seen Colin? More likely he *had* seen him and wanted to show her how little he cared.

Whatever. She was hardly going to ask.

Then Will was back, looking around the rearranged furniture for what he wanted. He sat at the desk and a sound like animals scrabbling filled the room as he went through the drawers.

'What the hell—?' She rushed forward and set on his windmilling arms.

Will pushed her off. 'Get out of the way, Lara.'

'No, I won't.'

But the force of his determination sent her backwards,

until the edge of the sofa was at the back of her legs and she was forced to sit down abruptly.

She concentrated on the room, even while she hardly dared look into the corners, or behind the door, lest Colin come blundering in.

From Will came grunts of annoyance as he moved on and the contents of Lara's own chest of drawers came flying through the air, bumping on the carpet as they crash landed.

'Stop it, stop it!' she yelled, launching another attack at his busy shoulders. 'What are you doing?'

Again, she was elbowed away. 'If you would tell me what it is you want,' she said icily, 'then perhaps I could help you find it. And then you can go.' She contemplated the back of his head as he continued to rummage frenziedly, and considered embedding something sharp and fatal in the tissue and bone. All the dressing-table could offer was a rusting pair of tweezers and a nail file. Hardly enough to make much impact. So she sat down again, powerless as of old, and took in the spectacle. Let him do his worst; it was nothing to do with her any more.

On the floor a red wrapping ribbon had been transmuted into a stream of glossy viscous horror-film blood. Or so it seemed at that very moment.

He went to the dresser in the kitchen, bullishly, and wrenched open the door.

Lara crossed her arms. 'The cupboard is bare,' she said emphatically.

He gave no response to the echoing interior. Then he dropped to his knees, and made as if to go in head first. More rustling sounds emerged, and then a noise which indicated he had what he wanted. He backed out with an envelope in his fist and a vindicated expression which tinged his features with black.

Curious as she was, Lara sat tight as he began roughly

to pull out the contents of this packet. She was forgotten as he seized at his prize, absorbed and urgent.

'Old bills?' queried Lara after some minutes of silent wonder. She craned to see which ones they were. 'Now, Will ... I never took you for the sentimental type. I suppose it's quite flattering really ... something to remember me by. I should have spent more of your money!'

'Shut up, Lara.' He went on sifting.

'Shuffling memories,' mused Lara with a biting edge.

Still he was searching.

'Will, I would like you to go now. I'm fed up with whatever game it is you're playing. Just ... leave me alone now.'

He didn't acknowledge her in any way as he blithely picked out another fistful of old papers which he pocketed.

'Fine,' he said.

'Good.'

For a moment he stood by the back door, his hand resting on the knob. Was it her imagination, still on red alert, or did he note the changes to the garden with more intensity than might be expected?

'You didn't want me to go, did you?' he mocked.

'You are incredible, you know that.'

He proved that by taking it as a compliment.

She chose her words carefully. 'It doesn't seem to have occurred to you, Will, that I might not want you back.'

It was a fair appraisal of the situation. 'You want me,' he said.

'No,' said Lara, 'I don't.'

Still that did nothing to deter him. Or so his grin said.

'It's OK. I wouldn't expect you to understand, Will. Not someone with your inexhaustible self-regard.'

'You always wanted me. You were the one who made

the move on me, right in the beginning. You saw me,' said
Will, moving closer, 'and you wanted me.'

'Oh pul-lease.'

He put a hand on her shoulder so that it curled around
her neck. She felt his touch as a prickle of loathing.

'You are quite ridiculous, Will. It was the best turn you
ever did me, going when you did. The way you did. If I
haven't told you before – thank you.'

The smile he gave her was detestably smug.

They exchanged nothing further until he was at the
front door.

'You've changed, Lara.'

'You haven't,' she replied. 'You're the same jerk you've
always been. It just took me longer than it should have
to realise that.'

The door banged behind him like a funeral drum.

Lara knelt in the ransacked room, fenced in by spilling
papers, open books, strewn boxes kept to store unneeded
gadgets, old designer label bags and gaily painted
wrappings.

She could not cry; there was nothing left to feel.

Colin was bleary when he eventually discharged himself
from the bedroom, but his determination was undimmed.
If he had heard their angry voices, he said nothing.
Neither did he mention the disarray.

'Have you made up your mind yet?' he asked.

Lara played the only card she had. 'Have you been back
to the workshop lately?'

'I went last night.'

'And?'

'Annette didn't turn up.'

'Does anyone know where she is?'

He gave a shrug. Then hope was a sunrise on his

cheeks. 'You mean . . . will you come back to the workshop with me?'

Lara let him think what he wanted.

'Tell you what,' she said. 'You find Annette for me, and I'll *think* about it.'

22　The Weaver of Dreams

In the days that followed Lara had the distinct and uncomfortable feeling that she did not have the Garden Flat to herself. At any moment, she felt in her bones, there would be a knock at the back door and standing there would be a soiled woman. A woman who looked as if she had been dipped in chocolate, a person caked in mud who was pounding on the wood for retribution and, failing that, a hot bath.

It had not happened. Veronica had not risen; Annette had not reappeared.

Neither had Colin, with news.

But for days Lara waited, cleaning and scrubbing all the while at her floors and walls with automaton fists.

The forms she would need to complete as application for a place at law school had arrived in the post and lay catching tiny flies on the kitchen table. The telephone shrilled with ever more eager messages from a television producer who was keen to discuss her award-winning play.

But Lara, as she cleaned, was a woman on her knees, and one of a long line at that. For as long as she could remember the women in her family had worshipped one household god above all others: Ajax. This was how order was maintained, and chaos kept at bay. Lara had thought she was different but she wasn't.

So she cleaned some more. The wooden floor in the sitting-room gleamed like lacquer work. Straight lines of wood ran away from her with mesmerising directness as she crouched.

She could set her life back on track, they seemed to say. She was free; she could glide away. She buffed and puffed all the harder.

When she came to examine her own predicament and the moves she could make next, it seemed that none of it belonged to her. She was sneaking around in the wastes of someone else's life. That was the rub.

A life of her own, that was what that had all been about, in the beginning. And what had she attained?

It was the photographer's wife, of all people, who appeared when Lara was most in need of a balanced perspective.

Lara had abandoned the unequal struggle against dust. She was walking along the King's Road, aiming for nowhere in particular in the direction of the World's End. She was thinking while walking, because thinking while cleaning had not, in the end, had the desired effect.

She was trundling past Warehouse thinking about flared hipster trousers (and being nearly thirty-five) and how the last time she had worn such things they had to be two inches too long in order to hang stylishly over Dolcis platform shoes, when she saw Day's wife.

There was no time to take avoiding action.

'Penny!' cried Lara, as they came close to bumping head on.

'Oh! Lara – it *is* Lara, isn't it?'

A nod.

'This is a surprise.'

'Isn't it!'

After that, awkwardness set fast, yet still neither moved on.

At last, Penny said, 'Are you meeting someone? You look as if—'

'No . . . no . . .'

'You look well—'

'Yes, I—'

'Lara, can I talk to you?' asked Penny.

Penny had grown thinner. Her delicate face seemed almost luminous with the mass of faint lines over her pale tissue-paper complexion which stretched tight over her cheek-bones. Her cloudy grey eyes were large in their sockets.

She stood on the sanded beechwood floor of a trendy cafe they had entered; she was barely supported by legs in narrow trousers, and swayed slightly. In a glorious sartorial oxymoron, she wore a knitted sweater of shimmering greens and kingfisher blue, and vermilion and canary yellow, so that the effect was that of a bird of paradise freeing itself from a dull swamp.

Her long thin fingers fluttered and darted around the clasp in her hair, around her lip which was bitten ragged – she was reaching out and she had chosen Lara.

They claimed a table and sat down.

The young waitress was all teeth and the nineties version of platform shoes. Her thin opaque black legs were wooden in them, straight as a puppet's as she clumped towards them. They ordered cappucinos.

There were cinema posters on the pale cream walls, and blown-up reproductions of black-and-white stills from Fellini films in which the women all seemed to be suppressing terrible, hilarious secrets. Jazz music played, just a fraction too loudly, to make it clear that at this quiet time of day it was for the benefit of the staff more than the customers.

Penny seemed not to notice. 'You haven't been to the workshop lately?' she said hesitantly.

'No.'

'You didn't sign up for the next stage?'

'No . . . I . . . no.'

Annette . . .

'Have you?' asked Lara as calmly as she could. 'Been back to the workshop, I mean?'

'Not for weeks.'

There was an awkward pause.

'Cass and Sandra,' said Penny as if casting around for some other common ground. 'They've really come to life, haven't they?'

'Hmmm,' fudged Lara. What had they done now?

Penny, at least, had not just appeared without warning on Lara's doorstep and marched into the sitting-room. Penny was clearly not a person to hurl herself backward into the nearest cushiony chair without an invitation. Which made a change from the presumptions of most of Lara's recent visitors.

Lara began to feel happier. Perhaps this was a chance to put everything into perspective with a relatively *normal* person who had come into contact with the nice–nasty workshop.

It was still hard to make small talk.

'I hope you don't mind me dragging you in here like this,' began Penny again, even more awkwardly this time. Her voice was not much louder than a whisper. 'I thought . . . that I might be able to talk to you. Had you heard the workshops have been cancelled? No one can contact Annette. You know how it is . . . I can't talk to anyone about this – certainly none of the women at home, and none of the women who buy my work, of course, or even any of my normal friends . . .'

Normal friends? But in the instant that Penny's words pulled her up short, Lara recognised their essential truth.

The very mention of Annette's name made Lara's skin contract.

'Got to keep going. Can't disappoint,' continued Penny. 'Anything else would upset everything they hold true.'

'But *you*'re upset,' said Lara.

'Yes,' said Penny, 'but I don't think that counts.'

They considered each other across the marble top of their table. A clarinet solo from the sound system made a mournful counterpoint to confession.

'It seems to me,' said Lara, knowing she was about to make her first useful comment since Penny's arrival, 'that what you need is a good . . . outburst.'

'Oh, I've been doing that for years.' Penny overturned that theory. 'The time has come, as we all know, to stop all that and do something constructive.'

Lara's coffee tasted of dread. Here we go, she thought. Again.

'My life,' said Penny, quite vehemently now, 'is patchwork, through and through. Make do and mend.'

'I – I can understand that.'

'I thought you would be able to, although I didn't in the beginning.'

'In the beginning?'

'I remembered you, you see,' said Penny.

'Oh?'

'You came over at the fashion show to interview my husband. Another worshipful lady come to glorify . . .'

'You didn't say anything – before.'

'No.'

'I wanted to talk to you. I did recognise you at the first workshop, but you always seemed to slip away,' said Lara lamely. 'And I never did glorify him.' There didn't seem much point in going over all of that again.

'No, you didn't. He was furious. Not to say taken aback. Did he make a pass at you?'

'Er, well now, I . . .'

'He usually does. Especially when things aren't going his way. Never mind, I'm used to all that.'

'What are you going to do, Penny?' Lara wanted to know whether there were, ultimately, any solutions.

This time the woman wove an enigmatic smile.

'Hints for the modern needlewoman,' said Penny. She looked at Lara with an unmistakably sly look. Lara raised her eyebrows.

Penny's voice was softly informative. 'Make sure your hands are clean and cool before beginning. Your hands should be clean throughout, most importantly when the task is accomplished.'

She paused to let the full flavour of this float around the room and sink into Lara's consciousness. Then she continued in the same tone. 'Take immediate action if you prick your finger and blood falls on your work, for unsightly stains and an unprofessional finish could result . . . with unfortunate consequences.'

In the silence between them that followed, Lara heard the scrape of chairs and the creak of boots on the wooden floor as the couple at another table moved on, and the distant drums of her own pulse. Penny, by contrast, was a serene statue, her mouth an alabaster smile which was waiting and knowing.

One thing was sure. They were not talking about needlework here.

It took an age for Lara to ask. 'What . . . have you done, Penny?'

Penny came to life slowly. She *had* been careful. She was a mistress of invisible mending, after all.

'I have taken a lover and I have ordered more appropriate company for Day,' said Penny. 'Pigs.'

'Pigs,' said Lara.

'A herd of swine. Lovely, smelly, mud-caked, snortling

pigs which even now are trampling through his pristine, anal-retentive, fucking white house. And . . .'

Lara was laughing now. 'And you have a lover?'

Penny nodded victoriously. 'I have taken a lover,' she reiterated.

'Good for you.' Just so long as there were no *bodies* — well, apart from in the living, breathing, skin-on-skin sense, that was. Lara breathed her own huge sigh of relief.

'And he will die,' said Penny, 'when he finds out *whose* lover exactly I have taken.'

'Whose?' urged Lara, every vein singing — despite herself — with vicarious excitement.

'His, of course. You might have heard of her,' said Penny, head well up now as she stressed the pronoun. 'I fell in love with her picture on the wall.'

'Like a fairy-tale . . .'

'Exactly so. Her name's Agnetha.'

Lara remembered.

'Scandinavian?'

'Swedish,' said Penny, colouring proudly. 'As well as being extraordinarily beautiful and well known, she's far too nice a person for him.'

'Neat,' laughed Lara. 'Very neat.'

They left the cafe together and walked towards Penny's car. It was parked in an exclusive side street in defiance of all warnings and restrictions.

'We're going off together, Agnetha and me, into the sunset.'

'Good for you,' said Lara, meaning it.

'Somewhere warm, away from *him*, here . . . away from everything.'

Penny looked down at her slender hands.

Lara raised an eyebrow. Was there more? 'So . . .?' she said.

'I have done something truly awful. I've been *bad*, Lara.'

'No! No, you haven't! Listen to me, all you've done is what another person has been doing to you for years. All you've *done* is stop being so bloody nice about it for once!'

Penny was visibly trembling as she shook her head. They were at her car now, a chic little run-around for the Knightsbridge wife, and she leaned against the passenger door.

Lara had to ask. The question had been nagging at her, impossible to shake off. 'You mentioned, earlier . . .' she began, before finding the courage to come straight out with it. 'Have you been in touch with Cass and Sandra at all?' Somehow she knew they had something to do with it.

Slowly, Penny nodded.

Then she reached inside the woven bag which hung from her bony shoulder. She extracted a shiny black pistol. The barrel juddered in her hand as if it had a life of its own.

Lara felt herself pulled down through the pavement towards the earth's hot core. A gasp filled the startled silence which must have come from her lips.

The gun quivered now in Penny's open palm.

It was a while before Lara could ask, 'Is that real?'

Another hopeless shake of the head.

Right. Everything was OK. There was no crisis. Nothing to get worked up about. Lara was about to pass on these brave consolations when Penny told her, 'Although . . . it looked real enough for me to do the building society on Muswell Hill a while ago.'

The world reeled again.

'You . . . what?'

'With that friend of Sandra's,' said Penny, 'on the big motorcycle.'

23 Retributions

Lara planted immortelles in the garden, honesty and helichrysum, in the shady place where she did not like to stay too long. When they flowered they would look like stretched paper. True, they would have to be cut and dried carefully to be resolutely everlasting, but it was the thought that counted, wasn't it?

Maybe someone else would come along and do the necessary.

It wouldn't be Lara. She knew now that somewhere along the line she had mislaid the person she used to be. It was then she thought of Penny and her new love, southbound somewhere with a share of £10,000 in stolen used notes stuffed in her travel bag.

And she was pleased for her.

Lara had never been much of a conspiracy theorist. Now she was not so sure. Even the inanimate objects in her life seemed to be ranged against her, she fumed as she rubbed one shin bruised by the blow from the stone slab which had fallen (how?) from the rockery. Was it unearthed and hurled on purpose – and if so, by whom or what? Not that she believed in malevolent spirits. Or rather, she hadn't, until now.

She needed sanity, by which she meant Greg.

What with his move upriver and her complications they had not been in touch.

She dialled the number of his mobile phone with a mild flutter of nerves which she recognised were more to do with security than romance. He sounded pleased enough to hear from her.

There were no reproaches, on either side. This was the simple life, after all.

Lara made a date with normality for eight o'clock that evening.

She would go with Greg to a party in Earl's Court, full of ordinary people: madcap antipodeans, students, travellers, hard-drinking kangaroos, sheep-farmers' daughters in psychopathic pursuit of a good time in a metropolis as far from home as possible. Somewhere she would get pissed and have a laugh along with the crowd, in other words.

When the doorbell rang this time, it was touch and go whether Lara would stir herself to answer it. She put down a paperback she was failing to read and turned down the volume on the radio which was all the company she could handle. The news at midday had disappeared in the ether, and the weather was predicted to be cloudy.

The bell went again.

Muttering to herself, Lara slopped into the hall with her shoes only half on. If Cass and Sandra were on the doorstep they weren't coming an inch further in than that.

When she opened the door, it was to a man in a leather jacket and a woman in uniform.

The police.

'Lara Noe?' asked the man.

She nodded dumbly.

'I am DC Hames and this is WPC Blair. We have reason to believe that you can help us with our inquiries.'

Lara took root to the spot. The police officers seemed to exist in a different dimension from hers. They were far away and getting smaller, more detached from her. They were no more of this moment than some foul scene from a tortured imagination.

'May we come in?' asked the WPC.

Someone else's brain operated Lara's hand when she opened the door wider.

Then they were standing in her sitting-room, where all the others had passed. Who would have thought, in the weeks since Will had left, how many people she had never known before would come to her in this room?

The man was tall and dark with curiously flat coarse hair. Lara looked at his immense shiny shoes sunk into her rug, and then up gradually to what she didn't doubt was a hard-ridged torso like a tailor's mannequin under his coat.

The woman had a bumpy nose and cracked lips. There was a hard look below her short mousy hair, and stocky legs which emerged from the unflattering skirt. On her shoulder were shiny numbers, and shiny raindrops on her shoes.

They were both younger than Lara.

'We'll sit down, if we may,' said the woman, and they did so.

They appraised her sternly.

'Where were you on Tuesday afternoon?' asked the male constable.

Where was she? The days had melted into each other without the structure of work and commitments.

'I . . . I was . . .'

They knew. Of course they knew. Someone had seen her and Annette, and Cass and Sandra and the whole sordid, muddy, muddled episode. How could they not? But Tuesday afternoon? What was Tuesday afternoon to anyone?

At any moment Lara's heart was going to leap out of her throat. She swallowed hard. The room shrank around her as the police officers receded further into their own dimension, further from Lara's recognition of the here and now.

She could lie, but she could think of nothing to invent. 'I . . . was here,' she said.

'*Were* you, Lara?'

'Yes, I suppose so. I was here.'

'We have reason to believe that you may have been in North London on the afternoon in question,' stated the woman implacably. 'Would you like to tell us about that?'

Lara shook her head. It became a shiver she could not control. 'No. No, I wasn't . . .'

The man studied her intently as his colleague persisted. 'We think you were, Lara.'

'I was here . . . on Tuesday afternoon.'

'We have a warrant to search these premises,' he said calmly.

Lara was a ball of self-consciousness, shaking involuntarily.

The WPC took herself off towards the bedroom.

Lara and the other officer sat in silence. They could hear drawers being pulled out and cupboard doors opening. When she returned, he stood up and went through to the kitchen. 'Your garden – out through here?' he demanded, rattling at the back door.

She nodded. They both went out.

Lara closed her eyes to the view through the window and door. In her mind it was dark, with torchlight bouncing over the walls outside and the soft earth beneath their big shiny feet.

This was it then. Annette had ignored all her frantic messages and gone to the police. Was she saying now that Lara had tracked her down and gone to Islington to beg once more for her help?

What of Cass and Sandra, and Quiet Al?

So this is what it had come to, the big adventure.

Lara wanted oblivion.

The officers slammed the back door behind them. Lara, in a state of total separation, watched as though through the lens of a camera as they stamped on the coconut matting.

It wasn't me. I didn't do it. They brought it here. I didn't believe it had actually happened. I didn't know how mad and bad they were! I would have reported it myself but I left it too late!

Gravely they returned to her. 'By the way,' said DC Hames, 'we've found your car.'

Out there?

Lara blinked unseeingly at them. Still she could say nothing.

'Although you can't have it back quite yet.'

Lara was heat and ice, flushing on and off like an alarm. 'It's my car!'

'There's nothing worse than a misguided cover-up, Lara,' said Hames. His tone was brutal.

Stay calm. Stay calm . . .

'What's that supposed to mean?'

And now he was cajoling. 'Where *is* he, Lara?'

'Where's who?'

'He's got away from us once already. You'll make it a lot easier on yourself if you tell us now where he is.'

'I don't know! I don't know what any of this is about!' She was cracking. She could feel her sanity stretching.

'You *have* seen him, haven't you, Lara?' The woman took a turn.

'WHO?' she screamed. 'Who have I seen?' Were they talking about Quiet Al?

'Will Radcliffe. Your partner. He lives here.'

That threw her. It took a while before she said, 'My *ex*-partner. I haven't . . . We split up, months ago.'

'But he's been back. This is the address he gives.'

Lara stared. A bell rang, distantly, in her brain.

'We know, Lara. We're very observant. It's one of our most irritating characteristics,' said the man.

The shaking took deeper hold. 'He came back here the other day. Out of the blue. I had no idea. I was furious – I didn't want to see him and I haven't seen him since.'

'What did he want?'

'I don't *know*.'

'He must have wanted something.'

What was all this about?

How much had they seen?

'He must have wanted whatever it was he left here, Miss Noe.'

'I . . . There wasn't anything left. I'd already sent it back to him. Given some clothes away.'

They waited for more. Lara burst into tears. 'He took some papers. Some stuff, I don't know. That was all. I can't tell you any more than that because I don't know any more than that! I didn't want him to come back!'

There was a charged pause.

'No,' said DC Hames. 'Maybe you didn't.' But his tone suggested he was keeping a very open mind. 'Almost forgot. This is for you.'

Lara took the brown envelope and ripped it open. It was an invoice for the removal of a parking clamp and a parking ticket to pay. 'What?' she shouted. '*What?*'

'Found on the front seat,' said Hames. 'Your car. Your car *is* a dark green Rover Metro, registration M455 VGU? Reported stolen on 7 March? This is an invoice and ticket dating back to 5 March.'

'I can see that.'

'Wouldn't want you to incur any more penalty fines

than you have to, would we?' said Hames. 'Left it on a double yellow, I see.'

'What?' demanded Lara. 'But I never . . .'

They were enjoying this. Lara put the papers aside wordlessly as they made as if to go. She had begun to lead them back to the door when Hames said, 'And now we would like you to come with us. You do not have to accompany us, but if you do it may help your case should we decide to charge you.'

Charge her . . .

Her heart knocked at her ribcage.

Don't get yourself in deeper. Don't say anything until you have to.

They were waiting for an answer. She had no choice.

Lara grabbed her bag and slung it on like a guerrilla's kalashnikov.

There was a police car waiting, double parked, outside the main door. Lara was propelled into it. Another man was at the wheel and the engine was running, the sound counterpointed by the rhythmic drag of windscreen wipers. Gusty rain made the square a dank walled hole under dark clouds.

She could feel the first male officer's arm like a steel pin against her own thin sleeves as it guided her into the back seat. Then the woman constable took the front seat and he climbed in after Lara. The car moved off before his door closed.

For a moment Lara sat in mute indignation.

They crossed Ebury Bridge Road and she watched with absolute detachment as the streets unrolled through the rain-spotted window. The chichi antique shops of the Pimlico Road passed by, untouchable.

Let the world do its worst; the game was up.

This was what it had all been leading up to. She should have known better than to break the rules, to stray from the straight and narrow. It was not in her nature, and now she would be made to pay the price for daring. This was all she deserved. She was on her way to a police station for questioning.

Was *this* exciting enough?

The Royal Hospital warped behind Lara's glass view.

'You OK?' The man turned to her.

Lara had begun to shake. She nodded, shivering.

'Don't worry,' he said. 'You help us, we'll help you.'

They cruised further through the wet streets of Chelsea, then shot left at traffic lights to cross the bridge for Battersea. Lara still had no idea where they were heading.

Against all reason, she closed her eyes.

They came to a stop not long afterwards in a dark side street. The sky above was purple-grey. At the end of the road was the roar of some main thoroughfare, bright with rushing headlights. A double-decker bus lumbered along with the familiar whine and tick.

'Where are we?' she asked automatically.

And what has this place to do with Cass and Sandra and the body in my garden?

'Off Battersea Rise.' DC Hames opened her door and indicated that she should get out.

This was no police station. Outside were backstreet workshops: a garage, a tool-hire outfit, an upholsterer's studio. The buildings were more random, and the effect more ramshackle, than the uniform rows of Victorian brick which lined all the residential streets she knew were around them. At this end of the street all was quiet. Business had clearly seen better days. Lara became aware of the sound of her own breathing.

There was a dark car and another man waiting for them. He introduced himself as a detective sergeant. She barely looked at his face, saw only that he was not in uniform. He led her into a narrow alley between two of the buildings, followed by the WPC. A dank smell rose from the clammy black brick all around them as they hurried through. They splashed through lurking puddles. Lara felt him turn as if to check that they were not being followed, then he pushed open a door to their right. A side entrance to a shop, perhaps. She would never have noticed it was there.

She was shoved inside.

It was even darker in there.

'Up the stairs,' said the detective sergeant.

Lara's body obeyed as if someone else was driving it.

She reached a landing and was pushed forward. It was only then that Lara said, 'I thought we were going to a police station.'

He switched on a light. It burst startlingly from a bare bulb in front of her. The three of them were standing in a large unpleasant room.

'We wanted you to see this.'

The curtains were drawn, heavy full-length drapes of a dark and ugly fabric. Dirty plain walls showed patches of damp creeping up from the skirting-board. In one corner was a diseased outbreak of black mould. On the bare linoleum floor were the pockmarks of long-gone furniture and cigarettes.

The sum comforts were a table and two upright chairs.

'When was this place cleared out?'

'I don't know anything about this place. I've never been here in my life!'

The officer implied with an eyebrow that he was not born yesterday. He went over to the table. He was carrying a case, she saw now. He clicked it open, without taking his gaze from Lara.

She watched with the same sense of detachment she had felt in the car. She was watching through the wrong end of a telescope. Whatever was to come, it had nothing to do with her, not her real self.

The minutes ticked by. Was he waiting for her to crack?

Lara wrestled with her instincts for as long as she could. Her voice, when the words came out, was a barely controlled cry: 'What *is* all this? I don't know what this is all about!'

'Tell me,' said the officer in a voice as stark as the room, 'when he first rented this place and began to use it as a company address.'

The prickle of panic was giving rise to hysteria.

They stared at each other. The penny took far longer to drop than it should have done.

'*Will*! It's Will, isn't it?'

Lara thought she saw a change in the tension of his face, but then he was stainless steel again. 'Well now . . . we seem to be getting somewhere.' This was a sneer. Still the WPC said nothing.

'I don't know what it is you want to know. You ask me when he first rented this place. I had no idea that he *did* rent this place!'

Yet again her life was being rewritten. She knew nothing about this foul room – she had known nothing of this Will either. Which begged the question, too large for now: Who or what had she been during her years with him?

Lara's courage wobbled. 'You . . . you don't suspect me in whatever it is that Will has been up to? You do realise that I don't know anything?'

'Now, Lara . . . I have to ask myself – is that likely?'

Was Will still playing games with her?

'I swear . . . I know nothing about this place.'

'Take a look at this.' He produced a card folder from the briefcase and handed it to her.

Lara's fingers trembled on the flap. Getting a grip, she pulled out a sheaf of black-and-white photographs. There

were not many. She went through them numbly. They
showed a young woman, a pretty Kensington Emma with
her hair in a streaked blonde bob with hairband, wearing
loafers and short skirts – but never too short.

She was walking along a street.

She was with someone outside a cafe.

Lara glanced up quizzically but the officer's demeanour
was weighty and dangerous as a silenced pistol.

One of the photographs was a hazy close-up which
showed a pert nose and wide eyes.

The next showed her being greeted at a door by a foxy-
looking man.

She was locking a car by a parking meter.

She was walking away from a car – *from Lara's car*.

It was only when Lara went back to the shot of the
man by the doorway and scrutinised it that the shifty
features transposed themselves into Will's face.

She let the pictures fall into a pile on her lap. Hot
redness gripped her neck.

'You know who she is then,' said the detective.

Lara nodded. 'Janey.'

'Jane Anstiss. They're supposed to be getting married,
you know.'

That was a thunderbolt – but no longer the worst. Lara
steadied her voice. 'And that's my car.'

'Yes.'

'So *he* took it? Will stole my car?' Now the questions
back at the flat meshed together.

A shrug. 'Probably had a set of keys.'

That would be right. *Bastard*.

Lara was exhausted suddenly. She longed for her bed,
for a bath, for clean sheets and oblivion. She let her
eyelids drop. Tears had sprung from nowhere.

'Tell me what you think Will Radcliffe does for a living.'

She sighed. 'He's involved in films. He is a partner

in an independent production company called Narcissus.
They're based in Golden Square.' It came out pat and flat.

'And what kind of films are these? Films I could go to
the cinema to see?'

'Not feature films. Films for television.'

'What kind?' persisted the detective.

'I dunno . . . anything he can. One-offs. Travel films,
he's into all that.'

'And these films, do they actually get made?'

This was becoming more surreal. The tacky linoleum
was swimming now, or so it seemed in her brimming eyes.
'Well, you know how it is . . .'

'No I don't, Lara. Tell me how it is.'

'They don't always get made . . . They can't always get
the money together. Times are hard. That's what the
business is like. They can work for months on a project
that comes to nothing in the end.' Just like my life now,
thought Lara.

'Does he have money – personally?'

'No, not particularly.'

'Private income, that kind of deal?'

She shook her head. If she had been more on the ball
she would have seen where all this was leading.

'Yet he can finance a certain . . . lifestyle. Interesting,
that. What does the name Goldquest mean to you? And
Stare Productions and Bust Ltd?'

It was implicit in his tone. 'You still think that I know
what this is all about.' Lara put her head in her hands
and pressed her pounding forehead. 'And I don't. I just
don't. Why won't you believe me?'

Her words hung in the air.

'Because I never believe anything,' he said softly.

Even Lara was learning that was the only way to be.

'If . . . if you think I know something, then why are you
telling me all this?' she asked after another tense silence.

'We're just making sure.'

304

'You must be very sure I hate him.' Her gaze fell down again to the photos of Janey and her car.

When she looked up again, there was a moment of mutual understanding.

The detective sergeant smiled. 'Just making sure,' he said again.

There were so many questions, they stuck in her throat. She was shaking uncontrollably when she finally managed to disgorge the one she dreaded most because it would say the most about her.

'Just . . . tell me . . . what it is he's involved in.'

The detective gave her a one-word answer: 'Fraud.'

24 The Masquerade

After her months in the wilderness, Lara had renewed contact with old friends. She invited them to a party – a fancy-dress party. A farewell party.

An age after the burial ritual, she paid tribute to Rose.

Lara dressed like Rose for the party. She unfurled seven-denier stockings with lacy tops and rolled them on to her legs with butterfly hands. She gave herself a rosebud mouth.

The stage was set for Lara's great goodbye. Not that any of the masqueraders would know the extent of it – only that she was going away and she would be gone for a long time. They would not find her here again.

So Lara clothed herself in her former image.

It was goodbye for ever then to the sucker she had been: the person who had been so insecure about herself that she had never dared to look too critically at the man who gave her confidence simply by wanting her. Sure, she knew he lied to her; what she hadn't realised was that he did it for a living. It had been very lucrative, apparently, running a film company that never made many films.

It explained a lot.

And had he come back because now he wanted whatever it was he had left with her for safe keeping?

In front of her mirror, Lara backcombed her hair. She could bring this off: Filofax, mobile phone, shoulder pads, high shoes, big earrings, big hair. It was so effective when she was finished, so subtle, that there was the distinct possibility that no one would get the joke.

Entrances, as Val upstairs had said, were the important part of fancy-dress parties.

And *exits*.

There were fairy lights leading out from the back door into the garden, strung out like her nerves along the wall, then tangled in branches and the shrubs she had planted. It was the first time she had given a party on her own for years.

The lump-in-throat hour she was alone passed quicker than ever before.

Soon the guests had swooped on Lara; they were carrion on her missing months. They wanted to know where she had been. They needed to know what she had been doing. They demanded every detail, the better to judge themselves against her.

Lara posted an enigmatic half-smile.

She let her gaze wander over shoulders and slide away to the latest arrivals. The flat and garden were suddenly full of familiar faces made strange by neglect.

Val's knock-out scent gripped the innards of the house. Its epicentre was the kitchen, where the woman herself was swathed in black shreds as a nymph of the night. 'I am wearing a dress in which I died – in all senses of the word, unfortunately – in a new play at the King's Head two years ago,' she was telling a large man in motorcycling leathers. From the accessories he carried, including an already drunken Sandra, Lara deduced he may well have been the motor-biking thrash rocker known as the Grunt.

Annie arrived early. This was an event to mark Lara's re-emergence as a force to be reckoned with, as far as Annie was concerned.

'You look wonderful,' she told Lara. '*So* clever. The spirit of the 1980s!'

Lara smiled. Annie was about the only one who would get it, more or less.

Her former *Reflections* colleague had come as – Lara wasn't sure exactly what Annie had intended. She was attired in a silver-foil tube with slashes of red paint and dark lipstick over her bare arms and huge on her lips. She seemed to be coated with a malevolent vitality.

Or perhaps Lara was just being nasty.

Whatever was intended, it meant nothing to Lara any more.

'I hear,' said Annie, glittering under the lights, 'that congrats are in order.'

'Oh?'

'London Weekend TV?'

'Ah.'

'I didn't even know you were writing a screenplay. You never said.'

'No,' said Lara.

'Well done.' She seemed to mean it, too.

Lara felt bad, for about a millisecond. 'Word's out, then?'

Annie nodded. 'Friend of mine knows someone there, you know how it is.'

'News travels.'

'What's it all about?'

'You tell me.'

'I meant the screenplay.'

So did Lara. She improvised smoothly enough, though. 'It's about a woman who decides that she will no longer strive to be good enough.'

Annie pulled a puzzled face.

'There's no point, when she looks around and sees that everyone else has discovered the way forward is to ditch any stupid ideas of right and wrong and join the rats.'

'Tell me about it,' sighed Annie, conspiratorially now.

'I did once, if you remember.'

Annie gave her a hard little stare. 'So what happens to her, this woman?'

Lara grimaced. 'I don't know yet. We'll have to wait and see. Needless to say, it will contain the most demeaning scenes of sex and violence ever attempted.'

It clearly wasn't what Annie imagined. 'Oh. Demeaning for whom?'

'Who do you think?' asked Lara.

'Talking of which . . .' Annie grinned wickedly. 'Ella's having a God-awful time. The split with Skelton's been a *disaster*. Rumour is, her job's on the line.'

'Really.'

Annie nodded enthusiastically.

'Sad,' said Lara.

'Well, not that sad. You know what they say . . . lose an editor, gain a promotion opportunity!'

Lara didn't doubt that. She moved on.

Lara's old off-duty crowd, who for the past months had been only disembodied voices on the telephone answering machine, arrived with a triumphant fanfare on the door-bell and burst into the passage from the hall.

'Where is she?'

'Where have you *been*?'

'Why haven't you called before?' they cried.

Fi and Bea, and Sarah and Sue – together with a couple of men Lara did not recognise – had come as an assortment of schoolgirls and twenties flappers, a choice which implied they had delved into stock archives for the occasion, but that they had made an effort in deference to Lara's recent exile.

They swirled around her, kissing her cheeks, appraising, signalling that an explanation, privately, later, was expected. Sarah did not mention the balloon trip. Then, true to form, they swamped the drinks counter in the kitchen.

When Lara used to go to parties, when she would strive to be flip and fun, the people she met there always gave the impression they thought she was a lightweight through and through. So she acted that way, in self-defence. Don't think that I'm taking myself too seriously, her demeanour would suggest, although it never managed to convey the notion that her interrogators might be doing exactly that themselves.

Privately, she was confident that she was as bright as any of them – only less *pushy*. But in an arena where instant appraisals were so important, that was already something of a disadvantage. For Lara knew, perhaps better than most, how we are constantly defined by the unreliable eyes of other people, and that in those circumstances, appearances are the *only* reality.

More and more guests arrived. Lara had not seen most of them for far longer than her months of isolation, a few not since the previous summer. Inevitably, some asked about Will.

She told those who did, that she was getting married – to someone else.

Jo from the clothes stall had come as Marlene Dietrich, her eyebrows plucked and painted into thin haughty circles; she was beautiful and quite untouchable.

Colin was a sheikh in a sheet (he had surprisingly little flair when it came to wrapping himself in material for public show: the plain white was a dull choice). He had no news of Annette for her though he had tried and tried. He had been cornered by Cass, a strikingly effective Gypsy Rose. She was yelling cod predictions for show. Through the throng Lara saw Dora – dressed as her alter-ego Madame Isadora in plum velvet and beads – making her way towards the noisy impostor.

Even Greg had appeared. It was an age, in his terms, since she had stood him up the day the police arrived. He had forgiven her, it seemed. He planted an uncomplicated peck on her cheek, and introduced her to a pretty girl and a couple he had brought along. They all wore antipodean hunter's hats in deference to the occasion, and headed straight for the beers.

It was his way, she knew, of telling her it was over.

The realisation hardly touched her now.

The moon rose. Outside, the hoydens were dancing their way around what was left of Lara's circles of despair. Their miscreant jigs whirled on into the night. Sandra was having the time of her life; Lara was haunted by her laughter and certainty. She was mesmerised by the lanterns and the dark recesses of her garden, the black caves beyond the bushes which led to who knew where. Perhaps she could walk towards one, and then keep walking as it opened up before her, lured in by the promise of forgetting.

Sandra, her wild halo of hair whipped into snakes which hissed and darted in the wind, came spinning over to tell her that she had left her family for good, had moved into a house in Hackney with the Grunt and various of his acquaintances. The Reverend Barry had taken it badly, apparently, but his sermons had never been so heartfelt and unpatronising.

And she and Cass had gone into business, capitalising on the unsuccessful recipes they had developed while they were still finding their way.

A catering business.

'It's going rather well – all by word of mouth, you know,' said Sandra. 'It's a kind of speciality service . . .'

'Don't tell me,' said Lara.

'Oh, it's not as bad as you think.'

'Oh?'

'Not the full works, as it were. Just a few strategic upsets.'

'Meaning?'

'The odd horrible relative or unwelcome guest finds they aren't able to enjoy the party after all . . .'

'Yes, but . . .'

'But it can't be the food, can it? Because everyone else is all right!'

Lara shook her head in admiration. 'You've found your calling, then.'

'It is very, very satisfying,' pronounced Sandra.

'The parish lantern's up,' said Dora as she passed.

'Sorry?' Lara dragged her attention away from Sandra.

Her elderly neighbour raised her gaze high into the night sky. 'The parish lantern. The moon.'

'Ah. Yes.'

'Don't notice any of us tanning yet . . .'

'Um – what?'

Dora pinched her arm. 'No, not noticeably any browner, I wouldn't say . . .'

'Oh . . . you mean the moonb . . .' Lara couldn't say it. She couldn't let her eyes slide over Dora's shoulder either. Was this it then, the moment of truth?

'Only I *did* wonder, dear, at the time . . .'

'Sorry, Dora, I—'

'Whether it would work. Had my doubts, even as you told me, whether your moonbathing would do the trick . . .'

But the old woman slipped away before the sudden sharpness that exploded in Lara's head as a warning could subside and allow her to speak.

Cass planned to take time off when the catering venture was truly up and running. She missed the workshop sessions now that Annette was no longer there. They *had* tried to track her down, but not too hard. It was probably better to let sleeping dogs lie she said.

That was then, and this was now. The present was much more exciting. Cass had heard of an alternative lifestyle commune in New Mexico. A month there would reinvigorate her resolve, she had decided. There was also an interesting strain of cactus which grew in the region, which was worth investigating. In its sap was a poison which could produce the entire range of desired effects and was all but undetectable.

'And you?' asked Cass. 'I suppose you'll be going as soon as you can.'

'Sooner,' Lara assured her.

'Far away from here.'

'A long way.'

Cass pulled down the corners of her mouth. 'Change is as good as a rest.'

Lara heard it as 'arrest'. She did not answer. 'What about Al? Is a commune in New Mexico his style? Will he go with you?'

'He might. He has a few loose ends to tie up.'

'That's . . . nice,' said Lara.

Cass gathered her Gypsy Rose shawls tighter around her. 'We'll see about that,' she replied.

More drinking. Shouting. The music was turned louder and louder.

Loud and alien above the din, Lara's own voice rose at each of her guests in turn:

'I was offered a job at *Vogue* . . . but I turned it down.'

'I'm going into television!'

'Amazing chance – I'm off to New York with this screen-play I wrote, never thought it would come to anything, and then . . .'

'Married, yes! No – to someone else . . .'

How they admired her! Lara Noe had made good.

They always knew she would, in the end. All good things came to she who waited.

The bass of the party music was turned up like the heartbeat of the entire neighbourhood. It could have woken the dead.

Lara was wondering about that when the woman appeared, out of the gaudy night, in the garden at her shoulder.

Lara started, saw her through the hours of wine as though through the wrong end of a telescope.

'He asked me not to come,' said the woman without preamble.

Lara said nothing. She was immobile; the horror brought by her previous night visitors had seeped through her skin and she felt it now, cold in her bones.

'But I had to. Friends . . . you know . . . we heard this was on . . .' She gave up any explanation. 'Will doesn't know. I had to see you before it was too late and you'd gone.'

It was Janey.

She was not dressed for a party. Honey-brown hair – darker than Lara remembered from the time when she answered the door to her – sat sleekly on the shoulders of an expensive raincoat. Her fingers trembled visibly as she fiddled unnecessarily with a velvet Alice band.

Here she was.

Here was the woman who had made her feel so imperfect.

Except she hadn't. Lara knew that now. She had done that herself, with a little help from Will.

Lara stood her ground, in the harsh white light strung from the boughs of the sycamore. She made no inviting gesture. 'I see . . .'

'He didn't think it would help.'

Keep calm, keep calm . . . 'Oh. And you think it might?'

Janey gave her apologies in the form of a little shrug. Mainly, though, her discomfiture was writ large in the purpling shadows under her eyes, striking blue eyes smudged with too much eye make-up and darting nervously at and beyond Lara.

'I don't know.' It was a hopeless reply. 'I . . . this is rather awkward,' said Janey.

'I think we both know that.'

'Could I . . . speak to you?'

Wearily, knowing she would probably regret it, Lara nodded.

So here they were, past and present woman in Will's life, surrounded by the contrived madness of a costumed fete, and the two of them might as well have been in an isolation tank. The revellers faded from the picture, although the music still intruded. The words of the songs told them over and over they'd been fools for love.

Perhaps, thought Lara dispassionately, that is how I felt for longer than I knew.

There was no tiptoeing around the point. When it came – on impact as they sat down on the cold damp seat she had fashioned from the unwanted flagstones – it was sharp as shrapnel.

'It's Will and me. He's asked me to marry him and I've said yes,' said Janey, detonating her bombshell above the noise of a conga led by Sandra.

'I know,' said Lara.

A pause.

'Don't tell me that you wanted me to hear it from you,' added Lara. 'Or did you come to ruin my party?'

The light from the kitchen window made silver trails down Janey's cheeks. Her make-up began to run with the tears. 'Lara, I . . . I need you to tell me something.'

Lara closed her eyes against a fugitive reality. *'Me?'*

315

Lara imbued that with as much sarcasm as she thought the other woman's balance of mind would take.

'I *know* how this must seem. And the last thing I want to do is cause you any more pain over Will . . . although that's probably exactly what I'm doing, and I'm sorry, I really am, but . . .' Janey's bluebell eyes were brimming glassily.

Lara took pity on her at last – or rather pity finally overcame curiosity. Was Janey really this insensitive?

'I feel nothing for him now,' Lara said truthfully. As truthfully as could be, that was, without recourse to concepts such as hatred and revenge.

Janey seemed encouraged enough to go on. 'What I want to know . . . What I *need* to know – and it just seems to me that you're the only one who can tell me . . .' She faltered there and lowered her chin with a damp sniff.

There were further watery attempts to stem the dam burst.

Lara had learned so much in recent months. It seemed a pity not to use it. 'You can ask me,' she said, 'but what makes you think that I would tell you the truth?'

That was a blow which seemed to shrink Janey. She stood on the hard stones of the path Lara had made, and put her arms across her chest. It was a while before she said quietly, 'I'm sorry. This is all a horrible mistake.'

'Janey . . . I'll get us a drink.'

Lara didn't care . . . she just didn't care.

Janey shook her head. 'I just need to know . . . when you went on holiday to Greece last year . . .'

What was this? Was she about to be presented with yet another, truer, version of what the Greek interlude had been? Lara gave a strangulated laugh. 'If you're in an unhappy relationship, you don't have holidays. You have a change of battle scene.'

The other woman's clenching hands told her this was deadly serious.

'What's been bothering me, about you and Will, is that you had this disastrous holiday together, and still you came back and picked up the pieces and carried on living here together. I mean, why didn't you split up then?'

Lara sighed. Where was this leading? 'Do we have to discuss this now?' she asked.

Janey was deadly earnest. 'Why did you let it drift all those months?'

'You mean,' said Lara, 'why did *he* let it drift.' She approached the question as if it might blow up in her face. 'He was away a lot,' she replied at last. Maybe she did want to talk about it. Maybe Janey was more subtle than she gave her credit for.

'Travelling?'

'That's what he told me. He was in . . . South America for a while, and the Far East. There were loads of three- or four-day trips all over the place. I can't remember exactly.'

It wasn't exactly an answer, either. They both knew that.

'For the production company?' prompted Janey.

'What else?' said Lara sarcastically. Now there was the biggest question of them all. Lara thought of the police and the rotting room in Battersea.

'What I'm getting at is . . . did you ever suspect that he might not have been straight with you, about what he was doing and who he was with?'

That struck a chord, a nasty one below the belt.

The police had been to see Janey. They had told her that Will was still running two bogus companies using his old Eccleston Square address.

'Or are *you* still running companies with him from this address?' asked Janey desperately.

There was a long silence, interspersed with alien cries from the party, during which Lara went over the old

317

scenarios of terse words and candlelit promises. She tried
to feel Will's presence as it was in this garden, around
the flat, to see his face in her mind, but the only images
she could find were ugly ones.

'No,' said Lara, 'I am not and I never have done.'

Janey weighed that up. 'The fraud squad have been
through his office and the flat.'

'And the room in Battersea?' Lara couldn't help herself.

Janey did know about that. 'That was just a mailing
address – they can't find anything that *proves* he's guilty
of *any*thing. And he is still innocent until proven guilty,
isn't he?'

Janey was convinced it had all started as a mistake
which became harder and harder to correct. It was all to
do with accounts, pushing money here and pulling it from
there to give the impression that the figures added up.
There were sums from government grants, and European
enterprise schemes and the British Film Institute, and
they had all become tangled before finding their way into
Will's pocket.

Lara didn't take in most of it.

'But now the fraud squad have been round saying he's
bought up company names, and switched funds around,
then run up debts and let them go bankrupt . . .'

He had been busy.

'I don't really understand any of it,' said Janey stoutly.
'But I can't believe it's that bad.'

That took Lara aback. 'I think . . . you might have to.'

Was that why Janey had come – for confirmation from
the only possible person that this man she loved was
merely caught up in extenuating circumstances? How did
Will *do* it?

'I've got my father looking into it,' Janey continued.
'He's in business, he knows how companies work, has
accountants and lawyers. It *is* possible that this is all a
terrible mistake.'

Lara didn't need to know any more.

But Janey did. 'And Jennifer – is she involved?'

Jennifer. How inexorable it was. Lara was never happier to be out of it all. 'How would I know? I wouldn't put it past her.'

It was a winding path that Lara hesitated to follow – and yet even as she teetered on the brink she knew that her mind was half-way along and it was not possible to turn back.

'I thought she was a friend of yours,' said Lara. 'That she introduced you to Will.'

'I hardly knew her. We met at some charity do – I was on the committee and she was being glamorous and gracious.'

Janey was still asking the question. 'What I need to know, Lara, is: what *is* she to him? He says she helped put a couple of deals together but that he hasn't seen her for months . . . and then I find that he's *still* been seeing her . . . ! I mean, what's going on there?'

'I . . . really don't know,' whispered Lara. And never had pure shining honesty sounded so false. 'I don't know.'

'What do you *think*?'

It was a note of desperation which chimed so clearly with her own that Lara felt suddenly pure. Sane. 'I don't,' said Lara firmly.

The other woman misread her reaction. 'I'm sorry. So sorry. You must have feelings left for him.'

'Oh, yes,' confessed Lara. 'I think he's a prat.'

Janey was staring straight ahead at the house again, though the open door, through to the brightness of the sitting-room as if memorising the scenes of her lover's former life, imprinting his shadow by the mantelpiece, sitting in a certain chair, standing by the window, making the gestures by which she knew him and shared him.

'He was hardly ever here,' snapped Lara. 'And I've changed round all the furniture.'

'The thing is,' whispered Janey, 'that's not all.'
'No,' said Lara. 'I didn't think it was.'

Janey burst into tears again. And here was Lara, trying to comfort the woman who was going to marry Will.

Although she had to ask, 'Why are you going through with this, Janey?'

The unhappy bride-to-be gave one of her brave sniffles. The lines on her forehead crinkled into calico sails being let down. 'I'm pregnant, Lara. I'm having his baby.'

Lara was drowning. She could not breathe.

'Keeping it, then, the baby?'

'I'm not getting any younger,' said Janey.

Then Lara had to deal with hearing Janey tell her in turn, 'He's not a bad person, Lara. He's a chancer, you must know that. This time he may have . . . overreached himself, that's all.'

Conversation was desultory after that. Without knowing why, only that the reason she did so did not directly involve Will, Lara took his wife-to-be's telephone number as she was leaving.

Lara said nothing of importance – was it up to her to do so? – except one thing.

'By the way, that's my car you've been driving. I love that car. I hope you've been careful with it. In fact, I'd like it back now.'

25   Too Close to the Sun

The party had ebbed and flowed, then finally seeped away in the not-so-early hours. When dawn peeped over the scene in the garden as if hardly daring to look, the flowers were suffering, bent tipsily over empty wine bottles in their beds. A white paper plate was a discus in the hawthorn, and a thorny rose bush wore a sequinned eye mask.

Over the stones lay broken glass, shiny and brittle as Lara's party lies.

She kicked some out of the way.

She knew for certain now. No one could see how she had changed, and if they could, they did not care.

She felt a lurch to the stomach as she thought of the guest of honour and the woman who remained, apparently undisturbed beneath it all, under the soil. Then she gathered herself.

A bass rhythm throbbed in her head long after the music had been quelled.

Systematically, automatically, Lara pulled her belongings from the flat. Inch by inch she stripped the walls, the drawers, the shelves, the darkest corners of every trace of herself. Long-lost possessions were at last retrieved; never-wanted knick-knacks likewise unlost.

Cardboard boxes stood in one area, black rubbish bags

in another. Lara shifted the dregs of her years with Will, saving and casting off.

Inevitably, the envelopes came to light.

She examined their contents and knew that she was free and powerful at last. He had left them behind because there was nowhere safer – a place so safe that he had failed to find them when he returned to collect them.

Funnily enough, she remembered now that she had stuffed some of Will's old papers in with Rose before the burial ritual; just for show, they were in the jacket pocket. At the time Lara had done it in a daze, when it hardly registered what she was doing. Were they important? Would it look, if the sad, lumpy form were ever unearthed, as if Will had put them there, along with old clothes belonging to a woman he had once known?

It was fraud, then. Although Will – adventurous, glib, unfaithful Will, who put his money on chaos and knew it was a sure bet – would not have used such a brutal term.

No doubt he would argue passionately that it was all down to bad luck and oversight that he had received grant money and rarely used it for the purposes intended. And the purest good luck that he always managed to divert funds elsewhere in the nick of time before a business venture went bust due to commercial pressures.

Will could be so convincing.

He had hundreds of thousands of pounds riding on it.

It was passion and revenge that made her contact Janey.

The result would be divine justice, thought Lara. Surely Will would appreciate the irony.

The two women, his old love and his bride-to-be, met like spies in a corner of a tourist pub off Leicester Square. There, Lara told her all she had discovered, and perhaps a little more.

She knew now that a general revenge against the world could never work, that the only person likely to be hurt was herself. The only way forward was to be true to herself.

So it was the old Lara, the straightforward, honest-as-the-day Lara, who handed over the contents of the desk in the sitting-room, the papers which had fallen down behind the overflowing drawers, the creased and torn accounting sheets, the dated correspondence from a contact at a Swiss bank, and the cracked computer discs bizarrely labelled 'Goldquest' and 'Stare' and 'Bust'. Lara – orderly, cautious Lara – had already taken copies and sent them to the nice detective sergeant she met in Battersea.

Janey received the evidence with trembling hands; by the time Lara saw her she already seemed to know what she would find.

When she and Janey parted, they had come to an accord, knowing they had done the best they could.

Now Lara knew what it was that she had to do. She was a woman in charge of her destiny, a woman running a military operation. This was the moment when, history would judge, the worm turned.

Time was running out. The arrival of another bank statement confirmed what she knew would come. Ella's beneficences had been a temporary aberration: the *Reflections* money had dried up.

Lara was dancing on deck as the ship went down.

If she thought now of the gathered sheaths in Greece, the plastic curtains around the taverna by the shore which she had designated the ominous empty wedding-dress covers, then it was only with a sense of fatalism and a vague satisfaction of her own prescience. She had known all along what would happen, one way or another.

On the other hand, it might be argued that this

outcome would have been obvious to anyone who had cared to think about it. The point was, it had not been obvious to Lara, at the time.

That morning South Molton Street was a windy ghost town. The gold rush to its expensive boutiques and designer emporia had been tripped up by bankruptcies and new excitements elsewhere.

It made no odds to Lara. Once, a long time ago, she had determined that this would be the place, and Lara was nothing if not true to herself.

Never had the right choice been so crucial.

She wanted him to look at her and to realise his grave mistake. That was what she wanted, perhaps even needed. Only it would not be quite that simple, of course.

Her nerve endings jangled like jolly church bells. There was a Toccata playing in her bloodstream. For this was a timeless tale of love and deception and betrayal. And maybe they had not yet fully explored the last part.

Annette had said that what she needed was a ceremony.

Lara had held the one for the dead. Now this was one for the living.

The woman in the shop (very exclusive) wore a tight little jacket against the chill of the air-conditioning. A furry collar curled shaggily over her shoulders like a savage haircut that had not been brushed away.

She used a long thin nose to look down at Lara in her black combat gear.

'How may I help you?'

'Lara Noe, *Reflections* magazine,' said Lara, watching the words raise the saleswoman's demeanour like a face-lift.

Lara caressed the soft garments on the rails.

She chose the perfect dress, one that would leave a lasting impression. It was surprisingly easy.

Then, for the last time, she charged it to the fashion department at *Reflections*.

Lara did not leave the Garden Flat immediately. Instead, she embraced the sense of living on the edge, having her bags packed all around her, the telephone cut off. She savoured the emptiness.

The day came after an aeon of waiting.

The clothes hung ready.

What would be the most satisfying aspect of leaving, for that was what she had decided to do? Would it be tying up loose ends, or the knowledge that there were opening vistas, new horizons on which to set one's sights? When Lara walked out of the magazine tower that afternoon, did she think that she was leaving only for a day or so, until her irrational annoyance had receded? If she had had the faintest notion that she was exiting not merely an afternoon of irritation but indeed her whole life so far – would she have ridden the elevator down with such burning resolution?

Hard to know, in retrospect, where the point of no return came. If indeed, that mattered at all, except in the mind of a person who insisted that no loose ends flapped and flailed in her wake.

Did she even feel guilt – or was that strictly for the innocents these days? She pondered this, naturally, as she wiped the draining board for the last time and bedded down the last coffee mug in a bag.

The keys on the table to go back to the letting agency made her think only of other doors to be opened and passed through. It would be a kind of afterlife, after all.

The removal men had taken only a morning to crate her belongings, such as they were. She barely looked around the denuded rooms. She heard the gas boiler give a valedictory belch, and remembered only then to snuff out its light and turn it off.

She had settled all the bills – in Will's name. He had signed up for the flat with her; there was no reason to suggest that he had not been living there right up to the end.

The clothes she would wear, so carefully chosen for the final ceremony, were ready in bags on the bare bed.

She ordered a taxi to take her round the corner to a hotel at Victoria.

She would change there and leave her luggage.

She closed the door of the Garden Flat behind her, the door through which so many unwanted visitors had marched, and climbed the narrow stairs to the main hall.

'So,' said Dora, 'you're off then.'

Lara started like a blown light bulb. Her dangerous, observant neighbour ended her silent glide down the communal stairs.

Lara put a hand out to the big front door as calmly as she could. She could hear the insistent tick of the taxi outside.

'It's been a bit of a close call, hasn't it?' asked Dora, squinting at the packed bags on the floor.

'I'm sorry?'

'Oh no, dear, no need to be sorry. None at all.'

Lara was lost.

'All that went on ... out there,' Dora jerked a scaly hand in the direction of the garden.

What was Dora Allbright saying? What did she know?

'I wouldn't worry about it,' went on the elderly woman. She might have been speaking of the noise all night during the party – except that Lara knew she was not.

'No ...'

'And no need to worry about me. I won't be complaining. I enjoyed the excitement.'

'I see ...'

'I've had my bright day in the sun, dear – you get on with yours.'

For whatever reason – and there were many – Lara felt a fat globe of a tear roll slowly down one cheek. She was still holding on to the door.

'There, there . . .' cooed Dora. 'It's not so bad! It's just the moment of leaving, knowing you won't be back . . . to where it all happened.'

Lara struggled with a bag, avoiding her eye. 'Except that . . . what did happen apart from realising that I got everything wrong? Nothing was what I thought it was. Not the people I thought I knew, not what I thought was happening all around me . . .'

'Don't be sad, dear. No need for that.'

Lara could not help it. 'The man I loved is getting married this afternoon!' she cried.

Dora gave her a long enigmatic look. 'Is he?' she said.

Lara nodded solemnly.

'Well, it's goodbye then,' said Dora ambiguously.

'Yes.' Lara stooped to pick up another bag. 'Dora . . .' She did not know quite how to put this. 'If anyone asks . . .'

The elderly woman raised a hand. Lara noticed the scales on it, but not the lines of the palm. 'I saw him here. I had my suspicions.'

'Him?'

'Your young man, of course – well, not yours any more, I suppose, given the wedding.'

Lara was dazed.

'I saw him barge back in that time. Didn't like his manner, I can tell you now. He upset you, didn't he? Never mind, the police have already failed to find what they were looking for here. They won't be back.'

Lara assented, baffled. Bags in hand, she searched deep into the old woman's all-too-plausible demeanour.

'You were too good for him, by far,' said Dora.

'Thank you.'

'Anyone could see that.'

Lara sniffled harder.

'Don't forget, dear. You can't struggle against fate, but the show's never over.'

'You are a very strange woman, Dora Allbright.'

'Thank you,' said Dora.

One hundred and twenty guests were invited to celebrate the marriage of William St John Radcliffe and Jane Phyllida Anstiss on Saturday 6 July at three o'clock at the church of St Simon Zelotes in Chelsea.

Flowers and ribbons strove to give the austere brick interior an appropriate jauntiness. Hats bobbed and familiar faces smiled familiar smiles she had forgotten.

Lara drew up with her escort and walked the walk of her life into that church.

She clung to his arm as bindweed to a strong stem, swaying under the twin prospects of collapse and dread at what this day signified for her.

The groom before the altar was slick yet jumpy in his morning suit. She recognised the man next to him as a person she would not readily have thought of as 'best' in any sense. Lara took slow deep breaths and gave herself ample chance to study Will on what should have been the happiest day of his life if one were to believe all the hype. She studied Will defiantly, not caring who saw her doing so: his blondish hair, his darker sideburns, the back of his neck, the width of his shoulders. She was aware of all the eyes on her – how could they not be? The eyes of everyone who thought they knew their story seemed to stick like prickly burrs. Yet Lara managed to keep her head up.

She moved closer towards the man who had played such a part in her metamorphosis.

He had made her the woman she was now.

He should be proud.

Organ music pounded around the vaulted church as Lara glided to her place, head higher than ever.

As the bride walked up the aisle towards him, Will raked a hand through his wedding haircut and issued an encouraging smile. Though there was a tilt to one eyebrow, which Lara – watching him intently – interpreted as a sardonic query as to whether his intended might have overdone the full white wedding doll-on-a-cake number.

The dress *was* a cream puff.

And the veil was a snowdrift.

It was hardly possible to see the bride's face beneath.

The bride came to a halt by his side. Lara kept her stare riveted to his face. She did not want to miss a moment of this as the bridesmaid raised the bridal veil.

Will's face twisted, then crumpled ... then collapsed into ruins.

Lara was radiant as she pushed back the veil fully from her face.

'Hello, Will,' she said.

Will was turned to grey stone as his colour drained.

She would treasure for ever the expression of horror on his face.

Lara picked up her ball of white skirts and ran and ran. Back down the aisle she slithered on light slippers. As she flew past the incredulous faces – some of them unfamiliar; all of them frozen in astonishment and disbelief as the bride escaped – she had a dispassionate vision of herself as a billowing meringue on the run.

There was no sound except for shocked gasps from the grisly tableau. The guests in their pews stood blankly as the pad and slip of her soles on stone whispered past them. All she could see along the runway was a line of dropped mouths. She half expected someone to reach out and stop her but it was as if in breaking all convention she were insulated from the possibility of touch. She was beyond all of them. In the same trance an unknown usher opened the great wooden doors and she was free.

Outside she paused, exhilarated.

It was a beautiful day.

Leaves jostled lushly in the city trees.

Birds sang.

Lara threw her head back at the great blue expanse of sky and hurled the bouquet of creamy roses towards the sun with all her strength. Arms outstretched, she whirled herself around and around, a spinning doll on a musical box.

No wedding bells had ever sounded as sweet as the peels of her laughter.

She stopped, giddy. Astounded with herself, she looked back at the church porch. No one appeared from inside. She would never know when the stunned silence in there broke.

She could see the policemen poised at either side of the church, saw that the rush of traffic had been halted at the corners of the street by police cars. More officers waited at the side exit.

A fine reception for Will, on his wedding day.

She saluted them and ran on. She had had her day.

The groom would miss the champagne and food now. Shame. The caterers would be putting the finishing touches to the feast at this moment. Cass and Sandra had done him and his family proud. They said they would know who Jennifer was, from the television.

Then, up the empty road came a surge and a scream. Behind the wheel of the bridal white Rolls-Royce, Janey bore down as if she were driving a roller-coaster, terror and excitement distorting her face.

'Fre-eee-eeeee!' she screamed through an open window.

Some way behind, a uniformed chauffeur gave abortive chase as the car slid away from him.

'Do you want a lift?' she yelled at Lara.

'No thanks! This is much more fun!' bellowed Lara.

The chauffeur shouted too, red faced and puffing, but Janey did not stop. She blew a kiss to Lara and was gone.

Lara hitched up her skirts again.

Passers-by gawped as she ran on, alone but for a big white dress worn for an unmistakable purpose, and an even wider smile. She whirled to the end of the block and turned right, seeing figures at last at the church door as she did so, then waltzed in a lunatic pattern along the pavement.

Not a soul said a word.

Perhaps she should have waited for a bus. That would have been fun.

A hooting from the road matched her mood. She gave a victory salute without even turning around. She put up her hand to hail a taxi. Two screeched to a halt in tandem. She chose one.

'Beautiful!' the driver assured her as she arrived at his window. 'Beautiful bride!' He leaned back, urgency paramount. 'Where do you have to be? I'll get you there, don't worry!'

'I don't know yet. Anywhere.'

He didn't understand. 'Which *church* do you need to get to?'

She was effervescent, high on daring. 'Been there,' she said. 'Now I'm going to pick up my bags from Victoria, then you can take me to Heathrow. I'm going to stand in front of a departure board and not decide till then where I'm going.'

She climbed in. The cab was filled with dress; she was sitting atop a great white cloud.

The driver began to remonstrate, then shrugged with

both arms in the air as if to tell her he knew she was crazy.

Lara didn't care.

The cab moved off. She was on her way.